Happy Lightning

DONALD JORDAN

outskirtspress

DENVER, COLORADO

Outskirts Press, Inc.
http://www.outskirtspress.com

ISBN: 978-1-4787-0018-0

Outskirts Press and the "OP" logo are trademarks belonging to Outskirts Press, Inc.

PRINTED IN THE UNITED STATES OF AMERICA

To my wife Sara, without whose love——

Chapter One

The year Mr. Hightower fell and broke his neck Neal Austin was twenty-five and had no intention of living an ordinary life. He was a slender young man with slightly rounded shoulders, small bones, and a prominent forehead. He had strong arms and legs, black hair, blue eyes, and a thoughtful line that ran from mid-forehead over his straight nose and full lips. He could be taken advantage of. Clerks and day laborers cheated him in small matters. He experienced a moment of self-rebuke but then let it go. He was sensitive, too: An old woman trying to open her car door, a lost child crying for its mother touched him in piteous ways. He always noticed them, thinking someday it could be a scene he might write about.

He had just left the office and started across the yard when he heard a shout. He turned and saw Mr. Hightower step off the dock just as a truck inched forward. He twisted and tried to jump back, and though it was only a four-foot fall, the split second required for him to hit the ground seemed like minutes. Neal couldn't hear, but sensed the crushing of mortal bones as Mr. Hightower bounced slightly and lay still.

He ran. Two or three couriers who'd witnessed the accident also rushed to his side. Wilmore, the driver, caught a glimpse of the confusion in his mirror and leaped from the cab. As they all arrived at the same time, Neal cautioned, "Don't move him!"

He tore off his jacket and threw it over the unconscious man. Someone hurried into the office to call an ambulance. Immediately, Mrs. Hightower burst through the door, stood looking a moment with a shocked stare, then threw herself down beside her husband.

"Careful, Mrs. Hightower. Something could be broken."

He put his arms around her. The blood had drained from her face, but her expression was stoic. She was a strong woman, capable of taking control of most situations. But now her voice was unsteady. "What happened, Neal?"

"I'm not certain. He must not have realized the van was pulling away."

In a few minutes the ambulance arrived, and as Mrs. Hightower got in with her husband, she looked at him. "Neal . . . ?"

"Don't worry about anything, Mrs. Hightower. Just call as soon as you know something."

As the ambulance sped away, Wilmore, the driver, said, "I didn't know he'd stepped back into the truck."

"Of course you didn't, Willie. The best thing we can do now is get these deliveries out."

Hiding his anxiety, Neal took the manifest and began to call out instructions to the couriers. One by one, the vans and trucks raced out of the yard with their payloads of pharmaceuticals and electronic equipment. As they departed, he hurried into the office and buried himself in paperwork. All afternoon he pored over service tickets and bills, remaining at his desk until long after the last driver had returned to the yard. At last, he locked up and drove home.

His house was in St. Elmo, an old mid-Columbus neighborhood made famous by a novel of the same name. Across from his house was Weracoba Creek, which traversed Cherokee Avenue and in past decades fed a lake where girls in bonnets and parasols used to boat. South was Weracoba Park. This was where he jogged and sometimes played tennis. His house was a rambling old stucco with peeling plaster walls, old-fashioned claw-foot tubs, and a narrow kitchen. He realized two bedrooms, living and dining rooms, two baths, and a wide back porch were more space than a bachelor needed, but he benefited from a generous aunt who rented to him at a bargain price.

The most curious aspect of the old house was an added-on sunroom which was accessed by a glass door from outside but only by large, low windows from inside. These he usually kept open, easily slipping through them to water the few plants and ferns donated by friends or some girl he happened to be dating. Up a set of creaky, narrow stairs was a tiny loft with a dormer window, a slanted ceiling, and wallpaper which had faded into an ugly manila yellow. The former tenants had used this attic for storage, but adding a heater, a desk, a couple of lamps, shelves for books, and a throw rug for the wood floor, he'd made it an austere but relatively comfortable office where he could think and write.

He hurried upstairs to turn on the small electric heater and went back down to the kitchen for a quick meal of soup and sandwich. His hope was to write for an hour or two, but he was unable to take his mind off Mr. Hightower. He ate without much appetite, took a shower, and then sat staring at his typewriter as he waited for the phone to ring. It did at last and Mrs. Hightower said quietly, "He broke his neck, Neal. Had it been a fraction of an inch over, he would have been paralyzed, but they think he'll be okay."

"That's good news, Mrs. Hightower."

"You know what I'm going to ask you. There's no one else . . ."

"I understand. I'll do what I can."

He sat for a long time thinking. He had worked for the Hightowers through high school and college, and now full time for three years. He thought it as good a place as any to earn a respectable living while he tried to write his way to literary success. And their small courier service in Columbus offered a good location for a break if one could find the time to travel — to the north were Atlanta and the north Georgia mountains, to the south the glistening white beaches of Florida, the Atlantic coast east, and to the west Alabama, birthplace of space travel. He had no doubt that someday he would be hurrying from one city to another for book signings. In the morning he returned to the office before anyone else arrived, and with a sense of loyalty and perseverance prepared himself for the arduous task ahead.

After a couple of weeks, Mrs. Hightower stopped by the office to write checks and make a few calls, and to report on her husband's slow recovery.

"Are you really all right, Neal? I know you were never expecting anything like this."

"We're okay, Mrs. Hightower. You just help your husband get well."

One morning she said, "He's getting cabin fever, Neal, and wants to come in for a while."

"Good. We'll have a little welcoming party."

Neal picked up donuts, orange juice, and coffee, and held the couriers an extra half hour to greet Mr. Hightower. As their employer walked up the steps, pale and not entirely steady on his feet, there was applause. Wilmore, in a touching display of sympathy, put his arms around him. "Welcome home, boss."

There were tears in Mr. Hightower's eyes. "Thank you," he said. "Thank you all." Then with melancholy and relief he went into his office.

A week or two after that Wilmore, one of their best drivers, said to Neal as they looked over the manifest, "The boss isn't the same, is he? He's changed."

"Yes. In what way, Willie?"

"He used to be tough and hard-driving. Now he just sort of sits around with this look on his face. Haven't you noticed?"

"I have, Willie. I guess it was the injury. He could have died or been paralyzed."

One afternoon the Hightowers asked him to join them in the office. As he sat down, Mr. Hightower blurted out, "Neal, we think it's time you took over this company, if you want it. You're capable and honest, and we believe you can really make something of it."

Stunned, Neal looked for escape. He'd never seen himself as a businessman, especially to tying himself down to a long-term obligation. "I'm afraid you overestimate me, Mr. Hightower. Besides, why wouldn't you want to continue? The company's making a little money now."

"A little, yes," said Mrs. Hightower. "Tell us you don't see room for improvement, Neal, for growth . . . that you wouldn't make changes."

Realizing that there was a lot more that could be done, Neal sat struggling. He'd never intended to stay very long in a job whose only purpose was to sustain him while he wrote. With mild panic, he said, "I suppose if someone really wanted to throw himself into it . . ."

"That's just the problem, Neal. Since the accident, we've been just drifting. It's made us see we don't want to keep doing this."

"Then why not sell out? I couldn't afford to buy, of course, but probably you could get a fair price."

"We could work out a schedule for you to pay a little as you go along. We really want you to have our company, Neal. We believe it's a great opportunity for you."

"Well, I'm flattered. I don't know what to say."

"Why don't you think about it and let us know?"

As he walked out of the shabby office, Neal knew he should be excited but wasn't. He neither wanted nor expected an opportunity to run a business. It challenged his dreams. Neither was it an offer he should easily ignore. At an early age his father had had a stroke, there was no insurance, and they'd suffered financial hardship all through his life. Every morning Napp Austin had trudged off to work when he could hardly drag himself from bed, and nights and weekends moonlighted for extra cash. And Neal remembered his own long days too, when he'd grab any job he could find to put himself through school. He knew writing was unlikely ever to earn him much money, and the opportunity the Hightowers offered him opened one door while very possibly closing another.

During the day the Hightowers glanced at him inquiringly, and at night he lay half-awake, listening to the creaks and ghostly whistles of the old house. He realized he hadn't accomplished much yet but he felt that in another year or two, maybe three, he would make a splash in the literary world. A business enterprise seemed about as far removed from what he intended to do as it could be — not because there wasn't money to be made but because he knew instinctively it would mean long, arduous, draining hours.

On Saturday evening he drove over to his parents' for dinner. His father was out in his shop, puttering around. Following the stroke Mr. Austin had begun a small repair business, and often brought work home with him. Ornate lamps, turntables and broken carousel horses — junk to some but beloved by nostalgic owners — were his specialty. It was a craft he liked and he had all the business he could handle. Neal felt that for the time his father invested he never charged his customers enough.

Napp was bent over a vise, meticulously fitting an old walnut chair leg with a wood dowel. "Isn't it time you gave this up and came in?" said Neal.

"Five minutes," his father said. "I promised a customer I'd have this back tomorrow."

Neal folded his arms and stood leaning against the bare wall, watching. His father was a small man with thinning steel-gray hair, sinewy wrists and bunched shoulders which appeared a little out of proportion to his slender torso, and a slow, shy smile. The stroke had left him with a slight shuffle, causing some people to suspect he'd been drinking. Neal had inherited his father's skills and could fix just about anything once he understood its workings.

He went into the house, where his mother was preparing dinner. He put his arms around her and thanked her for having him. "There'll be plenty left over for you to take home," she said.

"You don't have to worry about me. I get enough to eat."

"It's no trouble to make extra, you know that."

He helped her by putting napkins and silverware on the table. Then he walked through the kitchen down the hall to his sister's room. He found Lori sitting on the floor staring dreamily at a half-opened book. She was in her first year of college, and having left behind the hectic halls and riotous rush of high school, she'd put on a little weight which benefitted her figure. Her cheeks were fuller, her raw umber hair picked up glints from the overhead light and her slender wrists and long fingers drifted across the half-read pages with rumative distraction. She looked up and smiled with the detachment of one who has never learned to laugh or cry with abandon. "You know what I wish, Neal? I wish I could hurry up and finish school."

"Why? You're supposed to be having the time of your life."

"I want to get a job so things won't be such a struggle."

He realized that if Lori had any idea he sent money to help with her college, she would never make such remarks. Still, by the look in her eyes, the clothes she'd laid out on her bed, and the photos of friends on her dresser, he saw how tight things were for her. She had her own car, but to save money drove home only about every third weekend. Lori's eyes were blue like his, her motions and gestures tentative, and her expression pensive, but she was no pushover. He was pretty sure she could hold her own with her well-heeled classmates.

"Unless some Prince Charming should come along and whisk me away," Lori said.

"I wouldn't count on Prince Charming. Even if he did show up it wouldn't necessarily guarantee bliss."

"I don't expect bliss."

Neal had done all he could to take care of Lori from the time she was born. His mother told the story of how one morning she had heard the baby crying, and when all grew quiet she decided she'd better go in and see why. She found that Neal, six years old, had lifted the baby from her crib and sat rocking her, whispering, "Now, now . . ."

All through adolescence and young manhood he'd worked to earn money. He had cleaned for a butcher shop, bagged for a grocery store, mowed lawns and washed windows and driven tractors on a small farm — and always with the first priority to make his baby sister's life a little easier than his mother and father could provide for her.

At dinner Neal ate quietly, contributing as he could to the conversation, and remembering the times his mother had collapsed in tears because she had exhausted her credit with the neighborhood grocery, the time his father had pleaded with an uncle for a loan to get electrical power turned on, and the calls from the doctors and hospital seeking payment following his father's stroke. He wondered what his father would have given thirty years ago for the opportunity to step into an established business with a solid financial base. With a stab of conscience he realized it wasn't only himself, his writing or his own future that he should be thinking of.

On Monday Neal received a letter from his agent Sam Harris. The publication of a couple of short stories in non-paying literary magazines and the sale of a story or two in the low distribution, low-paying pulp market had been his credentials to persuade this New York agent to take him on. So far the pickings had been slim, but Sam Harris seemed to believe in him. He never stopped trying, and had come heartbreakingly close to making some respectable sales.

In the large manila envelope with the letter were two stories in which they'd had high hopes. Not to be brutal but to show his client where the manuscripts had gone, Sam included several rejection slips. As Neal read these over, he felt a python grip on his stomach. How many of these cold little printed rejections had he collected? Probably enough to wallpaper a sizable room. Sam wrote, "Sorry, Neal. I've just about exhausted the possibilities for these. I know it's little comfort, but I do think we came pretty close again."

Each morning Neal went to work trying to hide his gloom and as much as possible to avoid the Hightowers, and trying, too, to be convivial with the men who were constantly jostling one another over some sports team or over some girl they'd seen on one of their routes. With some irony and faint envy he noticed how at the end of the day most of them went home, happy with their T.V. and beer and their little families, with no concern whatever with contributing to the general good of mankind.

"Come on, Neal," one of them would say, "there's a good Cottonmouth game tonight. Why don't we go?"

"Maybe next time. Thanks anyway."

Starved for romance though he was, he seldom felt inspired to go out on the town or to call any girl he'd dated more than once or twice.

In his little loft he looked over the short stories Sam had returned, trying to decide if they were worth resurrecting. These near misses were somehow more damning than outright failure. He could imagine himself toiling year in and year out to find the perfect paragraph, the perfect sentence, hammering away, jealous for time to write, trying to make a splash while other young men his age lived a regular life and his family needed money.

Long ago he'd received something he would never forget. "For actors, writers, and painters, there is nothing as crippling as anxiety about their livelihood. Money is like a sixth sense, without which you cannot enjoy the other five, without which half the possibilities of life go unrealized. Sometimes you hear people say poverty provides inspiration for an artist. They don't know how it clips your wings, how it eats you like a cancer. The artist who relies on his art for a living is pitiful indeed."

At the end of the week he walked into the office and asked the Hightowers to sit down. "Tell me," he said, "exactly what would be expected if I accept your offer?"

Chapter Two

Neal was jolted awake by the insistent peal of the telephone. He groaned and looked at the clock. Four a.m. He'd been in bed exactly five hours, and it seemed to him that after running his company for three years he would have become inured to such disruptions like this; but he wondered if anyone ever did. He threw back the covers and jerked the receiver off the cradle. Nate Nately, their nighttime courier, said, "Sorry, boss. I've wrecked the truck."

Neal swung his feet to the floor. "You hurt?"

"Shook up a little. I don't know what happened. Skidded into a pole, the doors flew open and packages are all over the street. The cops are here now."

His thoughts leapt to pharmaceuticals which had to be refrigerated, electronic equipment that couldn't withstand jostling, insurance claims, down time . . . He swore under his breath. "I'll try to get help, Nate."

He fumbled for the light, looked in his directory and found the numbers of a couple of other drivers. They grumbled but agreed to hurry out. He threw on some clothes, locked up, and drove to the accident. It was cold. Frost along the shoulders of the road glistened like crystal beads. Not a star could be seen in the sky. Every house and building was dark. People were sleeping, except for him. He couldn't remember when he had a good night's sleep.

The truck sat at a precarious angle against a power pole. Most of one side was caved in. A hubcap had reeled off and careened across the street. One headlight was pointing down like a lazy eye. All the packages were off the macadam now, stacked on the sidewalk by Nate and the police officers. The two summoned drivers arrived and began loading the parcels into another van.

Hangdog, Nate said, "Truck's pretty beat up, isn't it?"

"Don't worry, Nate. We'll use a rental until we can get it back on the road."

Neal called a wrecker and helped them load the van. "Nate, you'd better hang in here until the wrecker comes." He sent the other couriers home and then drove to the office. As he unlocked the gate the sun was rising and optimistic pastels tinged the east. He'd neither eaten nor shaved, but was too hyped up to give it much thought.

Around seven the drivers began to arrive and with deliveries doubling up the dock became a madhouse of couriers identifying unfamiliar addresses and taking on extra freight. Neal hurried back and forth from dock to office. About eight-thirty Tia McCormick, his bookkeeper-secretary, came in, plunked her purse down on her desk and fixed him with her steady gaze. "It's all right, Neal, we'll manage. Why don't you go home and rest."

"Too much to do."

"You look like death warmed over."

"I'll try to leave early."

Around mid-morning the damaged truck, wrecked but not a total loss, was delivered to a body shop and Tia stayed on the phone until she could locate a rental. When Nate Nately arrived she said, "Nate's here to help now, Neal. Go home."

"Okay. I guess you're right." He drove to his loose-jointed house in St. Elmo, showered, shaved, ate some cereal and toast, and lay down on the sofa. Rays of crisp sun slanted through the glass of the sunroom, making yellow-tinged pools on the ferns and cactuses. Even with the sun the house felt cold and lonely.

He closed his eyes and thought of what he had accomplished in these three years. His success was debatable. He'd accelerated his payments to the Hightowers, changed the name to NEA Couriers, moved into one of the new industrial parks with five acres of neatly landscaped facilities, worked twelve-hour days, doubled the number of accounts, expanded the territory, and made the small courier service that had been hobbling along three years ago into a prosperous business.

But as he lay with his arm across his eyes he didn't see that he was much closer to where he wanted to be. He was now twenty-eight. The competition between time to pursue prosperity and writing was so demanding it seemed to him those three years had gone up in a puff.

About a year ago his agent had been able to place a short story in one of the mystery magazines. The income from this wouldn't have fed a millipede, but it gave him a lift. He got Lori through college, provided money for his parents, sweated over an outline of a novel, *Samson's Revenge*, and suffered dismal failure of his romantic life. Women came and went, and he was sorry that he soon forgot them. But he was glad that things still stimulated his senses. His awareness had become more vulnerable and sharper. When the movie *Rain Man* came out, he remembered how touching every element of the human experience is. A third of Yellowstone National Park was destroyed by fire, reminding him how one little decision, one little flame, can alter the force of life's landscape. And the new Hubble Space Telescope promised to send back pictures from galaxies light years away — while his personal universe revolved around getting up every morning, rushing off to pull his twelve-hour workdays, and falling exhausted into bed at night while his mind refused to let go. He had the sense he was on a runaway train which allowed him only fleeting glimpses through its windows of much to be sought, much to be desired, but little to be touched.

He turned on his side and scrunched the pillow against his spine. Thoughts of a train reminded him of a story he'd written in seventh grade. His family was on one of those rare vacations they'd managed, to visit an aunt and uncle in Virginia. They were traveling through a small town, his mother and father in the front seat, he and Lori in back, when they were stopped halfway across a railroad track. They looked up to see lumbering toward them a dingy red boxcar, apparently a runaway.

His mother cried out and jumped from the car. With one hand clutching the door, she with the other waved frantically for drivers in front to move forward, drivers behind to back up. But traffic was halted bumper to bumper, and there was no escape.

His mother could easily have thrown herself out of harm's way, but she held fast to the car door, squaring herself off between the indomitable boxcar and her husband and children. At the last instant, right at the mouth of the intersection, the train came to a halt, apparently braked by some brakeman managing the wheel on top of the car, from which he could see the street without being seen by those below. Little did he know or perhaps care what terror he caused an innocent, helpless family threatened to be run down by a boxcar. His mother collapsed back into the front seat and the traffic inched forward.

Instinctively, Neal knew he had succeeded in capturing a mother's courage, her protectiveness, and her willingness to give her life for her children. The teacher read the story to the class, and his classmates applauded. One girl cried. At that moment he knew his life was to touch hearts and evoke laughter and tears. It was his calling.

He pulled himself up from the sofa, wobbled like a man half-stoned, then washed his face and drove back to the office. There was too much to do to lie around, though remembering his seventh-grade story sparked a moment of inspiration, and he was sorry to let it go.

A few days later, Lori came to visit him at his office. She wanted him to be the first to know she was getting married. She was just out of college and was eager to begin her own family. It was hard really to tell how Lori felt. She was a quiet girl, always thoughtful but with a quick sense of humor. Her expressions and gestures were habitually subdued, and Neal could only hope that she knew what she was doing, that she would be happy, and that this wasn't simply an escape from another life. Her fiancé appeared devoted to her, but Neal, who'd met him during her senior year, had reservations.

"It's hard to believe," he said. "Getting married. I remember you jumping off our porch into my arms as if it were yesterday."

"That porch was twice my height but I knew you'd catch me."

"I'd ride you on my bike down those steps. You were about four or five. It seems impossible."

"Can I count on you to help?" Lori asked. "It'll be a small wedding, at home."

"No big church wedding?"

"You know we can't afford it, Neal. Besides, I want an intimate ceremony with a few friends and family."

"Just tell me what I can do."

"I've always relied on your advice, you know that."

"I hope I haven't steered you too far off course. Sometimes I'm afraid I have my wires crossed."

"You have your wires straighter than anybody I know. I just wish you'd get married."

He laughed. "It takes two."

"Ever since I was a little girl, I've seen you go at things so seriously. But you do care for people, Neal. It's not as if you're meant to live alone."

"I may expect a little too much, though. The longer a person waits, the greater his expectations, I think."

"Well, I hope you'll find someone. You'd make a great husband."

He helped with the finances and then stood with feelings of pride and nostalgia as his sister was married in the living room of their family home, with about twenty relatives and friends present. It was amazing how truly lovely she looked with faith in the future in her eyes.

It was 1988. A young writer named Michael Chabon had burst onto the literary scene with his *The Mysteries of Pittsburgh*. After being grounded by the disaster of Challenger, NASA had resumed space flights; and golfer Curtis Strange had become the PGA's top money leader with over a million in winnings. A great deal was happening in the world and Neal had the curious feeling he was missing out.

For over three years now, he had worked arduously. Little by little, month by month, his bank account increased. He supposed he was fulfilling the American dream. But his original yearnings wouldn't go away. He wondered when he would be able to contribute one good lasting thing. Sometimes he experienced a robust sense of accomplishment, but mostly he stood on his dock as the cold, cruel sun crept up over the horizon to bring him another lonely morning.

Then he met Sandi Steele.

Chapter Three

Neal was riding with Brent Wilmore, one of his couriers, to deliver parcels and packages to various locations, something he tried to do a few times a year, believing that a personal touch was good public relations for his business. They dropped off a package at The Learning Room, a school for special needs children, and Willie introduced him to the various office staff and a couple of teachers. They were about to leave when a young woman walked in. With a shy grin, Willie said, "Miss Sandi, this is my boss Neal Austin."

Sandi Steele smiled a lovely, heartwarming smile, looked at Neal with twinkling, friendly eyes, and extended her hand. Almost at once something swept through him. It was not merely her startling good looks, but a tenderness, an aura mixed with a subtle compelling sexuality that set glowing shock waves — he felt almost giddy. She had delicate features, a slender curved nose, long lashes and perfect white teeth. She wore her hair long and there were soft waves in it which picked up glints of auburn and gold. Her eyes were earnest and so brown that as they caught certain lights they appeared liquid.

"Willie's mentioned you so often I feel I know you," she said.

"Really? What does he say?"

"How hard you've worked to take a little business and turn it around."

"I don't know why you'd be interested," said Neal.

"Oh, but around here we're interested in everything. You should hear the stories about our pest control man!" There was a spark of mischievousness in her eyes.

"And what about you?" he asked. "You enjoy your work here?"

"Very much. I love the children, every one is special."

They stood talking and Neal found himself wishing he was still holding her hand. Finally, Wilmore, grinning, said, "We gotta go, boss."

"I'm so pleased to meet you," said Sandi.

"Maybe I should drop by more often."

"Maybe you should. We'll introduce you to our children."

As they returned to the van Willie said, "She's some lady, isn't she? Those kids — they all have some kind of problem, but she never stops loving and caring for them."

"She isn't married?"

"No, but I don't know why not." With a wink, Willie said, "I'm glad you noticed, boss."

Neal fought the impulse to phone Sandi Steele. With his business, his writing and his family, he couldn't see where he would have any more time now for a personal relationship than he'd had these last three arduous years. To take out a girl for a casual evening of dinner or dancing was nothing, but while they'd just met for fifteen minutes he knew instinctively that Sandi Steele could never be merely a casual date. Still, for a week it seemed something happened to remind him of her soft smile and intriguing mouth, her forthrightness with beneath the surface a hint of intrigue. He knew he couldn't be the only man tantalized by her, but he couldn't leave it alone, and at last he phoned her.

"I know we've only just met, but I wonder if you'd like to have dinner."

"Oh, don't worry." She spoke gaily, swiftly, with an openness that came through over the phone. "You come highly recommended. Willie speaks well of you."

"Does that mean yes?"

"Yes. I was wondering when you'd call."

Neal sat by his phone wondering if this meant she was accustomed to men finding her irresistible, or if she had been as hooked as he was. He wondered, too, if she sensed his rarely felt excitement.

She lived in a one-bedroom efficiency apartment in a rambling upscale north Columbus complex directly across from the pool and tennis courts. He parked in the space out front, and walked between mushroom ground lights up to her front door. The buildings were

Spanish in style, with stucco and exposed wood beams and arches. He winced when he noticed a Spanish bayonet espaliered against the dove-colored wall, remembering as a child getting pricked by one of those needlelike spears. Ivy grew on the walls like whiskers of old men and there were lots of trees and grass.

He rang the bell and Sandi threw open the door. He was struck anew by how pretty she was. "Come in, I'll show you my little place."

The apartment reflected her personality, he thought, a sort of spontaneous design. There were Japanese screens, giant pillows, wall hangings of plates and sconces and porcelains. On her coffee table were scrapbooks from her classes, pictures of her pupils in Lucite frames, others of an older man and woman who had to be her mother and father, children's handprints stamped on framed cloths, floating candles in bowls, and a collection of music boxes — all cluttered but somehow curiously homey. It seemed to him that her touch was written on everything, and he suspected any home she made would have no cold rooms, no impersonal spaces. There was a scent in the air of flowers or potpourri or perhaps it was perfume, and the dusk falling on her window matched the dove gray of the outside stucco walls.

He wondered if his own home should be more intimate, closer, more touchable — but, no, he was something of an isolationist, he needed space, the very essence of his creative personality evoked a wandering spirit. He pinched himself, though, figuratively, wondering if he enclosed himself in some kind of make-believe world, colored with glamour, or the possibility of it, without lasting substance. Still, at this very instant he was immersing himself in real glamour — sometimes his inner contradictions distressed him.

"I used to have a kitten," said Sandi. "One day she got out and I haven't seen her since. I miss her."

"Why not get another?"

"I'm not ready yet. It takes a while to get over such things. You live with anyone?"

"No cats, no dogs. I live alone."

"Willie tells me you work all the time."

"Well, I guess he got that right." He noticed a guitar standing against the wall. "You play?"

"A little. Playing and singing is good therapy."

"Therapy for what?"

"Sometimes I'm sad for my kids. My father's been ill, too. I'm not complaining, though."

"You really like working there?"

"The school? Yes, very much. You learn to appreciate little things — a healthy mind and body, for example. And to be happy for small favors."

As she turned out the lights and gathered her keys, he had a better chance to look at her. It was her graceful gestures and optimistic attitude, he believed, and the little creases which appeared on either side of her mouth when she smiled that were most appealing. Her laughter was lighthearted and sometimes a little mocking, and she looked at him with amusement which he suspected could turn into cool disdain.

He asked, "Where would you like to have dinner?"

"Anywhere you choose."

"Okay, we'll try the Pagoda then."

They drove across town and entered the Japanese restaurant across a moat in which gold and orange carp drifted. The various rooms and levels were decorated with hanging lanterns and delicate curtains of tubed glass. Neal asked for a booth and was glad to get a table beside a tall potted fern, providing some privacy, where they could talk. Right away Sandi said, "Tell me about yourself, Neal. Your work, your likes and dislikes, your friends."

"I have a couple of friends. Pat Fuller and Rob Palmer. Crazy guys. They're both married. Mostly we canoe and hike together."

"And their wives? You like them?"

"I do. They stay on me about not getting married, though."

"What about movies? Books?"

And so it went. They talked as if they'd known each other a long time — about her work, her family, about siblings and music, about politics and food and expectations. She'd lived in Columbus all her life, but they had attended different schools and probably because she was three years younger their paths hadn't crossed.

"We must have had some mutual acquaintances," said Neal, but in response to everyone he mentioned she shook her head.

"I did know a weird boy named Spud Kinkle. He used to climb up onto rooftops."

"Yes, old Spud!" he exclaimed. "Anytime Spud got mad or wanted to prove a point, he'd climb onto some roof and sit right on the edge and threaten to jump if he didn't get his way."

"Yes," she giggled. "It drove his mother crazy. His father used to say just let him jump. You know what Spud's doing now? Guiding photo safaris in Africa."

"No kidding. That sounds like Spud. If you knew him, you must have known Jimmy Harris."

"Was he a little pudgy? Very light brown hair?"

"That's Jimmy. His father ran a small manufacturing plant. I used to have a motorbike for my paper route. When the gas tank started leaking, Jimmy took me over to the plant and undertook to solder it for me with an acetylene torch. His father caught us and ran out yelling, 'You're going to blow the place up!' We had no idea how dangerous it was." As Sandi laughed he was delighted with the little dimple in her left cheek. "Well, what about your old friendships? Have you maintained any?"

"Oh, a few from college," she said. "Mostly my friends now are new ones." She smiled with her eyes, which seemed to change with the light, sometimes green, sometimes hazel. "That's the way it is, don't you think? People pass in and out of our lives, and we hope someday we'll make a connection that we'll treasure the rest of our lives. You should get to know my kids at school. All they want is to be loved."

"And you give them plenty of that."

"Oh, yes. It's a joy."

The evening passed quickly. As they drove away from the restaurant Sandi said, "Show me where you work, Neal."

"Why? It's just an ordinary office."

"I don't care. You've seen my place. I want to see yours."

He drove over to the new facilities, five acres of commercial property with plenty of landscaping, fig vines growing on the fences, maple trees marking the perimeter. The gate was locked, the security lights glowing, and he just drove by slowly. "That's it," he said.

"It looks very prosperous."

"I really never thought I'd end up running a business."

"What did you think you'd do?"

He declined to mention his writing; it was too painful. Not knowing exactly how to answer he dropped it.

They returned to her apartment, driving by the pool where big round globe lights threw a pinkish aura over wrought-iron deck chairs and two girls sat wrapped in afghans with their backs to the lights, reading. As he pulled up to Sandi's unit they could hear music from a radio between the two girls. The sky was starless, black upon blackness all across the horizon. He came round to open her door and they walked up the mushroom-lit walkway. Sandi bent to insert her key into the lock, and as she stood again, he took her into his arms.

She turned her face away. "You can't kiss me, Neal."

"Why not?"

"You don't really know me."

"But — a kiss."

"A kiss is very serious business." Then she smiled and pressed his hand. "Thank you for a lovely evening. I really enjoyed it." In one fluid movement, she disappeared.

Neal stood in a kind of hypnotized dismay, then walked out to his car. As he turned back to look at her apartment he saw that she had drawn the blinds. It was just as well. Right now he had to work, to make the money to escape, to write something significant and worthwhile. A romantic relationship could only intensify the pressures he had already imposed upon himself.

But as he drove off under the starless night he knew that sooner or later he must kiss Sandi Steele and that she would want him to.

Chapter Four

"Is this some kind of rush or what?" Sandi laughed. "I feel I'm being swept off my feet."

It was true. For a week he resisted every impulse to phone her. When he finally gave in and called to ask her about dinner and a movie, she said, "Yes, I've just been trying to decide which night," as though she never doubted that he would call or when he would call.

Following this evening, when they skipped the movie and talked nonstop for three hours, he found out everything he could about Sandi Steele. She read prodigiously. "Everything from politics to inspirational to autobiographies, and fiction," she said. "I've had more fun rediscovering some of the old classics, *Pride and Prejudice*, *The Age of Innocence*, *Atlas Shrugged*, and the works of Charles Lamb." Strange, thought Neal, for a beautiful young woman in the spoiled rush of contemporary America. She liked to play softball with the kids at school who could run and throw. She went out with friends to movies, to dinner, but when he asked her about dates she half-closed one eye and cocked her head to one side. "I'm pretty careful about dates."

"You turn down hundreds."

"I wouldn't say hundreds. But I'm not about to get myself into any compromising situations."

He gathered she never found life boring. "What do you usually do at night?" he said.

"At night. Let me think. Go home, get barefoot, eat, talk to my parents on the phone, read, practice my guitar, write a verse or two of a song, bathe and put on my gown or pajamas, watch the news. Usually before bedtime I'll have a bowl of blueberries or strawberries. I have an addiction to fruit, but that's a good thing."

Sandi was considerate and sensitive, but she could be riled up. "There was this lady in the left lane. I was in the right. She put on her blinker and turned so suddenly in front of me I had to slam on brakes and hit the curb. At the corner, I pulled right up beside her and told her she'd almost made me have a wreck. 'When I put on my blinkers you have to yield,' she said. Now where did she get that? It made me so mad!"

He chuckled, hoping she'd never get any madder with him.

They went to concerts and shows, on bike rides and hikes, to restaurants, parks and gardens. It seemed that hours spent with Sandi infused him with more energy, which in itself complicated matters. Precious as his time with her was, his desire to be at his desk, to write and to cast every single element of his life in a brighter literary, successful light, seemed to hold them apart in some strange way.

"I majored in psychology," she said, "with a minor in education, then I returned to school for a degree in special education. I've been at The Learning Room for two years."

After a date they returned to her apartment, where she sometimes played the guitar and sang. Neal sat, eyes half closed, soothed by her innocent voice with its fluctuating passion and warmth. She smiled softly and lowered her head to look up at him through dark-caged lashes. Something kept gnawing at him and he finally asked her outright, "How is it that you've remained unattached so long?"

She frowned at the question. "I don't see how this is important, Neal. I've told you that I'm very cautious with my relationships."

"Why?"

"I had to break up with this boy in college and it was terribly painful."

"Why did you break up?"

"He drank. No — he was an alcoholic. I could never live with a man who depends on a crutch to feel right about himself."

She looked up at him across a face pure in sincerity and pragmatism. "I'll never hide anything from you, Neal, but this doesn't really have much to do with us. Unless you make it so."

"No. I just pity the guy."

They were lunching together in a small coffee shop halfway between her school and his work one day when a ragged-looking old man shuffled in. Neal noticed him right away. He had gray stubble, a soiled, old cap, worn sandals and a tattered sweater much too warm for the balmy noon. With a sweet and self-conscious smile he stood at the counter to order, counting his change to determine what he could afford — a cup of coffee, a honey bun. His countenance and gestures were duteous and deferential. Neal could not explain why he was sometimes struck by a gesture, a glance, a smile of perfect strangers in a way that he felt pity of self-likeness with them, when no word was communicated. He only knew that there was a strain of humanness or love which ran through him strongly and which he hoped someday to be able to evoke through his prose. It was frustrating to him that his emotional images were beyond his verbal articulation. Why did it matter, he wondered. No man could live very long all within himself.

He motioned the server over to their table. "See that man over there standing by the counter? Get him a decent lunch, will you? He doesn't need to know where this came from." He handed her ten dollars.

The waitress looked confused. "Why don't I just give it to him now?"

"Please wait until we leave."

"All right. Thank you." She took the ten and moved away.

Sandi half closed one eye and cocked her head. "That was very kind of you. But why didn't you go over to him yourself, Neal?"

"In something like this I think it's better not to make a big production."

"Very well as long as you're sure you're not hiding yourself."

"Meaning?"

"You're a compassionate man, but sometimes handing out the money is easier than getting involved."

These little bullets of insight were typical of her.

One Saturday she wanted him to go on a picnic. Neal guarded his Saturdays jealously, using them to plan and write. He shook his head dubiously.

"It's an annual affair for The Learning Room children, families and staff," she said. "You'll get to meet some of my kids."

"But not Saturday," he said.

"Oh, yes. We'll have fun. I know you'll enjoy it. I need to teach you how to relax."

"But Saturday — "

She fixed him with a defiant gaze. "Well, is this what I'm to expect, Neal? I'm good for some days but not others?"

"This has nothing to do with you."

"I see. I'm one corner of your life, do not invade other corners."

"You aren't being reasonable, Sandi."

"No. I suppose love seldom is."

This was the first mention of love and he couldn't decide whether within her was a shadowy element of possessiveness, which he instinctively resisted, or of jealousy for those spaces in his life he closely guarded. He was not oblivious to his own egotistical weakness and supposed he must endure some self-abnegation if he were ever to realize the full capacity of his romantic-erotic nature. So far the only fault he'd found in her was an insistence beyond the point of sheerly female obstinacy. Still, it amused him to see that as she made up her mind to a thing she was going to have it — a combination of admirable determination and indulgent stubbornness, which he'd never admired in a woman, or a man either.

On Saturday they drove south from town, through a countryside of rolling pastures, dense woods, streams and lakes, white picket fences, pecan orchards and planted pines. Sandi let the window down to let the wind blow her hair wildly, one leg curled under her, her jeans tight on the evocative curve of her legs. They smelled the grass and hay, whiffs of turpentine, and the piquant smoke of a controlled field fire.

At the country place of one of the school's trustees, they were greeted by open-sided barns and rail fences circling riding and jumping rings. Neal pulled into the shadows of a tall sycamore, parked and took in the lake, the maples tipped by new greens, the barns and trees all in one sweeping glance.

"Pretty," he said. "Well kept."

"We all look forward to this each year." Sandi leaped from the car and took his hand. "I know this isn't how you choose to spend your Saturdays, but you can have fun if you want to."

"What makes you think I don't want to?"

"What I think," she said, "is that you need to see we don't have to kill ourselves trying to charge through life. The world can't be conquered all at once." Another probing bullet.

They were surrounded by squealing, animated children, some of whom couldn't run, could hardly walk, some who had trouble speaking or controlling their motor reflexes. As Sandi left him to go help prepare food, he noticed two or three boys who'd discovered a steep, rocky incline where a small pine sapling tilted out over a drop of about five feet. They'd found they could plunge forward, pretend to fall over this cliff, and save themselves by catching the sapling and swinging back to safety, something like soaring Tarzans in a daring jungle-like adventure. Another small boy, whose nametag said "Reggie," and who was obviously having trouble with his legs but clearly wanted to join in the challenge, contrived to climb the incline. Neal stood fascinated as the child dragged himself up, arm over arm, using his legs as best he could. None of the others offered to help. When finally he reached the top, flung himself over the edge, and catapulted himself back to safety, there was a great change in his expression. What tenacity! Neal thought. What courage! He felt humbled, inspired, a little awed. It was difficult to resist the temptation to rush up the jagged incline and swing out on the sapling himself.

He told Sandi about the incident and how it gave him a lift of inspiration. "Isn't that wonderful?" she said. "That's how things are, you know. We just drift along and suddenly something happens to pump us up. An act of kindness, a friendly smile. We call it happy lightning."

She hurried off. The next time he saw her again she had in tow a little blonde girl with startling blue eyes, fair complexion, and a pretty smile. "I want you to meet one of my favorite people. This is Lucy. Lucy, Mr. Austin."

As Sandi spoke, she looked directly into the little girl's face. The child then turned her attention to him and he saw that she watched his lips with extraordinary concentration. Her large, round, clear eyes were full of curiosity, slightly clouded by a lingering trace of sadness. They talked for a moment and then as Lucy ran off, Sandi said, "She's going through a difficult time. A few months ago she contracted a virus which destroyed all hearing in one ear and left the other about eighty percent impaired."

"What are her chances for recovery?"

"Hardly any. It's fortunate that she's as old as she is. It helps tremendously when they can already talk. Isn't she a beautiful child?"

Sandi herself was beautiful with the bloom of the outdoors on her. She wore blue jeans and sneakers, a casual, poppy-colored shirt, her hair falling loose, with a childlike pleasure adding a cheerful rosiness to her cheeks. He'd never seen her more comfortable than she was in this environment. The love she had for these children was obvious and extraordinary. As she returned to the barn where the food was to be served, he walked down to the lake fed by a stream running over natural blue and raw sienna rocks. Beside the stream stood the largest shaggy bark hickory he'd ever seen, its alligator scales catching small, spear-shaped points of light and its canopy at least eighty feet across. A small island had been established in the lake, and on it stood a great blue heron, with its long neck stretched out watchfully. The streaming branches of weeping willow formed a little copse of rock and shade, and for a moment he assumed the heron's perspective, looking across at this human incursion with haughty indignation.

Finally a bell sounded and they collected their lunch of fried chicken, potato salad, lime gelatin salad, potato chips, drinks, and a small banana pudding dessert. They sat together under the swaying pines.

"Are you having any fun, Neal?"

"I'm enjoying it."

"I have to teach you to treasure every single day."

"That would be something."

"I can do it, though." She spoke as if she'd made up her mind.

The afternoon drew to a close and Sandi helped gather the pupils and herd them into the vans and buses. Neal returned to the lake to watch the sun go down. It fell slowly at first, then descended with breathtaking speed, backlighting the trees with an orange-crested glow. The pines stood motionless as if in reverence, scarcely a leaf stirred. The earth was settling in to rest. You could almost feel it closing down. He registered it as one of Sandi's moments to be treasured.

As they drove back to town, she asked, "Do you mind if we run by my parents'? I haven't seen them all week."

The first time Neal met Sandi's parents about a month ago she introduced them warmly. "This is my mother and father. My friend Neal Austin."

Mrs. Steele clapped her hands together. "I'm so glad to meet you."

Mr. Steele poked one stick-like arm up from where he sat in his lounge chair. "So you're the fella she's been talking about."

"I hope she's painted an acceptable picture."

"Maybe, maybe not. I'll say she's right picky."

"Don't be giving away my secrets, Daddy."

From their expressions and gestures Neal had tried to determine whether they were pleased that their daughter had brought home a presentable boyfriend or fearful he'd be the one to take her away. His reading was indecisive but of one thing he had no doubt — whatever was best for Sandi would receive their total love and support.

The Steeles lived in a modest, old-fashioned home with a porte-cochere, hardwood floors, and a porch swing, not much different from his house in St. Elmo. Sandi knocked loudly and called out as they entered through the unlocked front door. Mrs. Steele met them in the living room and clapped her hands together. "I'm so glad you came!"

They walked through the house and out onto the back porch, which had been enclosed to make a sitting room for Mr. Steele. Neal surmised that it was from her mother that Sandi had inherited her bright outlook, and from her father her square-facing practicality. In her plain gray dress, dark stockings, and her coil of gray hair, Mrs. Steele talked freely, yet with one ear tuned to her husband's testy remarks. Mr. Steele hid nothing he felt or thought. "There's not one thing on this television that's worth a damn except the news," he grumbled. He was nobody's fool. Neal liked him and found his observations amusing and to the point.

"Look what measly interest the bank gives, but you just try to borrow a dime from them."

"You need some light in here, Daddy," Sandi said. "That old floor lamp's on its last legs." She flipped on the overhead, then another lamp. "Now maybe you can see."

"I could already see," he grumbled. "What you're doing is blinding a man."

Mrs. Steele clapped her hands together. "It's so quiet and peaceful!"

Neal asked, "So how are you, Mr. Steele?"

"I'm not crippled yet." He pushed himself up in his lounge chair to light his pipe, which had a sweet, pleasant aroma. "They just want me to think I am."

"You run out of breath so quickly," said Sandi. "We have to be careful."

"That don't mean I'm going to keel over."

"Is there anything I can do for you?" Neal asked.

"You might give me a shave sometime."

"I can do that." Then just to devil him, he said, "I'll bring some polysporin and Band-Aids with me."

He followed Sandi and her mother back to the kitchen. "Everything's all right?" Sandi asked. "What do you need?"

"We're fine," said Mrs. Steele. "He has a good appetite and still goes out to tinker with his car sometimes."

"He isn't thinking about driving again?"

"Oh, no, I don't think we could allow that."

Sandi began opening cabinets and drawers, checking things out to see what they needed. Then she put her arms around her mother. "Do you want me to do some shopping for you? Or I can stay with Daddy while you go."

"Oh, no, he's fine for an hour or two. I just have to watch he doesn't try to do something he shouldn't."

"I know it's hard for him. He's always been so active."

"It's the emphysema," said Mrs. Steele. "Sometimes he can hardly walk to the table. But he still has to have his pipe."

"I'm afraid it's too late to take that away. But if it gives him a little pleasure, I wouldn't have the heart."

They said goodbye to the Steeles, and as they drove away, Sandi slipped her arm through his. "Thanks for coming, Neal. I have to keep an eye on them."

"You do a good job."

"You never know when something might happen, and I don't intend to have any regrets."

Her brown eyes were earnest and brave, and her expression bright. But what gave her a glow, he thought, was her deep sensitive nature coupled with an objective practicality which brought both feeling and a touch of mockery to her pretty mouth.

"Their lives are different now," she said, "but they still have so much to live for." After a moment she added, "You know what I think, Neal? Life is an attitude. We pretty much choose how we view it."

"Does that make it easier?"

"Yes, because the choice is up to us." She looked closely at him. "We can't always have everything arranged just so. Nothing ever turns out the way we plan."

"But that doesn't mean you don't plan."

"No, of course it doesn't. There are things I'd like to have — a family, a good education for my children. Every woman would. If I never have them, though, it doesn't mean I can't treasure life."

He started to say something, then changed his mind.

She leaned closer to him. "You have to work things out for yourself, Neal. You know I love you."

This was the second time she had spoken of love, and the words came to him so quietly and innocently it gave him a jolt. It also forced him to realize just how deeply and quickly she'd become part of his life.

Chapter Five

Tia said, "You need to get some help, Neal. You're working too hard."

"That would mean more overhead."

"You're driving nails into your coffin."

"Think what it would cost, though."

"Stop taking on so much work, then."

"Look at it this way. Work like mad now to have full sails later."

"What if the sails are too ripped apart to function?"

Tia had a point, Neal knew. She did everything she could to spare him pressure. Grumbling among the men she tried to deflect sternly. Disgruntled customers she brought to him only as a last resort. Loyal, stern and efficient, with thin features, penetrating eyes and a brisk air, she barked orders like a sergeant or clamped her mouth tightly. The men liked her, but if they committed the same sin twice they could expect scalding excoriation. Neal had come more and more to rely on Tia, but he realized there were limits to what she could do.

Also he felt his relationship with Sandi was becoming more turbulent. Between running NEA Couriers and starved for time at his typewriter he was tense and stressed one moment and energized by his time with her the next. He'd always found it difficult to divide his loyalties, throwing himself wholeheartedly into anything he took on. Even back in school, when he was playing ball, nothing raised his passion at the moment more than that one homer, that one touchdown. It was for this reason that he took on almost no civic or charitable duties. The rare times he came home from work and fell exhausted on the sofa he felt guilty for letting his typewriter sit idle for yet another hour. To Sandi he spoke little about his writing, feeling the pieces he'd published of minimal significance, and the rest pathetic failures. Sandi felt this wedge between them and called him on it.

"I guess most writers are isolated in a way," Neal defended himself. "The work is a solitary process. At least for me, it is."

"So is having a baby. That doesn't mean you can't derive joy by sharing it."

"In one respect the artist is trying to get his very soul onto paper or into the sculpture, in another he has to separate himself from himself."

She said with disgust, "I don't know what you're talking about, and I'm not sure you do either."

"All I'm saying is, I can't seem to divest myself of this creative urge."

"Don't, then. You can be loyal to more than one cause. Maybe it *is* a calling, but I don't think you have to struggle so hard."

Several times she said, "Neal, you've never let me read anything of yours. Why not? I feel left out."

"You don't understand."

"No, I don't. Is it really that *sacred?*"

He was skeptical about lending much weight to non-professional critics, but one evening as they sat in his den with a fire blazing he handed her a story. "You have to be honest and you have to be objective."

Her glance was faintly mocking. "That depends."

For half an hour she turned the pages as he silently paced the floor. When she finished, she didn't look up at once. At last she turned her eyes to him. "She should have married him, you know."

"But why?"

"It would have made all the difference. What he needed was a centering, a focal point in his life."

"Well, that would have been nice and snug," he said, "but his heart wouldn't have been in it."

"Who knows? Hearts change. The way you've written this, she loved him so much it was bound to have become a dynamic force."

"Or a destructive force."

"It seems to me he might have been a bit too self-centered."

"Self-centered! He's always offering a helping hand."

"But he thinks a lot about himself."

Now he wondered if she were connecting his character to *him*.

"How can you have so much insight yet be so blind!" she demanded.

"I don't know. Why don't you tell me?"

"Don't you see that you've written about yourself?"

"Well, that's just the problem with allowing people to read your material. They always see the author in it."

"I'm not people. I'm me. And whether you admit it or not, your own struggles show up here, and the only thing you miss is bringing it to a satisfying conclusion."

He said irritably, "It's not supposed to be satisfying. Life seldom is."

"Maybe you need to rethink your character's priorities."

He saw that her shoulders were set with determination, and the small indentation above her lip deepened. Then, evidently seeing his irritation and deciding not to push it too far, she said, "I understand about creative people, Neal. It becomes an obsession. It becomes addictive. So why don't you drop everything else and do it?"

"How creative can you be if you have to worry about money all the time?"

"There are many ways to be creative. If you're looking for sunshine and it rains, you say, 'Isn't it lucky that we're inside while it's raining?' And if you're dying for rain and the sun cooks down, you say, 'What a glorious day to be outside.' Sometimes when you adjust your thinking this way, you're startled to find things better than you expected — happy lightning."

"That sounds a little too simple," he said glumly.

"Maybe it is. But you can usually discover something to treasure if you look hard enough." She gazed at him with her clear brown eyes. "So often we think we're better suited for another life when the life we have is really the best one for us."

He took the story and hurried upstairs to put it away. Then he leaned against his desk waiting for the tension to subside. Sandi didn't understand, he thought. Who *could* understand? It wasn't enough just to escape into his loft to extract the deepest passions of his heart. His need to touch someone, to make a difference, was quite apart from Sandi or his love for her. Sometimes he spent hours on a single page. Reducing ideas and emotions to the written word was often joyful and excruciating. He wondered if his vision was beyond his capabilities of expression, and if what he had to say really mattered to anyone. He felt that if he could just get one thing right, just make one worthwhile contribution . . .

He went back downstairs. Sandi was sitting on the floor, leaning against a chair and strumming her guitar. He stood in the doorway listening. Her voice was clear and sweet and quite unexpectedly a startling warmth flooded over him. He rushed across the room, fell down beside her, and took her into his arms. He buried his face against her neck and as the chair slid away they tumbled down, laughing. All the time he kept kissing her neck and mouth, her hands moved up and down his back and their legs linked together. He reached for the buttons on her blouse. Tenderly she shoved his hand away. "I can't tonight, Neal." He felt a moment of brutal letdown and then they sat up straight. "It's the wrong time," she whispered. He put his arms around her and waited for his heart to stop pounding. She took long deep breaths then rested her head on his shoulder.

"Neal," she said quietly, "do you see yourself ever getting married? Do you want children?"

"Yes, of course."

"You'd be such a good father."

"Children change everything."

"Maybe they do. But sometimes we discover the things we thought most important aren't so significant after all."

He knew Sandi wanted to get married and have children, and he wondered if he were being absolutely honest with her. Part of himself seemed to live apart from her and his love for her in anticipation of accomplishing some lasting legacy that could justify the years he'd poured into it. He supposed he might live one day with tender love and passion, and the next as a prisoner of the demands of business and his relentless desire to experience a creative life, but he doubted that anyone could live like this very long without giving up something, and perhaps a great deal.

Two days later he was no less solemn and uncertain when Tia walked into his office with a registered letter. "This doesn't look like good news."

It was from a law firm in the Northeast advising him that one of their largest clients had filed for bankruptcy. Neal read the letter over three times, then tense with disgust asked Tia to bring him a printout. Sitting at his desk he calculated that their losses would pretty much wipe out most of the past year's profits. There was a python grip on his stomach. What a wasted year! Month by month he'd managed to bring in new clients, generating more income but also heaping more work upon himself. All that effort, all that precious time squandered! God only knew how that year might have been translated into some literary achievement.

He took the letter to his lawyer Bruce Irwin, then waited three days to receive the news. "It happens all the time, Neal. Corporate bigwigs make themselves fat, cook the books, then bail out. Most of them have left the company."

"Any chance of getting anything at all?"

"Maybe a few cents on the dollar. The banks have seized all assets."

Neal said morosely, "I guess I'm just too gullible to have seen something like this coming. What drives men to steal and sacrifice innocent victims?"

"Pure, unadulterated greed," said Irwin. "I wouldn't blame myself too much if I were you. Erring on the side of trust is still better than a life of suspicion and distrust."

Neal kept the news of this setback to himself. He and Sandi went out to dinner Friday night and he tried to sustain a cheerful front, but he knew his voice sounded glum. After dinner they returned to Sandi's apartment and as they sat down together she said, "I want to know what's bothering you, Neal."

"How do you know something's bothering me?"

"How do I know. Because I'm sensitive to all your moods."

Finally he told her about his losses, and the year down the drain.

She listened sympathetically, then said, "I'm so sorry, Neal. What a disappointment! You're so honest it's hard for you not to trust everyone."

"It'll take a while to recover from this."

"Which I suppose means you'll have to work harder than ever, but even with this setback, you're doing all right, aren't you?"

"I suppose so."

"I admire your determination, but remember, just because you haven't reached one goal doesn't mean you're a failure in other areas. You touch many lives and should be happy with that."

"I don't know how many lives I've touched, really."

"Your mother and father. Your sister. And you've certainly touched mine. But I don't intend to play second fiddle forever."

"But you don't," he said.

"I do in a way." She fixed him with a long steady gaze. "I won't keep on though, Neal. What happens to us now is up to you."

Neal shifted his feet uneasily. This was an ultimatum, he realized, there could be no doubt. His hundred-hour work weeks and his writing took so much out of him he couldn't see how he could invest much energy in anything else, especially the commitment and responsibilities of marriage. And he knew Sandi deserved no less than the best.

"I would never force you into anything," she said. "But a girl would be just crazy to wait forever. By now I think you should know enough about me to make a decision."

Their goodnight kiss wasn't so lingering as she drew away and whispered, ever so formally, "Thank you for this evening."

It was as if softly but firmly she was returning their relationship to those nights when they first met and hinting at the beginning of her withdrawal.

Chapter Six

Neal woke disconsolate and confused. He'd never been in love, not even in high school and college, when everybody was supposed to have a best girl and even a promise of future marriage. His love for Sandi was solid, he knew, but before he could devote much of his life to the art, the complications, the conflicts, and comforts and domestications of marriage he felt he must get his business on an even keel, he must stop delaying and complete at least one worthwhile novel, he must figure out where he was going with his life and what kind of future he could make with a beautiful wife, and how much money they'd have.

Sometimes when Sandi kissed him goodnight now, her lips lingered and she held him tightly, her head on his shoulder as though he were about to be shipped off to war. Sometimes she offered him no more than a brush of her lips on his cheek as she turned away, as if their imminent parting were too sad to contemplate. He'd never put into words precisely his love for her. He knew when he did she would say, "If you love me, what are you afraid of?" He knew she knew he loved her, but she had reservations, too. Until she was convinced he could make her the most important thing in his life she was too square-dealing and realistic to think time alone would change anything. When he imagined another man taking her into his arms he became furiously jealous, but he was determined not to give her less than she deserved and was resolved to have, and he knew, too, he would never cease to be sorry if he let her go.

He blinked himself awake, got out of bed and dressed. He dressed fully, even down to shoes and socks, before walking into the kitchen to make himself a cup of coffee. Cup, coffee and spoon were always laid out the night before, and within thirty seconds he was able to pour a cup into the heavy mug his sister had given him one Christmas when she was taking some kind of arts course in college.

He stepped through the floor-to-ceiling windows into his sunroom, where along with a jungle of ferns and plants he kept a simple upholstered chair and a small side table. It was still early. Daylight was just beginning to tinge the east, and in this almost totally glassed room first light appeared, glinting on the edge of pots, printing a bright wedge on the tile floor and warming the prickly leaves of cactuses. His pebble-dashed stucco was just two or three blocks from the great white mansion St. Elmo, alter ego of the famous romance, a monstrous mausoleum, he imagined, to heat and paint, and whose expansive grounds had through the decades been subdivided into oak-sentineled streets with neat brick and wood and stucco houses, with detached novelty siding garages. Outside the sunroom and across the backyard was a tangle of unkempt shrubbery, a tumbled-down brick dividing wall and an upper rear yard where there had once been a fish pond, which now was dried up and cracked, attractive only to lizards and toads and undesirable vines. From time to time his aunt, who owned the property, sent over a man to swing blade and weed-eat the backyard, with the agreement that Neal was to keep up the front and close rear yard where there was grass and azaleas and trimmed walkways.

Sipping his coffee, he wondered if Sandi understood that there were corners in every person's life which were never meant to be turned, depths which were best left unexposed. He assumed she rightfully protected her own chambers which no one ever entered, and would never press him for more than he was willing to give, while concurrently hide as little as possible of her life from him if she had anything to hide.

As the sun rose, shadows began to emerge outside the sunroom, pale and dense. Something about the house, the gable or chimney and weathervane perhaps, made shapes across the backyard like a cathedral. The shadows were violet and indigo. He was reminded suddenly of some of those childhood Sunday School teachers he'd earnestly followed as a child, who spoke of faith and prayer in passionate conviction, when everyone knew that the only thing that separated them from an intoxicated night before was a quick shower and a smart blue blazer. He wondered if he were too self-centered, if Sandi meant it when she said his character thought too much of himself.

He drank slow, small sips from his mug, half expecting the phone to ring summoning him to some conflict or mishap. A day that passed without unexpected complications, most of them costly, was a rare pleasure. His couriers — not only Nate and Willie and Brent, but the more recent ones, almost all of whom were older than he — came to him with just about all their problems, from money to domestic quarrels to conflicts with workers. Even Tia, tightlipped and businesslike as she was, shared with him her increasing alienation from her teenaged daughter and appealed to him for advice. He never speculated about why so many people chose to share their troubles with him, what it was about him that encouraged them to ask for his wisdom and his sympathy, when half the time he felt he himself needed a shoulder to lean on. From the time he'd begun to write, people became his medium, his instructors, his pupils, his concern. If he knew them they were his responsibility, his outlet for vicarious emotional discharge. Perhaps in an inexplicable way the deflection of other people's upheavals was enough to keep his own conflicted life subdued, and his embedded passion for love postponed, and they drew from this reservoir of emotion.

The phone remained silent, neither his mother nor father nor Lori, all of whom he'd never ceased to tend and protect, and who always needed things like a new freezer or a good second car or money for a root canal, called, so he stepped back through the window into the house, made breakfast, ate alone, then shaved and went to work.

Under this cloud of uncertainty Neal thought he must do something, even if it were something desperate, and after much deliberation he decided to go up to New York to see his literary agent Sam Harris. From time to time he spoke to Sam on the phone and they communicated by letter, but in all these years they'd never met face to face. He hoped that a meeting might work magic in their relationship and on Sam's success in marketing his work. Foolish though this idea might be it propped him up a little to think about it. He could now afford a trip to New York, with which a few years ago he would never have indulged himself, and he felt something might happen which at the least would enlighten him about how he was to continue and if he should continue. He arranged his plane ticket and hotel with more apprehension than excitement.

Sandi was encouraging. "I think you should do this, Neal. Maybe it'll settle something in your mind. You can see the sights, maybe catch a play."

"My plan is to stay one night then fly back. This is purely a business trip."

Sandi smiled and nodded agreeably but she was subdued. He wondered if this were because she could imagine that this trip might bring about a change in his life which could adversely affect their relationship.

"Will you call me tonight? Or will you be too preoccupied?" She spoke with palpable irony.

"When have I not called you at night?"

She started to say something but changed her mind.

"I'll call," said Neal. "Let's just hope some little good will come of this."

He drove to Atlanta tense with anticipation and caught an early flight to New York. He'd always believed his debut in this magical city would be to celebrate his acclaimed novel that would be featured in the windows of Doubleday and other Fifth Avenue bookselling giants, but instead as they made their final approach he looked down on the skyscrapers with the conflicting emotions he imagined a foreigner must experience when descending upon an alien country. They taxied up to the terminal over what seemed miles across highways and around many turns, he retrieved his one overnight bag from the overhead compartment, then out on the street caught one of the thousands of yellow cabs and gave the driver the address.

They drove into Manhattan and straight to Sam's office on Fifth Avenue. After the open spaces back home, the monoliths of buildings standing shoulder to shoulder felt to him choked and compressed, as though at any moment they might implode from within. Simultaneously, the little murmur of excitement became stronger as he sensed a heartbeat, the pulsating throb of a city where everything human intelligence could imagine or invent underwent conception, pregnancy, tumescence and birth, not just occasionally but over and over again.

He exited the cab and negotiated his way beneath a half-opal canopy which had seen its best day. The glass door was opened by an utterly superfluous doorman dressed in an ashcan burgundy coat, and he passed into the dank and faintly sour smelling hall of a multistory Fifth Avenue office building. Inside the scruffy hall were a few potted ferns, a fading burgundy carpet of a design which suggested the fetus of an unborn octopus, and people. Instinctively from his southern breeding, he nodded and spoke, but registering quickly how incongruous such conduct was he clamped his mouth shut, lest someone scream and run as though assaulted. Despite his sense of alienation he found something magnetic about this old-world, magnificently expensive atmosphere and assured himself how quickly he could become absorbed by it. He took a rickety elevator to the fourth floor, walked down a dim and faintly musty hall and entered through an opaque glass door into a cramped, cluttered office filled with stacks of books and manuscripts. He was surprised and slightly reassured. No one would ever imagine that the quarters of a highly successful literary agent could evoke so little drama and glory. His own office at NEA Couriers was much larger and well-appointed. Unlike so many of his colleagues in the nineteen eighties and nineties, Sam had a soft spot for the struggling writer, even if it meant little or no commissions, and Neal felt fortunate to have landed him.

As soon as he pushed the door open Sam jumped up from a rickety desk chair and offered his hand.

"Neal, hello. It's good to meet you at last." He was a slight man with sparse, graying hair, deep-socketed eyes, and a straight, hawk-like nose. He wore a white shirt with a faintly iron-burned collar and no tie. His gestures suggested an energetic robustness, implying that he never had a minute to spare. He swept books and papers off an old straight-back chair and motioned for Neal to sit down. This cramped little office was big enough for no more than a desk, two chairs, an upright pigeonhole bookcase, and one dingy window looking out on Fifth Avenue — not even half as large as Tia's office back home. It was amazing to Neal that from such squalid environs literary successes emanated, and probably small fortunes as well.

"Have a seat, Neal. Pardon the clutter."

"Looks like you have a lot going on."

"We try. How're things going? Your business doing well?"

"Very well. It takes a lot of hours out of the day."

They exchanged a few banalities — the flight up, how long he'd be in New York, all the while Neal hearing a phone in another room ringing, answered by a machine. He had schemed to spend as much time as possible with Sam Harris, without distraction or interference, and this pealing phone began to grate on his nerves. "Can I take you to lunch?" he said. "You name the place. This is my first visit to New York."

Sam shook his head no. "Not today, Neal. Sorry." Having declined lunch, he in no other way indicated that he was too busy to talk. Neal noticed, though, that Sam was monitoring every call with a small caller I.D. instrument on his cluttered desk. "Tell me about your novel," Sam said. "Started it yet?"

Faintly rebuffed, Neal tried to muster enthusiasm. "I think I have a pretty good working outline."

"Many novelists never use outlines, you know."

"I know."

"What's your story about?"

"Two brothers who were very close, became estranged, and finally just before one's death found healing."

"Okay." Sam declined to speculate. "Got a title?"

"*Samson's Revenge*." Neal shifted his feet. "It's hard to start a long work when you have no idea if it'll be accepted."

"All I can advise you," Sam said, "is to believe in what you're doing and stay with it." He paused. "I sold a story by a new writer to *The New Yorker* recently. She was thrilled to death."

Neal fought a spasm of envy.

"I tell you this only to assure you that it does happen sometimes. You just have to keep trying."

The visit lasted all of twenty minutes and produced none of the results Neal had hoped for. He wondered why he'd flown all the way to New York just for this disappointing letdown. All around the office were stacks of books, author's and agent's copies, and despite his efforts he could scarcely resist the envy pressing on him. He was only thirty, but he'd been writing and working so long he felt older — he felt as he imagined young men must feel who went off to war just past school age and returned two or three years later with the shoulders of old men. He realized he was depriving his agent of precious time. Still, Sam slouched in his straight chair as though the success and fortune of those who had arrived and paid him large commissions could wait.

Summoning up an element of self-assurance — after all, he was a successful businessman back home — Neal squared his shoulders, then stood. "I just wanted to meet you and ask with what you know about my writing so far, if you think it makes sense to try a novel."

"Send me a few chapters and we'll see." Sam looked as if he really wished he could offer something more encouraging. "These are very difficult times for the serious writer, Neal. You'd have a better chance with some of the formula fiction. But I know that's not what you want to do." He held out his hand. "You write very well. Don't lose heart."

Neal left the agent's office dragging his feet. So much for his grand splash in New York. He wondered if he'd ever write anything notable. In the past five years, he felt the only thing that had happened to him of real value was Sandi Steele.

He had scheduled his return flight for the following morning. His plan was to spend the afternoon visiting some gardens, Chinatown perhaps, or the Metropolitan Museum. Now he didn't feel up to any of these. He had never ridden a subway so from Sam's office, still carrying his overnight bag, he mustered the courage to catch the closest train and then take a return subway back to the Waldorf Hotel, where he had reserved a room. The rest of the day he spent walking through Central Park, which was the best thing he'd seen so far in Manhattan. After a solitary early dinner in one of the hotel restaurants, he returned to his room.

Looking out the window, where the busy street was now half-deserted, he thought just what a vibrant city New York was — an art, music and theatre capital, thriving, vibrant, ingenious, disingenuous, erudite, depraved, romantic, magical. He thought by now he would have long since conquered this fiefdom; instead, he felt estranged and isolated. He pulled out a sheet of Waldorf stationery, and wrote down the impressions which for the moment did not encourage him to return:

He was a man who had stood in the center of a city packed with people, in blistering monoxide-poisoned breathless New York, and felt it to be the loneliest place in the world. He'd ridden the subway, traveling through black caverns inhabited by cave dwellers whose faces were equally impenetrable, as bright blurbs of light, skeletal framing, slim black wires, more faces, oncoming subways howled by; and directly overhead, in polluted sunlight, an upper canyon between mountainous buildings peopled by theatrical performers, half-dressed boys painted with impressive originality, heavy-lidded and wigged girls, eyes that held metaphysical statements: one cave symbolic of the other, both furtive, alien, hurried, impacted, beautiful. He had been in the city of romance, heavy and blue in the dusk, almost Mediterranean, dined alone, retired early, and fled as quickly as possible . . .

It was too dramatic and ornate, but the sense of loneliness was real. Then it occurred to him what a profound difference it would have made had Sandi shared it all with him. And what a huge difference, too, if those stores with books in the windows included his own titles. And now he was thinking all about himself again. Was it possible that a man might give up much of his youth, strive to support his parents and sibling, keep the welfare of others close at hand, yet remain self-centered? He wondered if his ambition to write a book that would touch others was just an excuse for an esoteric desire for a glamorous life. Sleepless, he felt indeed like a fish out of water — the water of his own skewed impressions of life.

In the morning he skipped breakfast and caught a cab to the airport. At LaGuardia, his flight was delayed, and he drifted aimlessly through the terminal. When his flight was finally called he flew to Atlanta, then drove an unimpressive hour and a half home, physical and emotional fatigue heavy on his shoulders. He telephoned Sandi at The Learning Room, perked up a little by her bright voice, and though there were still a few hours left that he could go to the office he decided to stay home, think, reevaluate, take apart and put back together this adjunct forage which he hoped did not spell an omen for things to come. Eventually, he collapsed into bed, then in the morning he ate a solitary breakfast and drove to work.

Neal expected that he would pay for his absence from the business with doubled demands and he was not disappointed. He'd been away only two days, yet the workload awaiting him seemed like four. Sandi was tied up in some performance and awards activity for a couple of evenings at The Learning Room and hungry as he was to see her, he had to settle for quiet talks on the phone. He sat down at his typewriter but couldn't compose a word. It occurred to him that between running a company and pursuing his literary ambitions, his energy was all used up in some vision, but not in living. And this was so different from Sandi, who was so alive in the moment, who so much believed in living for small pleasures and making the best of circumstances, in believing that where you are is where you are meant to be.

Neal thought about this. To Sandi every person, every experience was a gift, and she made a conscious effort to see everything to be just as it was supposed to be. How he'd become a part of her life, he could hardly imagine. It occurred to him that his desire to do something noteworthy, to be loved, to leave a legacy might be ill-advised when compared to day-to-day life, with its ups and downs, its disappointments and joys, and taking hold of life as it had been dealt him. He knew at least this is what Sandi believed. But his writing and what he meant to contribute through it had always held a separate place, apart from the other life he led or wanted to lead. Sandi saw through this too, and it humbled him to know she loved him in a way more lasting than any creative vision he contrived for himself.

He also knew that she wouldn't keep waiting. All through two lonely nights and days he kept thinking of her, of the way she tilted her head to look up at him through her dark lashes, of the tiny dimple that appeared in her left cheek with certain smiles, of the turn of her hips when he fell behind as they jogged together. It was easier to think of her sweet, heartfelt voice when she played the guitar and sang in a way that always calmed him and sent erotic signals through him — it was easier to think of this than of the less real dreams that might never come true. But he knew that to have this he must make changes that terrified him.

On Tuesday they finally went to dinner, and afterward took a walk in Weracoba Park. "Tell me about New York," Sandi said. "Anything."

"I was all choked up with jealousy and envy."

"Don't be so self-effacing. You write what you write. Even if the world never notices, you have to be yourself."

"Still, it's not a contribution if no one notices."

"Selling books doesn't necessarily mean the world will love you, Neal. Besides, would you quit if you realized you were never going to break through?"

"Probably not."

"You wouldn't, because you can't. What you can do, though, is try to lead a more balanced life. I don't think all the wealth and fame in the world settles those things our hearts really seek."

They walked out onto the bridge where water swept through the grass like flowing green moss. He put his hands on the rail and looked down on the tiny fish, slivers of silver.

"Plenty of people teach school," he said, "manage insurance agencies, drive trucks, have a family and still write. Why for me it's always seemed like two separate worlds I can't explain."

"That's something you'll have to figure out."

"Y' think you could help me?"

"I don't know, Neal. That's something you'll have to figure out, too."

Beneath them the school of silver fish suspended themselves perfectly still in the rushing current.

Gravely he said, "I never believed love and marriage could be divided. It wouldn't be enough."

He felt a faint tremor pass through her body.

"But I know we can't go on like this. I don't want to, and I know you don't intend to."

She remained silent.

"I mean, knowing all my shortcomings I wonder if you're willing to marry me."

There was another tremor, then resolutely she said, "I would never marry a man who asked me in confusion or desperation or out of fear of losing me."

"I am afraid of losing you. I'm more afraid of that than of anything else."

"I would never marry a man who couldn't love me wholeheartedly."

"You can't imagine how much I love you."

"Oh, I can. Sometimes I wonder if you know. Or at least if you're prepared to release yourself to it. Totally."

"I'm not getting this right, am I?"

"No. But you do know how."

"Yeah." He stood straight and took her hands into his. "Sandi, will you marry me? Now. Soon?"

"Do you promise to love me more than anything else? Anything but God?"

"Yes, I promise that." Her eyes were so beautiful he thought he could die in them.

She answered as soberly. "Then, yes, Neal, I will marry you."

She squealed and threw her arms around him. A jogger crossing the bridge jumped, then ran on, leaving them in the wake of his laughter.

Chapter Seven

Neal's shabby old stucco in St. Elmo was too primitive for a bride, and neither of them wanted to live in an apartment, so they delayed setting a date until they could find a house. New developments were divided into lots about the size of a postage stamp, and older houses were in such demand only the most dilapidated failed to be snapped up within days. Finally they heard about a promising place that had just come on the market in Peacock Woods. The original founders of Columbus, Georgia, had laid out the settlement in near perfect grids, avenues running north and south, streets east and west. As the town expanded east from the Chattahoochee River a network of veins and arteries crossed aberrantly, sometimes in confused non-patterns of greater imagination. Peacock Woods was one of those early old-fashioned neighborhoods of lanes and ways with sweeping curves and steep hills whose character was distinguished by stone chimneys and twisting ascending driveways. They hurried over and found a brick and stone one-story with a spacious yard, great oaks and maples, an octagon-shaped gazebo, and mounds of shrubs and hedges all about.

Sandi was excited. "I love it. Can we afford anything like this?"

"We'll see. It'll take some fixing up."

"We'll do it together. It'll be fun."

He made the deal and within a week or two carpenters and millworkers, glaziers and roofers and tile setters were busy at work. Somehow Neal managed to get by nearly every day to check on their progress. He found Sandi in jeans and loose shirt, sun visor and sneakers, her tongue caught between her teeth and her jaw firm with determination, pitching in to help scrape and refinish cabinets, then going out to select new hardware, wallpaper, and paint. On Saturdays, she arrived early and spent the day with the men in the yard, reconfiguring flowerbeds and pruning and planting new ones. Neal was amazed at her talents and her enthusiasm. She usually approved of what the workmen did, but if one of them got sloppy with his brush or saw, she demanded correction without compromise.

Neal happened to walk in one day when she was in an argument with carpenters and cabinet makers over her plans for tearing out part of a wall and creating an octagon-shaped bay window for a breakfast nook. This would look out over their back garden but the effect would be obscured by the L-shape of a perpendicular outside wall.

"But, Miss Steele," said one of the men, "isn't this going to look weird?"

"It'll look fine. It'd be a shame not to take advantage of the view."

"Besides, we can't figure out how to frame it without an interior gutter. And these are notorious for leaks."

"I have no doubt you can work it out," she said firmly.

The man looked at Neal in appeal.

"Sandi," he said, "I think he may be right. Maybe we could establish a breakfast area on one end of the kitchen. It's large enough."

She planted her fists on her hips and looked not at him but at the men who first stood firmly then began to shuffle their feet. "I want this right or not at all. I know you can do it. Would you like me to draw it for you?"

She got her way and after it was done carpenters and cabinet makers grudgingly admitted it worked out pretty well. Once Sandi made up her mind to a thing argument was almost always futile. To Neal this was both a source of endearment and of perplexity.

Neal reckoned this to be about the best time in his life so far — at least the happiest since his childhood on his grandmother's farm. The failures of his personnel were less momentous and the troubles they brought to his shoulders less pathetic. He was excited not to just hurry through one part of his life to get to another. Stabs of uncertainty barbed him at unexpected moments, but Sandi buoyed him up on her wings. All brightness and music, she never complained when she had a headache or menstrual cramps.

What he liked most about the new house was the large wooded lot, the separate garage connected by a lattice brick wall, and the privacy provided by shrubs and ornamentals planted decades ago. At night after their day's work was done, he could walk out under the moon or sprawl on a deck chair and listen to the night sounds as if civilization were a long way away.

When all the renovations and decorating were completed at last, they had a private celebration, by candlelight, on their sun porch. Sandi hung flowering plants, there was the new view of the yard, and on their round rattan sunroom table she placed a yellow print tablecloth and a bowl of floating blooms. She looked exotic and beautiful. "To us," she said, lifting her glass, "for a long and happy life. And to the world and all its people. And to our children."

"Children? We're not yet married and already we have children?"

"Oh, yes. Three."

"Of what species?"

"Oh, I think maybe two girls and a boy."

"Then I suppose we should set a date."

"Yes! But I need a little time to get my trousseau together."

A Saturday date was chosen and the wedding took place in a small chapel, with only a few guests. Their parents and siblings, Neal's friends Pat Palmer and Rob Fuller and their wives, friends from Sandi's school, and Tia McCormick and her husband and some of his couriers made up the wedding party. Like Lori, Sandi insisted she didn't want an elaborate ceremony. She wore a lavender dress, a white corsage, the pearls he'd given her for Christmas, and a heartbreaking smile.

Mr. Steele struggled into the little chapel, then stood aside talking with Neal's father before the wedding began.

Lori came over to Neal. "I'm so glad you're marrying Sandi, Neal. It's what I've always wanted for you."

The ceremony was brief and simple — a little mingling before, a little afterward, a toast, handshaking and hugs, and the traditional vows which Sandi believed could not be improved on. Exiting under a shower of birdseed, they ran out to the car, drove to Atlanta and flew to San Juan for their honeymoon. They held hands and talked all through the flight. At the airport they collected their bags and took a car to the Princess Hotel. As they turned off a relatively unscenic highway onto the grounds Sandi caught her breath. The entrance was double-laned with a medium pulsating in flowering shrubs, trees and grass. The front of the hotel sprouted plump and opulent at the end of three hundred yards, and the scents of flowers and sea air greeted them. A rainbow of sprinkler spray was caught by the afternoon sun, hovering over hedges like rubies and sapphires. "Look at this!" Sandi exclaimed. "The royal palms and hibiscus. A castle for the newlyweds!"

The doors of the fat hotel lobby were thrown open and through them they could see extended landscapes of palms, shrubs, winding walkways, pools, multicolored umbrellas, thatch-topped cabanas. Massive beams drew pastel dust up from the tiled lobby and tall vertical cages inhabited by brightly plumed parrots, parakeets, and macaws were interwoven with green vines. Calypso music came from behind the broad-leafed palms. Deeper scents of the sea and flowers emanated from large hanging pots and floor urns.

The striking beauty was marred when they walked up to reception to check in. The man behind the desk who turned to assist them was tall with wiry hair, sculptured features and a smear of mustache smartly clipped. "Oh, yes," he said, "the Austins. Welcome to the Princess." He shifted his gaze to Sandi and Neal registered the double-take. The four-hour flight had not diminished her radiance. "My name is Harley. We have a very nice garden room for you."

Neal's ears perked up. "Garden?"

"Yes. A beautiful view of our gardens and walk paths."

"I reserved a balcony ocean view."

The man frowned. "Well, let's see. No, I'm afraid we have no ocean views available."

Swift anger flushed through Neal. It was as if a cold bath had dropped down upon the setting. "I beg your pardon. These reservations were made months ago. We were told the honeymoon suite would be under renovations and were given one of your best ocean view rooms."

"But, Mr. Austin," said Harley. "I'm afraid the hotel is full."

"I don't give a damn about your overbooking. This is our honeymoon and if we don't get the accommodations I paid for I assure you it'll cost you a hell of a lot more than the price of a room."

Harley looked down, looked up, looked away. His mustache twitched. "Just a moment, please," he said.

He left the desk, went through a door and closed it behind him.

"Neal," said Sandi, "I'm sure a garden room would be lovely."

"Absolutely not. I talked to the reservation desk myself. It was quite clear to everyone we wanted the best room in the hotel."

In five minutes Harley returned. His frown had been wiped away and he smiled broadly. "I apologize, Mr. Austin. There was a mistake. We do have a lovely oceanfront balcony for you. One moment and I'll have your keys."

They stood silently waiting. In moments he handed them the keys in an envelope including some hotel promotions. "The room is ready. You're welcome to go on up and your luggage will follow in a few minutes."

"Thank you," smiled Sandi.

"My pleasure. I hope you enjoy your visit."

They walked across the lobby to the elevator. No other passengers entered the car and as soon as the door closed she put her arms around him. "You know, don't you, that I'd be happy with you anywhere. The basement even."

"It's a matter of principle."

"But not enough to upset you."

He smiled at last. "But you're the one who won't take no for an answer."

"In certain cases, yes," she said.

They found their room and went in. On the bed tables were pale pink orchids in trumpet-shaped vases, with bowls of fruit in the breeze of scented fans. The French doors were open and they walked out onto the balcony just as the sun slipped into the sea.

"This is really all right?" he said.

She came close and put her arms around him. "It's beautiful! The waterfalls, and the coconut palms — it's just enchanting."

She went in to shower and dress and Neal sat on the balcony trying to think as little as he could. She emerged wearing a sleek, flowery garment showing her legs. With pure, helpless lust he reached for her, but with a smile she eluded him. "Wait, my love, the moment will come."

They went down to an extravagant buffet dinner on an open-air terrace illuminated by tree lights and bathed by Calypso music. The servers wore brightly printed shirts emblazoned with flowers and moons and dancing maidens. Late swimmers in bathing suits ran up the winding paths, towels wrapped around their shoulders, and disappeared into the lobby.

Across the table Sandi took his hand. "Did you see the orchids growing right on the trees over there? Awesome!"

After dinner they walked down to observe the crab races on one of the lower terraces. As the guests circled about, cheering and making bets, the boys in charge, using long sticks, encouraged the crabs to scurry toward the finish line, making a big show of it.

"Go, one!"

"Naw, one's nothing! Do it, two! Do it!"

"Naw, naw, seven's my man. Run tall, seven, run tall!"

"What do you think, Neal? Should we bet?"

"Why not? Here."

"Oh, no, I'll gamble my own dollars."

After betting and losing a couple of dollars Neal slipped his arm around Sandi's waist. "You about ready to go?"

"Indeed I am."

They drifted through the lobby and took the elevator up. Their balcony opened onto a large silver moon, and from the beach drifted the sounds of the band's homemade rattles, drums, and kettles. "You go first," Sandi said, "then I'll get ready."

He showered and shaved, then sat on the bed as he waited for Sandi. She emerged from the bath in a pale blue gossamer gown, bringing with her the exotic scent of some tantalizing perfume. She came straight into his arms and they fell back onto the bed. With tender pleasure he slipped the gown off and as she responded with shameless passion, there was a cataclysmic crescendo, a tightened intensity, an uttered cry, and their wedding night was consummated. Breathless, Sandi said, "I love you."

"I love you too."

This first evening set the tempo of the week. They sat on their balcony looking out over the towns and cities of coral reefs, and ate shameful breakfasts of cheese eggs, sausages and fried bananas, pineapples and sweet rolls. On the beach Neal could hardly keep his eyes off her. She carried her chin high, her shoulders erect, and moved in sweeps and swirls like a plumaged bird. He was excited by her walk, too — this consciousness of her figure or of the sexuality he aroused in her, which must be the source of some heightened stimulation. For now the world was far away, his business and writing were far away. They lay in the sand, claiming their space among the towels and beach chairs and tilted umbrellas.

As Neal half-dozed Sandi ventured out into the surf, then ran back and fell beside him. "Is that water cold!"

"How can it be cold with the sun blazing like this?"

"You just try it."

She tugged him up and as they walked out together he saw why so few guests left their padded chairs. The water was icy. After the first shock, with great bravado they willed themselves into a running attack, fell headlong, splashed, went under and came up together, her legs locked round his waist. They played until the water became too cold and they retreated to the beach where under the blistering sun they dried quickly.

"Is this the way to live," said Sandi.

"I'm afraid I could get used to it."

"But then what would you ever do that's special?"

"I don't know. Maybe follow the seventies crowd. You know who the seventies are?"

"I don't," she said.

"The fabulously wealthy who live in houses only where the temperature is around seventy."

"Well, that would be some lifestyle. But I like things just the way they are."

After a couple of days they began to make forays into town. At the straw market, Sandi bartered for things she didn't need, because dark women with flashing eyes appealed to her. "Me lady, me lady, just twenty dollar. Fifteen. Give me twelve." She haggled, enjoying the game, then when they reduced the price, paid the original amount. She purchased baskets, wood carvings, T-shirts, and coral jewelry, and a whole assortment of trinkets for her students. In the stores on Bay Street, she bought perfume and gifts for their parents, and he bought a black coral bracelet which he fastened on her wrist with a kiss.

They took a cab over to the old fort, where they first joined a tour then drifted around on their own. Life in the barracks must have been tough, Neal thought — stifling hot, putrid, and the officers' quarters not much better. It was interesting, though, how the engineers had designed the emplacements, the strategic pivots for riflemen and gunneries. They climbed the worn stone stairways to the highest level of the fort where the cannon positions in the thick walls allowed only enough room for the barrels to turn and raise and lower their elevations.

"Look at this, Sandi," said Neal. "How do you suppose they could hit a little ship way out there with an iron ball? Probably it was more luck than skill."

Thinking of all the men and women who had died in so many wars on so many continents so that his generation and the ones before and after could enjoy the freedom to walk these streets and the opportunity to indulge themselves like this, Neal felt his throat tighten.

Sandi slipped her arm around his. "These things touch you, don't they, Neal?"

"It's silly, I guess."

"No, it's not. I'm glad." She looked into his eyes with dead soberness. "This has been the happiest week of my life."

At the end of the honeymoon they flew home, and when they drove up into their garage, she exclaimed, "My house! My dream! I love it!"

They brought their bags through the latticed walkway and set them down on the lower patio. He unlocked the door, swept her up and carried her across the threshold the old-fashioned way. Day by day they talked and made love gratefully and greedily, and with experience and familiarity began to shape their lives together.

Chapter Eight

Following the honeymoon they spent a couple of days getting used to the house. They moved things around, set up his home office, cleaned the floor and benches of the gazebo. Then one morning Sandi woke, stretched and said, "Ah, glorious day. I have to go to work."

"Work? What's work?"

"I know my children miss me." She pressed her body against his, kissed his cheek and nestled her face against his arm. "Now that you're a married man, what are your plans?"

"My plans. To grow the business, retire at an early age and write something worthwhile."

Neal had declined positions on various political bodies but finally accepted a seat on the planning advisory board, and another on a non-profit youth council.

Sandi always concluded her day with an air of excitement. She spared him little in detail, and even the events he would have found irritating she took into stride.

"Is every moment precious to you?" he asked.

"Oh, yes. Everything that happens is an opportunity for growth." To him this was both endearing and perplexing. How could any sane person maintain an optimistic attitude all the time? She went off to school in the morning and in the afternoon sustained a busy and energetic schedule. Two or three times a week she reported to him, "I went shopping for Mama and Daddy today. They needed a few things." Or, "You remember one of our teachers Betty Fieser? She's moving into a new house and I know how hard it is. I spent a couple of hours this afternoon helping her." Or, "Guess what! I took flowers to one of Mama's friends in the nursing home. That sweet lady was dear to me all through my childhood."

Almost every time they were in the car together she said, "You drive too fast, Neal. Slow down. I don't mean just in the car." But behind the wheel she herself had the tendency to wait until the last minute to brake, as though she almost forgot every time.

All through the day they telephoned one another. "Will it be okay if I'm a little late? Reggie's having trouble with his reading and I'd like to stay and tutor him."

"Of course," said Neal. "It'll give me a chance to catch up on some things."

One of her coworkers told him, "It doesn't matter if a child is in Sandi's class or not. She's concerned about all the children."

Neal found this to be true when Sandi said one morning, "There's a little girl in Julia's class I want to take shopping today. She needs a pair of shoes. Is that okay?" She had money of her own, of course, but always checked with him before spending on any extraordinary expense. He always concurred. On helping out those in need they seldom disagreed.

By the time Neal came home Sandi had usually arrived, changed clothes and headed out into the yard to spade flowerbeds or pot plants, or into some room of the house to rearrange things. Sometimes in the evening she settled into long leisurely baths, washed her hair and painted her finger and toenails while he sat hammering out a paragraph or two on his typewriter. Sometimes she arranged to meet a girlfriend for tea or coffee just to give him the extra time. She seemed to realize that when she was in the next room waiting for him to join her it placed some pressure on his work. She was sensitive to everyone, but Neal soon saw that she was no pushover. Against a bullying parent, which was rare with special needs children, she stood her ground.

"Absolutely not, Mr. Whaite, your child is capable of understanding and obeying our rules."

In one touchy situation Neal offered to speak to a father. "No," she declined, "I have to do this on my own." More than once he heard her say, "I have to take care of this myself." The set of her pretty mouth and the pulse beat in her throat told him she could handle just about any situation with the children and parents.

One of her coworkers confided in him, "If Sandi's not busy with her own work she's always helping someone else. She seldom just does nothing."

Once as they walked around their yard together she lifted her arms and cried, "I love my house! I love my garden! I love you!" Then she turned to him soberly. "I love you so much it scares me. This is more than I ever asked." There was a faint quiver of her lips. "Girls dream but they never know who they'll marry or what circumstances they'll find themselves in. It's scary to have found you and be this happy."

"Scared? Happy? Isn't that an oxymoron?"

"No. Because nothing like this can last forever."

"And how can you make it last?"

"All I know is you plant every precious moment in your heart and never let it go. Then when it's needed, you tug it out and live it all over again."

Each morning Neal rose early and slipped out to the gazebo with a cup of coffee while Sandi slept an extra hour. His thoughts about work and writing would steal in and he wondered if he would ever give birth to *Samson's Revenge* and if Sandi would ever get used to his necessary interludes of solitude, this other world he had to live in at least for a brief period every day. Peripherally, he realized she was filling gaps in his life he'd scarcely been aware of, but inevitably thoughts about his writing and about how little he'd accomplished so far cast a shadow over their intimacy. Sandi wanted to invade this shadow by reading things he wrote, but lacking the professional confidence that only public success brings, he was guarded with his work. He knew she felt this distance and was hurt by it.

Late one afternoon after they'd jogged together they sat on one of the narrow benches in the gazebo. "Perhaps you're trying too hard, Neal. Nothing seems quite natural and convincing when it's forced."

"It's a character flaw, I guess. There's this thing in me that just won't let go."

"Or maybe you just brood too much. In almost anything, the most successful is usually the one who appears at ease."

"How do you do that when nothing comes off quite right?"

"Who says it's not right? Don't judge yourself by the criteria of others. The only one you have to be honest with is yourself."

He knew she'd learned to live this way, to accept things as they were without comparing herself with others. In her heart was no room for jealousy or for covetousness.

"And what about your business?" she said. "I know it takes a lot out of you. We could manage on less."

"Could we?"

"You know we could. All the money in the world isn't going to free you in the way you've always imagined. Besides, perhaps you're made for another purpose."

"I'd like to know what it is, then."

"You will, when the time comes." She then said, "Do you really think changing your circumstances will make you happy?"

"Well — yes."

"It won't, though. Happiness is circumstantial. It fades with time. I believe you have to look into yourself to find true joy."

As they started down from the gazebo, she stumbled. He caught her, she laughed and swung away, and he held onto her arm. They began to engage in a tug of war. She broke loose and ran, and he chased her across the yard. Each time she felt him about to catch her, she squealed, ducked, and darted back the other way. At last he pinned her against a tree, her face flushed, her laughter light as leaves, and her mouth irresistible. He kissed her until their lips ached, then pulled her shirt out and slipped his hand under.

"Neal, we're all sweaty." Giggling, she whispered, "At least let's get into the house."

From time to time he dropped his struggles with *Samson's Revenge* to return to short stories. Sam Harris finally sold a second story, written under a pseudonym — he was determined to reserve his name for those masterworks he was yet to produce — to one of the mystery magazines, for which he was paid the magnificent sum of $800. They went out to celebrate.

"To my husband, a man of many talents," toasted Sandi. His successes were her successes, his pains her pains.

But she never hesitated to stand her ground. One evening they were invited out to the Fullers' country place. Sandi drove out first, then after work he followed. They rode golf carts and four-wheelers, splashing through shallow creeks, and had a good time. It was almost nine o'clock when they left to drive home in their separate cars. He followed her for a few miles, but Sandi was driving too slowly and he passed her, tapping the horn to let her know. He assumed she would speed up and follow close behind but instead she dropped further back. Just as he reached town, his cell phone rang.

"Where are you!" she demanded.

"Almost home. Where are you?"

"You're ahead of me?"

'Yes. You saw me pass."

"I did *not* see you pass. I've been just crawling, waiting for you to catch up. I thought something might've happened."

"Before we left the Fullers, I told you I was in a hurry."

"You're always in a hurry." After a moment of black silence, she said, "You left me out on this dark road alone."

"Sandi, it's a four-lane highway. There are cars everywhere."

"I don't care. You should have stayed close to me."

When they arrived home, she didn't let it go. "I can't believe you left me. Most men would want to protect their wives."

"There was no danger at all."

"You don't know that. I certainly was not about to leave *you*."

Frustrated, he said, "You've lived this long without me and nothing's happened."

She murmured, "A woman wants to feel protected and cared for, Neal."

He thought all this overblown, but he saw that she was hurt and he took her into his arms. She resisted at first, then gave in. "Next time I'll stay close even if you crawl."

Sandi continued to work at The Learning Room. Her love for the children, for his parents and for his sister Lori made her a part of the family as though she'd been there all along.

Lori had been married three years now and had a baby daughter, a curly-haired, blue-eyed girl named Brandi. The child seemed to enliven their lives, but Neal and Sandi suspected her husband Cloud had been a disappointment to her. Cloud had an outgoing, winning personality and was always willing to help out, but he had no ballast, no center. He drifted, stuck in a kind of adolescent abstraction. In high school and during a couple of seasons in college he'd been a football hero, and he evidently yearned for his days of glory. He was a boisterous, often loud man with a desire to please — to please others, not necessarily his wife.

One night after they all had dinner at his parents', Neal walked into the living room to find Sandi and Lori sitting close together in deep conversation. They'd been wondering if Lori and Cloud would be drawn closer by their child or if their lives would be disrupted further. At first it seemed to be a shot in the arm but with a man like Cloud infusion of adrenalin was short-lived.

As Neal came in, Lori was saying, "Do you know what Cloud's mother tells me? That as a child, whenever he felt bad, he blamed someone else. I don't think he's ever outgrown that."

"But other people aren't responsible for our feelings," said Sandi.

"Cloud tries hard but never seems able to make anything work."

"But he's a good husband, isn't he? He seems to love you and Brandi."

"He'd be ideal if I could open up his head and pour some contentment into it. When he's miserable, we all are. Not long ago I was in the hospital with a kidney infection. Do you know he wouldn't even come to see me?"

"Lori, no! Why not?"

"He can never accept that I'm sick. I have to be whole and present for him. When anything shatters his personal world, he falls apart."

Neal sat down on the chair across from them. "When were you sick, Lori?"

"Oh, a few months ago. I didn't want to bother you with it."

"It makes me sad to think you couldn't come to me with your troubles."

"Cloud envies your success, Neal. The independence and the money, too."

"And he thinks that would make him happy? Everybody isn't cut out for business. That doesn't mean he couldn't have a good life."

Backing off, Lori said, "I don't want you to condemn him, though. I just wish you could help him see he's not a failure."

"I wouldn't say he is at all. He's always ready to pitch in and he has a kind heart. But he's wrong to treat you like this."

"He admires you so much, Neal. I know I shouldn't talk about our difficulties, but sometimes I can't help it."

"I think you *should* talk about them," said Sandi. "At least then there's a chance it might make a difference."

As they heard Cloud and Mr. Austin come in from outside, Lori broke off the conversation and smiled. "I don't want to worry you with this. Probably I'm painting a bleaker picture than it really is. Cloud's a good man and loves his family."

They walked into the kitchen, where Cloud was offering to help Mr. Austin on some project. No one would ever know he'd become so demanding of his wife, and so accusing when things failed to go his way. He was beginning to bald at a young age and to thicken around the waist. Big as he was, he walked lightly on his feet. As he spoke, he lifted his brows, radiating minute horizontal lines across his forehead. Most people thought well of Cloud, Neal knew he would never impress anyone as a domineering husband. "I was telling your father about a hoist," said Cloud. "You can do just about anything with a hoist. A hoist makes your life so much easier." He repeated himself. "Your father needs to get him a good hoist to help move those engines around." Of course, Mr. Austin knew more about hoists and ratchets and come-alongs than the other two men put together.

As they drove home, Sandi asked, "Is there anything we can do to help Cloud, Neal? Lori's a sweet girl. I hate to see her so distressed."

"I do, too. I don't know about Cloud, though. When a man blames someone else for his troubles, especially his wife, he just needs some sense knocked into his head."

"Well, let's think about it. Maybe you can give him some direction."

Neal hardly knew how he could help. It wasn't a matter of financial support. He'd learned that benevolence of that sort had a way of turning sour. Besides, he'd already propped them up twice — once when he paid off credit cards for Lori and a second time when he lent them money he knew wouldn't be repaid. It occurred to him that sometimes, in some peculiar way, the beneficiary resents the people whose fortunes are greater than his own.

"I see such a difference in you and Cloud." Sandi lay her arm over the armrest and touched his shoulder lightly. "You've always taken care of Lori. Your mother and father, too. I don't know why you see your sensitivity to others as a kind of burden."

"What makes you think I do?"

"It's just like your writing. You have a vision not everyone has. And because you haven't realized that vision you think you've missed out. But to strive means everything, Neal. To succeed may or may not add another dimension." She turned in her seat to look at him. "You may never write anything great or even get noticed. I wish you could see that our lives have to touch only one or two other lives to make all the difference we need to make."

He laughed mirthlessly. "I guess I want to touch the whole world."

"I know you do. But sometimes if you influence one life *that* life may be the one to touch the world. All we really need to do is try to make the world just a little better than we found it. We can all do that."

Conversations like this made Neal feel better; but honest and open as they were, and as reinforcing as Sandi was, he knew she remained vulnerable to the separation his single-mindedness wedged between them.

One night he came home charged with one of those rare moments of inspiration and fired up to get to his typewriter. Sandi was in the bedroom dressing.

"Changing at this time of day?"

"It's time to get ready." She looked at him in the mirror. "Nan called and said Pat isn't feeling well and probably won't go. We can still go with the Fullers, though."

"Go where?"

"Don't you remember, Neal? We're all going out to dinner."

"Damn. Do we have to?"

"Well, yes. This has been planned for two weeks."

"I really have some work to do."

She raised her brows. "If you want to let the Fullers down and abandon me, go right ahead."

"I'm asking for an hour. Just one hour!"

"That's all *I'm* asking. All you think of is sitting at that damn typewriter!" She dropped her head suddenly. In the mirror he saw that her lips were tight with disappointment. The fight went out of him and he put his arms around her.

"I know we can't walk away from a commitment."

"I want you to want to even when the Fullers aren't involved," she said. "This is our night together."

So the inspiration was dropped into a mental box, maybe for revival another time, maybe not.

Sometimes Neal wondered about himself. Could it be just a *feeling* he sought — merely some romantic notions about being a writer? Fame and fortune were important to a man who'd seen his father struggle all his life, a man who at the age of twenty-five took on the responsibility and commitment of two men. But he doubted that *Samson's Revenge* would bring him fame or fortune, either. A story of two estranged brothers who finally reconciled just before one's death was about love, life, spirit, self-reliance — the things he believed in and wanted to share, but hardly evoked the excitement people paid money to read. And it was hard. He sweated over every sentence, over the right voice, over the subtle detachment. He could scarcely imagine those favored writers who had fun with their work. Nor could he rationally defend these nights after two or three hours of struggle when he jumped up from his desk, swearing, and slammed crumpled sheets angrily into the wall.

Still, nearly every turbulent breath was calmed by Sandi. No matter how stressful his day, everything was made right when they went to bed and she wrapped herself trustingly in his arms, making little adjustments of her back and legs as though she intended to be there forever. He wondered if his ambition might ever be translated into a contented life. It seemed to him creativity was a driving force much like falling in love. One might hope for it all his life, and if it never came that life could be lived, but always with the sense of something missed.

Chapter Nine

Sometimes Neal would find a vase of flowers on his office desk — Sandi had slipped away from The Learning Room during her lunch hour. Sometimes on his home office desk he'd find a small gift — a chapstick, a fingernail clipper, a hairbrush. She delighted in giving him little surprises.

She made it a point to call Lori nearly every night. "I'm worried about your sister," she said. "She just doesn't seem at all happy."

"I'm afraid she might have married a loser."

"I don't know. Cloud is such a personable man. Maybe his eyes are too big for his talents."

"Could be. You have to be careful with how much you prop people up."

Neal's inauguration into Sandi's intimate self was first one of awe, wonder and unabashed lust — her beautifully shaped legs, her heart-tugging smile and the tantalizing curve of her narrow hips. Physical beauty transcended into something deeper and more intimate and opened elements within himself he hardly knew existed and was a little afraid of. Most of his life he'd spent thinking, working, writing. Turning himself over to her two strong arms, the work of her hands and of her heart was something new and slightly scary to him. Through the worst days he heard her gentle warm voice. Hard as he'd tried to write about true emotions he began to wonder if the extraordinary nature of pure emotion is discovered by only a few in a lifetime.

"What are you doing today?" she asked at breakfast. "Anything momentous happening?"

She always woke vivid and alert. He wasn't especially grumpy, but what he most wanted in the morning was silence. He wanted to get up, grab a cup of coffee and go to his desk for half an hour to think, to make notes, to plan. If she came into the kitchen too soon to make breakfast he felt short-circuited. Still, he couldn't be dull with brightness all around. She insisted on making his breakfast, then seeing him off and kissing him goodbye. Most times on the breakfast table were cuttings from her beds and gardens. Seldom did she appear in the morning without her hair brushed, her face washed, her skin glowing. Before hurrying off to The Learning Room, she made the bed, brought in the newspaper, washed the breakfast dishes. She hated to come home to a disorganized house.

One night she said, "You remember Lucy, the little girl who lost most of her hearing? I'm so excited! Some of her hearing is restored."

"How?"

"No one knows. It's a miracle!"

Another night, "I feel so sorry for Reggie's family." He remembered Reggie as the child who on the day of the picnic had with great determination catapulted himself over the edge of the ravine with the pine sapling. "Reggie's father lost his job and they're afraid they can't leave Reggie at The Learning Room the rest of the year. And he really needs to be there. There's not another school like ours."

"You mean another teacher like you. You're the miracle worker."

"All I can say is that love makes all the difference, and we make sure those kids get plenty of that."

"Why don't you see what it'll take to keep Reggie there the rest of the year?"

"You don't mean we can help?"

"We might manage a few dollars."

"Oh, I was hoping you'd say that!"

In fact there was always somet genuine need like this he felt compelled to contribute to, usually anonymously. There were his parents, too, his sister, her ne'er-do-well husband.

Sandi could hardly get her mind off Lori. "Cloud just can't seem to settle on anything. He wants to start his own business."

"With what?"

"I don't know. I feel sorry for little Brandi. She's such a sweet child. You think we could have her over to spend a day or two with us?"

"Fine with me. Might give Lori and Cloud some time together."

Sandi wanted a baby but Neal knew he wasn't ready. "We'll have children," he said, "but not now."

"Why not now?"

"I don't think I can handle a baby."

"I'm twenty-six, Neal. I don't want to be thirty when I start my family."

"Plenty of women do. Just give me some time."

She gazed into his eyes. "What exactly are you afraid of?"

"Children change everything."

"Yes. They bring joy that isn't all about yourself."

"They bring responsibility," he said. "Maybe more than anything else."

She looked at her hands and asked softly, "Neal, I'd like to understand why you think you can't work and write and live a regular life. Most authors I've known anything about have to do other things to make a living and live a normal domesticated life, too."

"Maybe they're blessed with more time."

"Or is it me? I sometimes wonder if you see this marriage as just an experience you must pass through to reach the life you really want to lead."

"Don't be ridiculous," he said irritably. "Nothing means more to me than you."

"But I want children."

"I didn't say we wouldn't have them. Only that I need more space."

She walked away, her head high, her back rigid. Then she came back and looked at him steadily. "I would have married you anyway, you know. I guess we need to start taking precautions."

"Why don't we just see what happens."

Despite the demands of work Neal made time for them to do things together. They went antique shopping or drove up to Calloway Gardens to hike or ride bicycles, or joined the Palmers and Fullers for a cookout. The three couples were good friends and were more or less always included in each other's guest lists. Everyone liked Sandi.

Sandi tried to get home ahead of Neal and bathe and dress before he arrived. If he came home early he'd find her at her dressing table, a robe thrown loosely around her shoulders, smiling tenderly at him in the mirror.

"You're just beautiful."

"Thank you."

One night he walked in to find her standing in the kitchen staring at him with a look he'd never seen before. Her cheeks were stung alive and her lips were parted expectantly. He realized at once that it had happened exactly as she had expected and as he'd hoped it wouldn't happen. "You aren't?" he said.

"I am!"

"You're pregnant."

She ran into his arms. "Oh, happy lightning!"

He lifted her and swung her around, but a shock of uncertainty quaked through him. His smile was dutiful but false. How he'd fit in another responsibility he didn't know.

"You've always wanted to do remarkable things, Neal. Well, now you've helped create life. Doesn't that mean something?"

"I don't know."

"I ask only one thing. You must find time to be with me more."

He struggled to grasp it all, the tiny embryo, part of him, his genes, his personality planted in her belly, and found it almost impossible to imagine. But he knew now he had to prepare himself for another life, another involvement, and the radiance in Sandi's face cast his uncertainties in a shabby light.

"Listen to this!!" She had already surrounded herself with baby books. "At five weeks the baby has a heartbeat. At twenty-eight days, arm and leg buds are forming. At six weeks, eyes and ears are developing. Soon afterward, toenails and fingernails emerge."

In some curious way all this remained part of her, but not of him.

"You should see the things they're making for babies now. And the baby books, hundreds of them. What a mother should know, what to expect at every stage. Did you know when a healthy baby's ready to be born, it turns to come out headfirst? Isn't that fascinating!"

Neal pushed harder than ever to hammer out a few chapters of *Samson's Revenge* to send off to Sam Harris. Some passages he struggled with mercilessly, beating himself up over them. Some he felt rang clear as a clarion, and others he felt missed in a way that suggested he simply did not have command of the words. And about still others he was never certain. It was the subtle emotion, the inner conflict, the true origin of drama that he wanted to capture. In one scene he had one brother pacing up and down his den:

He was back home now among familiar things that spoke to him about enthusiasm and hopefulness. The remembered shouts and laughter of his brother's children resounded through the lively energetic walls. Yet, underneath the image of love and optimism and well-being ran an unnatural restlessness. With memory bathing him in its resurrecting light he suddenly shuddered and started as if some cruel pain had struck his chest. Something broke loose in him which he could not describe or identify but only knew that despite his courageous efforts it seized him and wrung him, torturing all the memories of what could have been. As he walked the floor with this visit of his relatively happy young adulthood, it seemed impossible that things could have gone so wrong, that even memory was threatened and distorted. Still, when he heard his daughter and his grandchildren enter noisily and robustly through the side door he had the sense of a quickened life, of stimulating optimism . . .

Passages like this took a lot out of Neal, not because of the words but because he was never convinced words could evoke the inner turmoil he tried so hard to express. And he was never convinced there weren't ways to show this turmoil through action not description.

Somehow Neal found time nearly every day to walk with Sandi, and once or twice a week they jogged around the park. Sandi's step was snappy and happy, and as her face grew fuller and her lips redder, her voice and mannerisms assumed a lighter quality.

"I felt the baby kicking today," she said.

"Really? How do you know it wasn't indigestion?"

"Oh, no, there's a difference." She assumed a position on her back. "Put your hand here. Now wait a minute. There! Feel that?"

"No, I don't feel a thing."

"Well, you will. She's very active at times."

"How do you know it's a she?"

"I just know. It's a feeling I have."

He called the school to check on her several times during the day, and he could hear giggles in the background, little children watching their teacher's tummy grow.

The drivers began to address him as "Daddy." "Hey, Daddy," they said.

Tia teased, "Don't worry, Neal, it won't hurt that much. Not you, at least."

"Sandi feels the baby, it's all part of her chemistry, but to me . . . I don't know."

"What's wrong?"

"I just don't know if I'm ready for this."

"You will be."

His days were as hectic as ever. He spent hours on the phone, all the while trying to imagine this little human being curled in the womb, stretching, kicking, yawning, and turning. At night he sat stewing over his typewriter, unable to articulate emotions which he feared were about to undergo dramatic change.

As her belly grew and her bouts of nausea subsided, Sandi continued to teach and to report how intrigued the children were. "It's so fascinating to them. Of course some of them have little brothers and sisters, but that's not like Miss Sandi having a baby."

One night she said, "Listen. I'll bet you can hear the heartbeat now. Put your ear here."

He lifted the gown on her stomach as she pressed his ear to her cool, taut skin, and with a jolt he heard the brave flutter of a personality determined to burst into life. "I hear it. Another heart beneath your heart."

"Beating from my heart. I'm her lifeline, for now. And soon you'll be."

"It happened so fast."

"Well, I don't know about that. Nine months is a long time for a woman. Oh, Neal, do you think you could possibly go and find me some lime ice milk?"

Neal did his best to hide his apprehension and he chastised himself for his inability to share her happiness. She was in another realm, looking forward to the future, while he thought about separation and responsibility and the dead reckoning of time.

One evening they were leaving the gazebo when Sandi fell. He leaped forward to catch her, but wasn't quick enough. She struck the ground hard, the extra thirty pounds or so bringing her down awkwardly, twisting her leg. She gave a cry, the breath was knocked out of her and she lay stunned. Frozen in horror, he couldn't move. Then he fell down on his knees.

"Sandi . . . !"

"It's okay, I'm all right."

"That was a nasty fall. Something could be broken."

"I don't think so."

"Move your hands and feet."

She wiggled them, then pulled herself up into a sitting position.

"What made you fall?"

"I don't know. It happened so quickly." She reached her arms to him. "Help me up."

He slipped his hands beneath her shoulders and drew her to her feet. She steadied herself against him a moment. "I'm okay."

"What about the baby?"

"I hope she's all right." Her face was pale, and as they moved toward the house she limped a little.

"Should we go to the hospital?"

"I'll call the doctor."

He helped her to the bedroom. As she lay down, color returned to her face and her expression was concerned but not panicky. "Get me Dr. Carver's number, will you? It's in my index."

"Want me to call?"

"No, I'll do it. Don't look so scared, Neal. I'm sure we're all right."

He dialed the number and handed her the phone. Of course, her doctor wasn't working. The answering service would page the physician on call. She explained everything and put down the receiver. "I think the best thing is for me to lie still for a while."

By the time the doctor contacted them, she was half-asleep and Neal was pacing the floor. He stood poised until she finished talking and hung up.

"It's exactly as I thought. He wants me to lie still and watch for spotting. If nothing develops, he says everything's fine."

"When will we know for certain?"

"Oh, by tomorrow, I guess."

"You have to be more careful. Promise me."

"I know. It scared me, but babies are really pretty resilient. She's kicking right now."

He left her resting and went out to the gazebo. It was nearly dark, but there were yard lights and he had a big cordless floodlight. This was the second time something had tripped her. Down on his knees, he saw what it was. There were two wood steps from the gazebo, one a little shorter than the other. He'd never noticed this before.

He went to his shop, collected a hammer, saw, and crowbar and returned to the gazebo. It was dark by the time he tore into the old steps and ripped them out. Shattered boards wrenched loose with an echoing groan. In the night air it was a tortuous sound. These steps would never trip anyone again. He worked with a vengeance, sweating, swearing. He collected the splintered boards, hauled them to the trash, and tied a short rope across the opening as a temporary barricade.

With these pent-up emotions expended, he went in to shower. As he passed through the bedroom, Sandi sat up. "Neal, what were you doing?"

"Tearing out those steps."

"Are you crazy? You didn't have to do that tonight."

"They'll never make you fall again."

"You sounded like a madman. What will the neighbors think?" She rolled over and smiled. "I love you."

Her last day at school was filled with tears and kisses. He went down with her to say goodbye to the children. They had agreed that she would stay home with their child. The children made farewell posters and cards, and one by one hugged her, kissed her, and cried.

"We'll miss you, Miss Sandi."

"I'll miss you, too."

"Bring your baby to visit us."

With tears in her eyes she said to Neal, "I hope they find a replacement who'll love them as much as I."

Pregnancy gave Sandi another element of beauty, Neal thought, even with chubby cheeks, swollen ankles, and a middle too big to reach around. But she was miserable, too. Every step required effort, she could hardly get comfortable, she threw open windows and sat in the cool breeze. If she didn't feel the baby kick for several hours, she became nervous. But when she kissed him goodbye in the mornings and when he returned home in the evenings, she was all smiles, making every effort to hide her discomfort.

At night she exclaimed, "Has your baby been active today! I think she must have done about a dozen somersaults."

"Why don't they get tangled up in the umbilical cord?"

"That can happen, but it's usually because something's wrong. Nature has a way of taking care of such things."

Even in the ninth month it was still hard for Neal to grasp the idea that something of himself, some vital part of his flesh, his personality, his thoughts even, would become another living being.

But on the day of Eddi's birth, a burst of life emphatically protesting yet insistently searching, he received her cautiously into his arms and was shocked to see eyes like his and hands like his, his fingers, his toes. In that instant he knew that nothing would ever be the same again.

Chapter Ten

When the baby cried out Neal groaned. If only she'd let him sleep through the night. He closed his ears, turned over. But something else tugged at him. Sandi stirred, slipped toward the edge of the bed. He caught her shoulder. "No, it's my turn to go. I'm not letting her get the idea you're the only one who comes."

"Ha." Sandi fell back, her voice husky with sleep. "Be my guest."

He shook himself awake and yawned himself into Eddi's room. The nightlight illuminated everything in a pastel stillness. A mobile suspended over the bassinet, little birds on strings, drifted to and fro. Eddi lay on her stomach, her baby cries like muffled hiccups. "You hungry again? How many times? Three? Four?" He lifted her out of the bassinet, changed her, cradled her in his arms, and took her into the kitchen to warm the milk. He returned to her room and sat in the rocking chair. As he fed her, he looked around to make certain everything was safe. Room warm enough, nursery rhyme wallpaper, golden lampshades, and a miniature phonograph which played "Me and My Teddy Bear." As she nursed her bottle, Eddi looked straight into his face, her eyes wide.

It was strange to Neal how just weeks ago this perfect little person had been floating in her mother's womb. Her little fingers grasping his finger, her elfin toes, her eyelashes, her pretty mouth — everything was there, perfectly formed, thriving, breathing, trusting, dependent. Dependent, yes, as so many of his other loved ones seemed to be. A sharp noise made her tune up. Her lower lip turned under as if she were terribly wounded, and a moment later she began to cry. They laughed at how sensitive she was.

"She looks just like you," said Sandi.

"Well, not entirely."

"Oh, yes. You'd think she'd at least have some of me."

Eddi fell asleep nestled against his chest. He held her a while, then put her back in the bassinet, wondering what he could do to keep the world from seeming to her like such a harsh place, wondering if he could measure up. He had to run his company, he had to make money, he had to write, and now he had this new little creation to try to tend and nurture. Sandi seemed extraordinarily happy, everything she had dreamed of was hers, and his determination to be a good husband, a good father, must somehow fit into the patterns of his long subterranean yearnings.

He went back to bed. Sandi didn't wake, but made little adjustments to fit her body snugly against his. "You should feed and bathe the baby as much as you wish," she'd said. "These are the strongest bonding experiences." She laughed at the care with which he handled Eddi. "Babies aren't that breakable, you know. You just have to be careful to support their heads."

When weather permitted Sandi made a light cool dinner and they took Eddi out to their gazebo where he'd built new steps, for a picnic. It was evident that Eddi liked the outdoors, her big, blue eyes taking in everything.

"You aren't sorry we had a baby, are you, Neal?" Sandi spread a blanket on the floor. "I hardly gave you a choice."

"No, of course not."

"I know you didn't see children in your future just yet."

He answered carefully, "The important thing is that she has a good mother to be here with her."

"I'm happy I can stay home, one of the rewards of your hard work. And you're so good with her. You can never know beforehand — some men — some women, too, just can't relate to babies."

"I thought everybody loved babies."

"Oh, no, not necessarily. Wait until about age two, when she'll begin expressing herself more forcefully. Then you'll see." She took his hand. "I thank God every day for you and my baby, Neal."

Neal left the house early, arrived ahead of everyone else, and threw himself into work. At the end of a never-dull day he drove home half-discontented and exhausted, but the odors of a good meal greeted him, and the baby, reclining in a padded chair on the counter, turned her wondering eyes up to him. "How are you, little one?" Sandi put her arms around him and kissed him, and then they sat down to a dinner. Afterward he gave Eddi her bath, comparing their images in the mirror. It occurred to him that only one precise union in one precise moment in time could have brought forth this exact little baby, and that struck him in a strange way he was unable quite to grasp yet.

As Eddi fell asleep and Sandi sank into a chair at last, he walked out under the panoply of stars, through the green-white pastel shadows of windows and patio chairs, and stood looking at the sky. It was said that the human eye could see about ten thousand stars, with billions, perhaps several billions, indistinguishable, but all in their assigned orbit. A single event, a missed turn, a fateful decision could knock the human star out of orbit in the blink of an eye. He wondered what he felt guilty of. Embracing the known, but giving up some of that for the unknown. He wondered if he would ever learn to live not in the future, but to live, as Sandi did, in the orbit of presence.

Chapter Eleven

From the large windows in his office Neal could track the seasons, and they seemed to rotate incredibly quickly. The winter rains whipped down and the path of spring's sun could be followed across the gravel yard, the first sparkle of light on the rail fence, the final glow on the horizon changing from crimson to pale yellows and blue-whites. His moods and responses were affected by scents, by sentimental love songs, by an unexpected touch of wind on his cheeks, sometimes melancholy, sometimes with an aliveness quite removed from the hectic commerce which began an hour later, when the couriers arrived and he sent his vans and trucks racing around the city.

With the men there was always something. Brent Wilmore had the habit of flirting with the girls in about every office he visited, and when one of them took him seriously and began calling his home he came to Neal for advice, panicked over the risk of losing his wife.

"But, Brent," said Neal, "I've warned you about this flirting before. What were you thinking?"

"Aw, it was just in good clean fun. How was I to know she'd just split with her husband and was on some sort of rebound?"

"That's the point. You have to learn you can't say everything that comes into your head."

"But what should I do, boss?"

"Tell her you made a mistake, you're happily married and please do not call your house again. Be gentle but firm."

Russel Wysdeck let a slick, fast-talking stockbroker persuade him into putting his money in a high-risk stock, and he lost just about all his kids' college funds. Wysdeck's depression caused such gloom around the office Neal was obliged to sit down with him and try to structure a plan that would help him dig out. "This won't be easy, Russel. And there's a limit to how much I can help. You're going to have to cut back on everything."

"Boy, is my family sore at me."

"How'd you get into this anyway?"

"A friend introduced me to this broker, you know? The deal sounded too good to be true, but I fell for it. Big profits quick. I know I should've known better."

"Never have I known any get rich easy schemes to work," said Neal. "There are plenty of con artists that'll sell out their mother for a dollar."

Neal himself was the victim of some of their antics, too. One morning the drivers were horsing around and let a dolly stacked with expensive electronic equipment roll off the dock. "My God!" he cried, "what am I working here, a bunch of clowns!"

The world news wasn't much inspiring either. In 1991, the Exxon Valdez had spilled millions of gallons of oil in the pure coastal waters of Alaska. A new war called Desert Storm was supposed to evict Iraq from the oil-rich country of Kuwait. Until then, who'd ever heard of Kuwait? The movie *Robin Hood*, one of the year's big grossing films, provided some reprieve, and the good news as far as anyone knew was that the Cold War was ending with the collapse of the USSR.

Maybe it was a good thing he had a wife and child to come home to.

One evening Sandi said, "We need some quiet time together, Neal. I think we should go to the beach. I've already arranged a condo and spoken to Tia."

"Tia?"

"As I see it, she can handle things a few days."

"So you and Tia are conspiring against me?"

"She'll manage very well."

"How much time do I have?"

"We're going next Friday. Do whatever you need to get ready. I don't want you agonizing over work all weekend. I think it's become a habit."

"Yeah, it's strange how some people believe in making a living."

"That's fine, but you have a family now, and we're going to have fun together."

She brought in two new bathing suits, one tiny fragment of a thing for Eddi, one for him.

"I don't need a new bathing suit," he said.

"Oh, no, you could keep wearing the one you had in college."

In her tiny suit, Eddi, with her chunky little legs, her dark complexion, her dark hair and striking blue eyes was a beauty. She was an alert child with an eager smile. She wriggled her arms and legs wildly to demonstrate her excitement at the simplest things. Sandi always manipulated schedules so that when he came home Eddi was awake and ready for playtime.

Sandi tried the new swimsuit on Eddi. "We have so much to look forward to. Just imagine, Eddi's already trying to crawl. She's a determined little thing and she loves being outdoors. She gets that from you and me, too."

Neal knew that when Sandi made up her mind there was no sense fighting her. With amused obedience, he made a quick trip to the office on Friday, then at Tia's insistence, finished up and returned home, where he found Sandi with several bags of food ready for the car. "What's this? You aren't planning to cook?"

"Breakfast and lunch. I know you must have your quiet time in the mornings."

"But you need time off, too."

"Oh, we'll go out, all right, for big, sinful dinners."

They took 431, south to Florida, where they were greeted by open meadows and tall pines, by pasture fences strung on vine-choked posts. A washed-out blue sky led them all the way, and somewhere along the line they slowed down to watch a yellow-winged crop duster swoop down over a field, skim across the crop, release its spray, and rise again in a steep climb. What an acrobat, he thought, this daredevil flying.

Sandi brought her guitar and strummed and sang as Eddi, in her car seat, listened with her eyes opened wide. Four hours later, they hit the coast, checked into the condo, threw their bags in, put away the food, and changed. Then they plunged out onto the beach. With a double beach towel underneath and Eddi investigating the white sand with her tiny toes, Sandi hugged her knees to her chest, tilted her visor down over her brown eyes, and smiled up at him. "Go on into the water, Neal. I'll stay with the baby." She'd lost all the pregnancy weight and her legs were tan and shapely. He dropped down at the towel, stroked her thigh with the back of his fingers, and kissed her.

"We'll take Eddi in tomorrow," she said, "when the sun's high. It's a little cool now, I think. Go on, you should work up a big appetite."

He went down to the water, investigated the temperature with his feet, then moved on out into the surf. After a moment, it began to feel warm enough. He stood looking toward a sandbar where the first line of breakers formed, rolled and re-gathered as they neared the beach. After a moment of adjustment he took a deep breath and dived in. There was a shock, then it became exhilarating. He dived a few more times, swam fifty strokes and splashed around by himself. Then he ran back to the towel, swept Eddi into his arms and hauled her to the water and dipped the tips of her toes in. "This is the Gulf, Eddi. Isn't it beautiful? See the fish? The birds? How do you like that?" She wriggled her hands and feet.

He took her back up to the towel. Sandi laughed. "She loved that, didn't she? I could see from here. She's so excited about everything."

"Reminds me of her mother."

"I'm getting hungry. Where should we eat?"

"What about The Anchor out on the bay."

"Perfect. Eddi'll be fascinated by their aquarium. I wonder if they still have seahorses."

She dressed Eddi in a pink outfit and she wore a pale yellow dress and pearls with matching earrings. Her flawless complexion and striking brown eyes, and her long lashes and arms made her particularly lovely tonight, and he knew she was happy — a husband, a baby, a home back home, and a legacy of children in The Learning Room whose lives she had touched. Often she said, "I'm determined to show you that disappointments can be transformed into something positive. I believe circumstances are exactly as they should be in a particular place and a particular time." He could hardly understand it, but somehow she seemed to transform both simple and troubling matters into things to celebrate. In moments of sheer pleasure, her assurance brought a special radiance to her expressions. He hoped Eddi would be most influenced by her personality, not his.

They arrived at The Anchor early, and were able to get a window seat with a good view of the water and docks where boats were unloading their catch — small, low-sided fishing vessels, mostly white, able to accommodate four to six passengers. Neal noticed one in particular, painted teal green and called The Mermaid, which was rigged for scuba diving and snorkeling. Next to The Mermaid, two pelicans sat on barnacled pilings like wood carvings, and tall masts with flags of assorted shapes and colors flapped in a variable wind.

A nice-looking redhead with a French accent — probably a summer exchange student — took their order. "What a gorgeous baby. Would you like a high chair?"

"We would appreciate that very much."

"She looks just like her father."

"You see?" said Sandi. "All anybody sees in Eddi is you. Aren't you proud?"

"If she has my looks, I hope she gets your optimism."

"Better that she be kind and smart like you. Not too smart, though. It makes you miserable."

"Yes?"

"You see all these alternatives. I hope she'll be more simple-minded, like me."

"Simple, perhaps, not simple-minded."

"I must have some intelligence or you couldn't stand me for very long." She tied a bib around Eddi. "It's funny how it is with children. As they grow older they seem to drift away from many of the things they've learned. Then years later, it all comes back as if their heritage were there just waiting to resurface."

"That's a kind of immortality, I guess."

Their server returned to take their order. "I'm sorry but we're a little slow tonight. One of our cooks called in sick."

"Let's take a walk then," said Neal.

"You go ahead," Sandi said. "I'll just sit and enjoy the view."

He took Eddi and strolled along the pier looking at the boats and their catches. At the end of the pier was a fish market where a young girl was pitching buckets of crushed ice into the deep windows. The fish were packed into the clear chipped ice, flat gray flounder, red fish, black crabs and lobster which seemed to be swimming upward through the smoking ice. Across the bay, the shore was heavy with big trees, the grasses and clinging moss as fixed as a picture postcard. On the ruddy-black water, which became paler and paler in the decreasing light, a few single-masted sailboats canted into the breeze.

As they walked along, he pointed out items of interest to Eddi. "Those are seagulls, Eddi. And look at the little doggie. Wonder if he sails with the captain." He knew her understanding was limited, but they had agreed to stimulate her awareness at every opportunity.

Sandi waved at him through the window and he went back into The Anchor and strapped Eddi into the high chair.

"Eddi was taking all that in, wasn't she?"

"Seemed to be."

"I believe she's going to be a very alert child."

After dinner, they stopped at the large aquarium in the lobby to show Eddi the seahorses. They then drove to Alvin's Island, where Sandi wanted to get each of their mothers a small gift. She always tried to share her experiences through some little present for his mother or hers, for his sister, or for some friend who needed to know she remembered them. As she looked around, he took the baby to the toy department.

"What do you think of this, Eddi? A pretty shell collection. And look at these snowflakes." He inverted the snow globe and as the granules fell, she watched intently.

He found a small carousel music box, carried it to the cashier, and had it put in a bag. Sandi was fond of music boxes. "We'll get this for your mother. It'll be a surprise."

When they rejoined, Sandi asked, "What's in your bag?"

"We'll never tell. What about yours?"

"I got these pretty porcelain birds. Think they'll like them?"

"I have no doubt."

They returned to the condo replete with a good meal and the bloom of the sun on their skin. Sandi put Eddi to bed, then went into the bath and emerged in a new shortie gown, baby blue with delicate ruffles. His excitement leaped like a leopard, but she held him at bay. "First we have to sit on the balcony and listen to the surf."

With the lights out, he fell into a padded lounge chair on the balcony and she curled up in his lap. She wore some enchanting perfume, and the restless surf and whipping salt breeze added to the erotic moment. They talked for a while before giving in to the passion that was alive all around them.

"All right, darling," he said.

"All right, darling," she said.

They went to bed and made carefree love.

Next morning, with towels and cooler, sunglasses and lotion, they headed for the beach. In a pair of deck chairs under a big umbrella, they sat back and relaxed as Eddi played with her bucket and shovel.

"You see, these family vacations are important." In her bikini and her white-rimmed sunglasses, Sandi looked ten years younger. "We have to take them often, at least two or three a year, I think."

"I don't know about that," he said.

"Oh, yes, those are my plans. It's important to look forward to things together."

While Eddi fell asleep on a thick beach towel, they kept a close eye on her and sat in the shallow water together. "I'm so thrilled to have a beautiful daughter," Sandi said. "*Your* daughter. I'd like one or two more, but not yet. I want our children spaced about two or three years apart."

Neal went back to sit with Eddi, allowing Sandi to venture out deeper.

He watched her floating on her back like a feather. There were dozens of swimmers out and all along the beach more chairs and umbrellas went up. The tide was coming in. He wanted to be out in the water with Sandi, he wanted to hear her laughter like the airy flight of the sandpipers, but he stayed close to make sure that when the baby woke she wouldn't think she was alone.

They spent a second morning in more or less the same routine, then drove home late Sunday. Eddi slept almost all the way. Sandi sat beside him, sometimes reading, sometimes dozing. He hadn't written a word in two weeks, but it occurred to him that their lovemaking was more tender and generous than they ever were on the eve of those hectic jungle days. And the freedom to do this as often as they chose was something to get rich and famous for.

Chapter Twelve

One evening when Eddi was about eighteen months old, the three of them were down on the floor playing together. Sandi sat cross-legged, Indian style, Neal lay on his side, his legs and torso forming a half circle. In the middle were toys of several kinds, none apparently so intriguing as the top of a shoebox, a ring of keys, a stack of scoured butter tubs.

Eddi was impulsively active, with a curiosity which took in everything. Spying something which attracted her, she'd rush like mad to reach it before one of them intervened. She enjoyed nothing more than starting toward some object, have Neal pull her back, start toward it again, have him sweep her back, start toward it, and have him flip her onto her back and bury his face in her stomach. This was when she laughed hardest. She had a keen interest in her storybooks and would sit quietly watching them turn the pages.

"She has your determination," said Sandi. "Isn't it exciting? I think it's during the early walking stage when their personality becomes most pronounced."

As Sandi said "pronounced," the word came out as a little cry. He looked to see her clasp her hands to her breast and stiffen her legs.

"What's the matter?"

"Wow. I just had this terrific pain in my chest." She released her breath slowly, and eased her legs forward to sit up straight.

"What do you think it is?"

"Must be something I ate. Oh, there it goes again!"

She reached toward him and as he grasped her hand, she clenched his fingers tightly. Her face became pale, then after a moment she relaxed, the color returned to her cheeks, and with a wan smile she murmured, "It wasn't so bad that time. I guess we'd better put Eddi to bed, though. I need to lie down."

"You go on. I'll take care of her."

He sat a moment, watching her pull herself up and leave the room. Then he took the baby into her room, read her a story, and started playing her music. As he tucked her into the covers, she turned her head to one side, her eyes searching. Sandi came in wearing a nightgown and walking with her arms across her chest, her step curiously fragile. Determined that Eddi shouldn't go to bed without her goodnight kiss, she bent with effort. "Good night, honey. I love you."

As they crept from the room, Sandi asked, "You coming to bed now?"

"Yes, I think so. How are you feeling?"

"Better I think."

By the time he was ready for bed, he saw that she was already asleep. As he slipped in beside her, he was relieved to find that she appeared to be breathing easily. Without waking, she shifted a little and fit herself into the cradle of his arms.

During the night, he woke to hear muffled noises in the bathroom. He sat up blinking and a moment later saw her in the soft glow of the nightlight returning to bed, leaning forward as though under the strain of a great weight. She sucked short, shallow breaths, and sank down as quietly as possible, then sat unmoving, exhaling slowly.

He put his hand on her back. "You still sick, darling?"

"I was trying not to wake you."

"Don't you feel any better at all?"

"I've never had indigestion like this. It's all in my chest."

"Maybe we'd better get to the hospital."

"No, not in the middle of the night. Maybe it'll be better by morning. I'd rather give it a while."

They lay down and she pressed her back to him, her knees drawn up, her hand holding his encircling arm. He felt the tension all through her muscles. It worried him that she was struggling against some persistent pain or that she was gripped by deepening fear. About an hour before it was time to get up, she spoke to him as if she'd lain awake all night. "I guess you'd better take me to the emergency room, Neal."

Something in her voice struck him with a sharp note of alarm. He was up at once, dressed, then helped her dress and get a few things together. "We shouldn't have waited so long," he said.

"It's all right." Her movements were labored, her face pallid. "Poor Eddi. She won't like being waked this early. I guess we can take her to Mama's."

"Should I telephone first?"

"You'd better. They'll still be asleep."

He phoned the Steeles, told them Sandi needed to go to the emergency room, and asked if he could drop the baby off.

"Of course you can, Neal. What's the matter?"

"We don't know. She's having pains in her chest."

"Why, Sandi's never been sick."

"I know. I'm sure she'll be all right but we just don't want to take any chances."

"I'll turn the outside lights on for you."

He went to Eddi's room and stood a moment, looking down on her profile, the delicately upturned nose, the rosy cheeks. She was at peace, trusting and secure. Then gently he roused her, slipping his arms under her. As she began to cry, he held her close. "I'm sorry, darling. We have to get dressed now."

She sat half asleep as he pulled clothes on her and gathered her into his arms. As she dropped her head down onto his shoulder, he carried her out and strapped her into the car seat. Back inside again, he collected Sandi's toiletry bag and then, his arm around her waist, he helped her into the car. She slumped back and closed her eyes. As he pulled out of the driveway, he noticed that lights were beginning to come on over the neighborhood.

By the time he drove across town, Mrs. Steele was dressed and waiting. He took Eddi from the car seat, and walked up the steps to the room and baby bed kept there for her.

Mrs. Steele asked anxiously, "Is she any better?"

"Maybe a little."

"Should I come with you? I can hold Eddi."

"I think it's better that she stays here, if you don't mind. I'll call you as soon as I know something."

Mrs. Steele touched his arm lightly. "Please do call as soon as you can, Neal."

When he got back to the car Sandi murmured, "Poor Eddi."

"She'll be fine. Just try to rest."

He sped to the hospital, turned into the emergency entrance and looked for a place to park. A man wearing a patch over his eye walked through the double doors and, guided by the woman with him, got into a car. Neal pulled into their slot.

"Here we are, Sandi."

She roused as though startled, ran her tongue across parched lips, and sat up as he came around the car. Carrying much of her weight as she leaned against him, he walked her into the emergency room, got her settled into a chair, then for half an hour endured the interminable registering process, during which she was more patient than he.

"It's all right, Neal, I don't really think it's an emergency." She clutched his hand. "I know you need to get to the office."

"Don't be ridiculous. I'm not going anywhere."

Fortunately, there were only three or four other patients in the emergency room. The ubiquitous TV was on, but no one was watching and the sound was low. He held Sandi's hand, glad that they could sit quietly. At last a nurse took them back to a tiny room, or actually the corner of a room separated by curtains. Here they waited another hour. Neal was becoming more agitated but trying not to show it. When finally an ER doctor came in, Neal was surprised by his youth. He had closely cut wheat-colored hair and boyish features. His manner, however, was brisk and efficient.

"What seems to be your problem, Mrs. Austin?"

"I'm having these awful chest pains."

"Sit up here for me, will you?"

He examined her chest and back. "I want to order an EKG and some blood work to see if we can find out what's going on here."

"Okay."

"It shouldn't take very long. Just try to rest."

She lay down and Neal drew a sheet over her then dropped into a hard, straight chair beside the bed. As she dozed, his thoughts were anxious and confused. He'd never known Sandi to complain about anything, or to suffer any kind of illness. He found himself opening and closing his fists and realized a quiet fear had gripped him. He was worried about Eddi, too. Never before had she been away from them. After what seemed to him an interminably long time, the doctor finally returned. "I think we'd better keep you a while, Mrs. Austin. I've asked the nurse to contact your family doctor."

"Oh, do you really think so? I have a baby at home."

"I want to put you in a room and run a few more tests. You can give us a night, can't you?"

"If you're sure it's necessary." She looked at Neal. "What about Eddi?"

"Eddi'll be fine with your mother. I'll keep checking on her." He kissed her then walked out into the hall with the doctor. "Is it her heart?"

"I believe it is." His eyes were sympathetic. "We'll let your doctor take a look and decide if we need to call in a specialist."

"You think it could be serious, then?"

"We'll know more when we finish the tests."

Neal was able to arrange a private room. All the way up to the fourth floor he walked beside the bed, holding Sandi's hand. If he tried to let go, she held on tightly. In the room, he helped her into a hospital gown and arranged pillows on the bed.

She smiled weakly. "I'm sorry, Neal. I know you have a thousand things to do."

"All I have to do right now is take care of you."

Finally she closed her eyes, relaxing her grip on his hand only as she fell asleep.

He walked to the window. It was mid-morning now. The sun shown brightly on rooftops and power lines. He thought about how quickly things could change. A few hours ago they were on the floor playing with Eddi. Now Eddi must be wondering why her mother didn't come for her. It made him sad to think about it. As Sandi fell asleep, he slipped out of the room, telephoned Tia at the office and told her he wouldn't be coming in.

"What can I do to help, Neal?"

"Nothing here that I know of. Just handle things there. We'll have to see where this takes us."

"Give Sandi my love. And please don't worry about anything."

He looked back in on Sandi and found her sleeping, then hurried down to emergency parking and drove to the Steeles. As he pulled into the driveway, he sat quietly for a moment, tense and uncertain. Then he got out and went up the steps. Mrs. Steele met him at the door. "How is she?"

"Resting now, but we've checked her into a room. They're running more tests."

"She'll be all right, won't she, Neal? You don't think anything's really wrong?"

He shook his head. "They just have to find out what's going on and tell us what to do."

He found Eddi sitting on a blanket playing with the toys kept there for her in a big jack-o-lantern container. He dropped down beside her and took her hand into his. "Hello, darling. You doing okay?"

She began to give him things — dolls, cardboard blocks, books — then take them back. Then she climbed into his arms and he held her a while. "I have to go now, Eddi. Mama will be home soon."

"Mommy," she said.

He put her down and she didn't protest. It was too soon, he thought, for her to realize something was wrong. He kissed her and left her with her toys.

Mrs. Steele walked him to the door. "If it's okay, you'll have to keep her a little longer," he said.

"It's all right, Neal. Eddi'll be fine. Just get Sandi well and bring her back to us."

He drove home, rummaged through Sandi's drawers, and selected a couple of nightgowns he knew she liked. He tried to think what else he should do, but nothing came to mind. He was about to leave again when he realized he'd neither showered nor eaten anything since the night before.

In the kitchen, he made toast and poured a glass of orange juice, not hungry but forcing himself to eat. He sat at the breakfast table, looking through the window at the back yard. Pebbled walkways curved to the gazebo. Sandi had always kept them raked. Through a knot hole in the wood fence, the morning sun drilled a single shaft to strike the face of a sasanqua, exactly as if nature had planned it this way. The green leaves shone like crystals. This somehow only made the house seem more empty without Sandi there to share it with.

He put the dishes in the sink, locked up, and drove back to the hospital. This time he parked out front and walked through a maze of corridors, where janitors were mopping and waxing floors. In the brightly lit nurse's station on the fourth floor he noticed a big bouquet of floating balloons tied to the back of a chair. A nurse was bent over a clipboard at the desk. He passed by and entered Sandi's room.

As he crept close to her bed, he was startled by how pale she looked. She was sleeping, her mouth drawn, even her eyelids sunken. Less than twenty-four hours ago they'd been happily playing with Eddi. Now she lay in this alien bed, so helpless and silent it was terrifying.

Chapter Thirteen

She woke, took a moment to focus, then said with concern, "Neal, you aren't still here?"

"I left and came back."

"Go home, darling. I know it's hard for you to sit around."

"I'm not leaving until we see what the doctor says."

"How's Eddi?"

"Fine. She's still at your mother's."

All afternoon he gave her water or tissues, adjusted her bed and pillows, and worked cramps out of her legs. The rest of the time he stood or half sat on her bed, holding her hand and talking when she was awake. In the early evening Sandi's family physician Dr. Houser came in, shook hands, spoke to her, then listened to her chest and back. They liked Houser, a middle-aged, stout, no-nonsense man who took every patient seriously. His approach was silent, thorough, and professional. Finishing his examination, he said quietly, "Sandi, I've called in a cardiologist. We're going to move you to the C.C.U."

"Oh, do you have to?"

"I think you need special care right now."

"I hate to be away from my baby so long."

"I understand, but first we need to get you well."

"It's my heart, isn't it?"

"Yes, it appears so. Did you know you have mitral valve prolapse?"

"No. What does that mean?"

"The mitral valve is like a little door that opens and closes to allow blood flow in the left side of the heart. When the valve doesn't seal or fails to open and close properly this is called prolapse. It's not uncommon. Many people have it from birth and never know the difference. Anyway, we'll get you into a room and see what our heart man says."

Neal followed him into the hall. "How bad is it?"

"She's a very sick young woman, Neal. Somehow, probably through a virus, her heart valve's become infected. If necessary, it can be replaced with surgery, but this infection's become severe very quickly. We have to bring it under control as quickly as possible."

"How? What will you do?"

"Antibiotics and diuretics. Time's the crucial factor now."

"How crucial?"

"I'll be honest," said Houser. "The next day or two will be critical." After a moment he added, "Let's stay optimistic. Sandi's a determined young woman and otherwise in very good health."

As the doctor left, Neal stood leaning against the wall, stunned and terrified. How could this happen? After all these years, perhaps all her life, how could an infection attack her heart now? Where did it come from? Throughout her pregnancy she'd bloomed with vitality, and now with no warning at all . . . Sandi, of all people . . .

As he reentered the room, she murmured, "I don't want to be in intensive care. They won't let you stay with me."

"That's the hardest part," he said.

"Oh, Neal, why don't we just say no? Why don't we go home?"

"You know we can't do that."

"But I want to see my baby. She needs me."

"It won't be long. Just a couple of days to get this infection under control."

"I know Mama will take good care of her. But it'll be hard, with Daddy sick . . ."

"Eddi does them good though," he said. "You know that."

"She does, doesn't she? Such a sweet baby. I know she misses me."

"She does. That's why you have to get well quickly."

Her lips trembled. "Neal, I'm frightened."

He bent and pressed his cheek against hers. "You're going to be fine. It'll just take a little time."

She drifted off again and he stood by the bed, leaning down to speak to her reassuringly as they waited. When the attendants came to move her, he gathered her things and walked with them. Along the way, he saw that her spirits lifted and she spoke cheerfully to the aides. Just before they went through a pair of heavy doors, one of the nurses directed him to the I.C. waiting room.

"Oh, but does he have to leave?" pleaded Sandi.

"I'm sorry."

He bent to kiss her and whispered with difficulty, "I won't be far away. I'll see you in a little while."

"All right. Thank you, darling."

As he watched her being rolled away, he leaned against the wall and sucked deep, ragged breaths. He walked into the waiting room but could hardly sit still. He paced, staring out the windows. The hour or so before they let him go in to see her was the longest hour he'd ever spent. When he finally did walk into her room, Sandi smiled, grabbed his hand, and all the tension seemed to leave her. But in a few minutes she fell asleep again and he stood beside the bed wishing with all his heart that he could lift her into his arms and carry her like a child to their own bed.

During the next couple of days, his actions were mechanical and dreamlike. None of the things that were happening seemed real or even possible. Sandi lay pale and helpless in cardiac care, where he was allowed to visit only a few minutes each hour. An iron fist had closed on his chest. He had never thought about anything serious ever happening to Sandi. And what about Eddi? What would she do without her mother? He walked to the window, to the bed, back to the window . . . then a nurse came and asked him to leave.

For two days he slipped away only long enough to make phone calls or stop by the house to change or get a bite to eat. As frequently as possible he gave his parents and Lori an update. "She's sleeping a lot but I know she's fighting with her spirit."

"Neal, what can we do?"

"Just stay on your knees, I guess."

"Sandi's been such a joy to us. We all love her."

Time meant nothing, eating, sleeping meant nothing. Regularly, he phoned Mrs. Steele and as often as possible hurried over to see Eddi. The first couple of times, she seemed responsive enough, but about the third time he walked in she looked up and burst into tears. He realized she had thought it was her mother coming. He drew her into his arms, knowing he couldn't provide quite the comfort she needed.

"Mommie'll be home soon, darling. Grandmama and Grandaddy are so happy to have you here with them."

He sat down on the floor and played with her. They arranged blocks and looked at books, and he swung her on his leg. She looked at him with wide, troubled eyes. As she raised her arms and appealed for him to hold her, his heart hammered harder. "It's all right, darling, we'll all be home soon."

She pressed close to him, her blue eyes searching and silent. Out of sheer courtesy he went in to speak to Mr. Steele. He sat in his half-dark room surrounded by newspapers, the sweet aroma of his pipe deceptively pleasant. "How are you today?"

"Just look at the miserable mess they're making of the world. I don't think they got a dab of sense." His grumbling was a poor disguise of his own worry.

Mrs. Steele walked Neal to the door, her eyes glazed with misery. "Is she better, do you think? How can we help?"

"She's getting good care and may have improved a little. And taking care of Eddi means everything to us." After a moment he asked, "Do you think Eddi's really all right? I know she misses her mother."

"She's become upset a few times, but we try to amuse her."

"I hope it doesn't wear you out."

"Oh, she brings joy into the house."

Mrs. Steele was such a sweet gentle person. Her hands were graceful, like Sandi's. She was a stout-hearted woman, but he knew at this moment she was hurting as only a mother can. He put his arms around her. "Thank you so much for bringing your beautiful daughter into the world."

"Please get her well, Neal."

He slipped back to steal a look at Eddi and found her staring straight at him. He hurried out, emotion all up in his throat.

At the hospital, he waited for each visiting period, hour falling upon hour with an almost numbing, disorienting effect. A day, a night, three, four, went by, reports from doctors and nurses neither pessimistic nor reassuring. Time was on the side of her recovery, Neal realized, but looking into Sandi's pallid face, the erratic flutter of her long lashes, the pulse beating in her neck, the curve of her long, slender fingers on the sheet, he was seized by uncertainty. How easily life could be reduced to one simple event, he thought, one crucial moment. And what could one do to prepare against this kind of occurrence? There was nothing that he knew of.

The Fullers came to the hospital, then the Palmers, his parents, old friends of Sandi's, people from The Learning Room. His sister Lori came and sat with him an hour or two. Except for Lori, none of them asked to go in to see her — they knew these visits must be reserved for the husband. But to Lori he said, "I want you to go in. It'll mean a lot to her."

"I love Sandi so much," said Lori.

"She loves you, too. We'll share the time."

The Steeles got a neighborhood friend to watch Eddi and came up. It was very difficult for Mr. Steele. Neal met them downstairs and helped him along. His breathing was so labored he had to stop every few steps. The nurses broke a rule and allowed the two of them to go in to see their daughter together. They emerged from their brief visit with pale drawn faces, shoulders slumped. They spoke little, but their eyes said it all. Mrs. Steele murmured, "I'm so glad Sandi has your love to depend on, Neal. If there's anything that'll help her it's this."

"I know it hurts her not to be there for you."

"We've come to depend on her, perhaps more than we should. Now we must try to do something for her."

But what that was, no one knew.

Neal welcomed everyone who came up to visit, but what he really wanted was to be alone. Most of the time when he slipped into Sandi's room her eyes were closed, but when she sensed him enter or heard his voice, her face brightened and she whispered hoarsely, "Hi, honey." She lifted her arm, black and blue from puncture bruises, and reached out for him to take her hand. Much as she wanted to talk, he saw how hard it was for her. He pushed visiting time to the limit and returned heavily to the waiting area to attempt to endure the unbearable hours in between.

Then one evening when he entered her semi-darkened room, an opaque glare from the silvering sky solid as mercury between a separation of the curtains, Sandi looked at him with eyes clearer than they'd been in days and grasped his hand tightly. "How's Eddi?"

"She's doing well. Your mother's great with her."

"Does she miss me terribly?"

"You know she does."

"She's been such a joy to me. So much like you I can't believe it." She turned closer to him and holding his hand even tighter to her chest, asked, "You aren't sorry, then, are you, Neal?"

"Sorry?"

"That I've given you a child to raise?"

"You mean to help you raise. It'll take both of us to get it right."

"No, I mean you, Neal. Will it be just maddening trying to bring up a little girl by yourself?"

"Why should you suggest such a thing?"

"I've thought about it a lot. You have so much to do, so many plans. I've wondered if getting pregnant was a mistake."

"Sandi, listen," he said. "Next to you, Eddi's the only remarkable thing that's ever happened to me."

She searched his face, then smiled. "Maybe I can be proud, then, that I've given you this precious gift."

"There's nothing that I'd ever change, but I know a child needs her mother more than anything."

She released his hand suddenly, caught her breath in a sharp, choked gasp and tensed her body against the treachery which attacked her so suddenly. Then after a moment, she exhaled and ran her tongue over her dry lips. She slipped his hand into both of hers again and held it tightly to her side, as if more than any doctor, any medicine, any support system, his closeness seemed to give her the strength she needed.

"Oh, I wanted so much to be a good mother. All those stages of her life she'll experience, the walking and talking, the learning and wondering, and her little pinafores and cheerleader outfits. With all my heart I believed it would be good for you, Neal. I believed it would make such a difference in your life."

"Sandi." He tried to keep his voice steady, to calm his own breathing. He pushed back a lock of her crumpled hair. "Sandi, listen to me. It's understandable that you're frightened now. All this medication is bound to affect your emotions. But don't let yourself think this way. Everything you planned will happen. It's happening now. In no time, Eddi will be riding tricycles."

"But I have this feeling, Neal. I'm not trying to scare you or be melodramatic. But I don't think I'm coming home."

"Sandi . . ."

"No, please let me say it. I know you never loved me as much as I love you, but that's all right. Usually one person loves more than the other. Most of the time I don't even mind you having this other life. I understood about your writing and accepted things as they are. People go a little crazy when they love someone so much. And I believed that in time, I still believe that given time you would . . . Anyway, we have Eddi now. No woman should use a baby to hold a man, but I've always seen something in you, something you maybe have never even recognized. I thought if we could have a child, if I could just give you another little me . . . and then she turned out to be you all over."

He tried to speak, heard only a rasp, then said sternly, "You are coming home. I don't know how I could manage without you."

"But you can, I know you can, darling. That's why I can feel at peace somehow. It'll be hard and your life won't ever be the same again. Some days you'll nearly die of frustration. But she'll love you so much, Neal. You'll mean everything to her. She'll trust you, cling to you, and come to you even when outwardly she seems to resist everything you say. That's why I can have peace, don't you see? I don't know where your life was going. Maybe you would have found what you wanted and that would have been the end of me. But now I know I've given you one thing that'll bring light into your life when nothing else could."

There was a look of sadness about her, a look of regret, yet strange and more touching, the presence of brave resolution. He started to speak, could form no words, then helplessly shook his head and held her hands, which had been so strong but now felt so fragile.

"You'll probably marry again," she said. "Of course you should. And you'll have other children. But when you look at Eddi, you'll never forget me."

"Sandi, please," he murmured, and the tears broke and rolled down his cheeks.

"I'd want you to have a good wife. Any woman would love Eddi. If she loved you, she'd have to love her."

"I can't even begin to imagine such a thing."

"I hate it. It's so sudden. I didn't have time to get ready. If only I could see my baby again."

"There's nothing to get ready for. You're going to come home."

"I had such a short time with her. If I could just explain things to her. But I'm so lucky to have you as her father." She began to cry, then said softly, "I'm sorry, Neal. I'm so sorry this had to happen to you. You're such a good man."

"Sandi, please, you're making it hard on yourself. You're making it hard on me."

"I don't mean to. You know that's not what I want. But please don't be impatient with me. I waited as long as I could to tell you this, but it's important that you understand now. Oh, I'd give anything to see my baby again! I'm a little jealous to think about someone else raising her. But I want you to know it's okay. You'll always do the right thing."

A nurse came to the door and signaled that it was time to leave. He shook his head, and she gave him a stern look.

"I have to go, Sandi."

"Oh, must you?"

"I think they need to come in." He put his face against her cheek, then kissed her on the lips. For a moment, their tears ran together.

"Do you think they might let you bring Eddi to see me?"

"I don't know. I'll ask."

"Then go home and rest. It's no use sitting in that awful waiting room."

"We'll see. About Eddi, I mean."

"But then . . . you'll be back?"

"Of course I'll be back." He kissed her again, softly, then held her close. "I love you so much."

"I know you do. I wish people could learn that if you just stick it out, love grows stronger."

"I think you're right. Why have you always been so much wiser than I?"

"In some things I really am, aren't I? But you're the smartest man I've ever known."

He drew away, then at the door turned and found her gazing steadily into his face.

"'Bye, Neal."

He left quickly, then stood outside her room pressing his handkerchief to his eyes, trying to control the tears. Through the glass he saw her turn her head away and lie motionless, quietly, as though peace had come to her and she was simply waiting. One leg was up and bent over the other, and he knew it would have made all the difference if he could just lie beside her a moment, just let her feel his closeness and his strength for a while.

Since their wedding night, they'd never slept apart. With all the anxieties and urgencies and doubts, they'd always fallen back on the comfort of sleeping in each other's arms. What hurt him most was that she was alone, and he could do nothing to get close to her. If he could just crawl into bed and wrap his arms about her somehow he felt she'd get well. As he stood drying his eyes and watching her through the glass he felt as if the world were collapsing under him. Her expression was calm, her lips slightly parted, and he believed he could sense what she was feeling. It was that no sorrows of the future, no remorse for time lost, could destroy the precious treasures of which she'd been a part.

Chapter Fourteen

On faltering legs he made his way to the nurse's station, a brightly lit island in the center of dark silent rooms and courageous hearts. He found her nurse, a stocky, graying, serious woman with strong arms and wearing a pair of old-fashioned horn-rimmed glasses. "My wife seems especially troubled tonight. Is there anything you can tell me?"

She gazed at him a moment, her glasses framing black eyes in which he observed undisguised sympathy. "It isn't unusual for people to try to prepare for the worst, especially when surgery's imminent."

"A premonition of disaster. Is that normal?"

"I wouldn't say so. Sometimes patients do just the opposite — set their minds against very real possibilities. But I can tell you this, Mr. Austin. Your wife's no quitter."

"That I know. But how is she doing really?"

"I believe her condition's improved a little."

He returned to the waiting room and collapsed into a chair, wrung out, too agitated to sit still and too drained to move. With all this emotion pressing down on him he needed to get away, he needed to see his daughter, but couldn't bring himself to leave. He paced the room, sat down again, paced. A large family came in, engaged in an ongoing dialogue, and became argumentative. Able neither to close his ears nor to tolerate this incursion on his thoughts, he finally left the hospital and drove over to the Steeles.

He found Mrs. Steele sitting on a hassock trying to involve Eddi in a stack of plastic building blocks. They had come once to see Sandi, but reluctant to deprive Neal of the limited visits, were quietly waiting for whatever reassurance he could bring them. Mrs. Steele bore her pain silently, but he couldn't miss the fear and suffering in her eyes.

"Sandi's resting quietly." He tried to bring her good news. "And the nurse seems to believe she's a little better."

"When will they put her in a room?"

"I don't know, but you must come again. She wants to see you."

She looked sadly at Eddi, her worry for the future apparent in every breath and gesture.

"Sandi wants me to bring Eddi to see her, but I don't think they'll let me."

"It would mean so much to her to hold her baby."

"I'll see if I can pull some strings."

Eddi continued amusing herself with the blocks then came and lifted her arms for him to pick her up.

"Hello, darling." He swung her up and held her close. "I've missed you."

He kissed her and swung her about. Then as he put her down, he felt certain she played more freely and contentedly because he was close by. He hadn't much time, but forced himself to take time to bathe her, read her a story, and prepare her for bed. "You're such a pretty thing." He used any words of reassurance he could think of. "Mommy and I are so proud of you . . ." Finally he had to leave. As he put her down, he could feel the resistance in her eager little arms.

"Daddy has to leave now, honey."

She wouldn't let him go. She clung to his neck, and he had to pull her arms away. "I'm sorry, darling."

He saw an expression in her face, something troubled and uncertain, and he hardly knew what to do. She appealed to him to lift her up again, and unable to resist, he allowed her to sit quietly in his lap. As she curled her small frame against him and pressed her head silently to his chest, he wanted to talk to her but dared not try to speak. He could only imagine how deeply her little heart missed her mother and how much she wanted to go home to her own toys, her own bed, her own music. Leaving her was more difficult this time than it had ever been before. He finally did, though, and with a sudden, urgent sense of responsibility he walked down the steps and out to the car. As he drove away the terror was so heavy his conscious self had to give way to some deeper part of himself which now directed his movements and thoughts.

He drove to the empty house that he and Sandi had made, the house which only promised a crushing silence. He wouldn't be allowed to see his wife again for a while, and hanging around the waiting room was torture. Sandi's car was in the garage, and as he swung into the driveway, the eyes of a neighborhood dog caught his headlights. The mutt had often been a nuisance, but tonight he was glad to be greeted by a familiar face. He paused on the walkway which connected the garage with the rear door and stood looking at their gazebo, the lattice brick fence forming a maze of light and dark shadows, and at Sandi's flowerbeds. Everything seemed different and distant. He fumbled with his keys and let himself into the house. Except for the few lamps he'd left on, the rooms were dark. He walked down the halls to their bathroom.

After a quick shower, he made himself a sandwich and sat at the table. He was addicted to quiet moments and a little time on his own, but now the stillness of the house, the spirit of him, Sandi and Eddi was like a living thing whose departure left in its wake something precious.

He was unable to finish his sandwich. He left the table and moved through the house to their bedroom, to Eddi's room, the kitchen and the den, checking things, making points of contact, reaffirming that it was still a good place. Sandi loved this house, and her love of flowers was evident, too, in vases all through the rooms. He inhaled the sweet-sour, faintly nostalgic odor of faded blooms, of dying stems gone unwatered. He touched nothing, some subconscious obstinacy refusing to concede that anything had changed. Finally, dropping onto the sofa, he sat with his head bowed, praying that God would intervene in this critical moment. He removed his shoes and closed his eyes with no intention of falling asleep. When he awakened with a jolt, he saw by his watch that he'd missed a visiting hour, and he swore to himself. But now there was a little time before the next. Without meaning to, he fell into a restless, fitful sleep.

The urgent peal of the telephone aroused him. Startled, he snatched it up, instantly awake, and felt a great sense of regret that he'd left the hospital.

A voice said, "Mr. Austin?"

"Yes."

"This is the hospital. There's been a change in your wife's condition."

"What is it! Is she all right?"

"I think you should come up."

He didn't stop to lock the house. He ran out the door and drove furiously those few miles whose turns and signs and lights had become so imbedded in his mind these past few days. He didn't try to find a parking place. He left his car on the edge of the driveway, keys in the ignition. He skipped the elevator, running through the halls and up the stairs. When he reached the I.C. floor, his lungs were bursting, his thighs throbbing. He stopped a minute, bending over to rest his hands on his knees, catching his breath. Then he ran on to the nurse's station.

The floor was practically deserted. There were two nurses behind the desk. They saw him coming and looked up with masked faces which somehow communicated to him the worst possible news. There was a man there who appeared to be waiting for him. He came around the counter and held out his hand.

"Mr. Austin? I'm Dr. Marshall. I'm on the staff here."

Neal didn't know him and after that night would not begin to remember even what he looked like. From that moment, everything became an insufferable blur.

"I'm sorry to tell you that your wife has passed away."

How long it took for the words to sink in Neal didn't know. A shock like this didn't register at first. He felt his knees about to buckle.

"We don't know for certain yet, but we think the infection of the mitral valve set off other complications and a blood clot formed. We had no warning, no time to do anything." Dr. Marshall placed a hand on his arm. "Your wife died without a struggle, Mr. Austin. There's no indication that she suffered."

"Did . . . did she say anything?"

"We believe she died peacefully in her sleep."

He realized that something vitally important had just gone out of his life. It was hard for him to remain standing. He had no substance, no ballast — all that had been taken from him. He said at last, "I have to see her."

"Of course, you can go in. She hasn't been moved."

He blundered down the hall, entered the room, and closed the door. Sandi was lying with her head tilted slightly to one side, her hair spread against the white pillow. The nurses had prepared her; there was nothing shocking about her appearance. She looked so still, yet so beautiful.

The instant he looked at her, the tears came forcefully, agonizingly. They came in such a flood he felt sick. He stood motionless, trying to get control. Finally he moved to the bed and took her hands.

"Sandi." He kissed her hands, her cheek, her mouth. He was able to half sit, half lie beside her. He knew if there were anything she could feel, it would be this, his lying close to her. For a long time he pressed his cheek to hers. All his senses struggled to capture something, recall something, drawing from her in these last moments the strength on which he'd come to rely. Her face was calm and he thought she looked as if she believed her life had not ended in vain. The most overwhelming emotion he had to fight was regret.

There was a quiet tap on the door, but no one entered. He knew he had to turn her loose. This part of his life was over. He stood, then bent to kiss her one last time. "You've meant so much to me, Sandi. I hope you know how much I love you. I hope you know how hard it's going to be to let you go."

He walked to the door, then helpless, came back, took her hand and pressed it to his mouth.

"Goodbye, my love. Goodbye, my life."

He staggered down the hall, down the steps, and out into the night. He wondered if he would ever take a happy breath again.

Chapter Fifteen

How he got through the next few days Neal didn't know. How anyone got through them he didn't know. The arrangements, the decisions and choices — only the human spirit could keep one afloat at such a time when all he wanted was to be left alone. He fought as tenaciously as a soldier in battle against regret, self-pity, and the inevitable "what ifs." Many people attended the funeral services. All the church pews were full. He realized he had to stay on his feet as those who respected and loved Sandi came to speak to him. It was helpful to know they cared and would absorb some of his sadness if they could.

The hardest thing was telling Eddi. He pulled her into his lap as she looked at him with wide wondering eyes.

"Mommy gone away?"

"Yes. She's gone away."

"When she coming back?"

"Mommy's in heaven, Eddi. She didn't want to leave us, but . . . but . . ." He tried his best not to break down, but he couldn't help it. She cried, too, as though her little heart would break. He knew she didn't fully understand, yet in a way she must have felt the terrible absence. Whenever he heard her whisper, "Mommy," to herself, he realized he could never totally fill her mother's place.

He wasn't the only one in shock. His parents, Lori, and especially Sandi's parents crept away into their own private corners of suffering. From the Steeles something had been taken away when they needed her most. Neal could almost envy their age — perhaps they didn't have many years to hurt, especially Mr. Steele, who in his characteristic way kept his pain to himself but who seemed to have more trouble getting out of his chair, more trouble breathing, than ever before.

When he was finally able to put Eddi to bed, just the two of them in the large empty house, Neal walked out to their gazebo where he, Sandi and Eddi had spent so much time — not nearly enough time — together. The stars winked and glinted through the spangled trees, some gauzy wisps like fog floated across the Milky Way. One thing he knew: he would never fall in love again. It was too painful. He would post sentinels before the door of his heart, those portals through which this kind of love would never be allowed to pass. He wondered if having a baby could have somehow precipitated Sandi's infection. He knew this wasn't reasonable, but his thoughts were irrational. His anger, his terror and sorrow alienated him from everyone. What was God thinking, to give them this beautiful child only to take Sandi away? If she had to die, why did they first have to bring another life into the world? Eddi didn't ask to be born, she was innocent, but now he had a child to raise alone. How could he be expected to nurture and care for her in the way that she needed? And the things he wanted to do — all he could see ahead now was a stultified life crusting over as year after year dragged by. And what did it matter? What did his writing, his business, success matter? Without his Sandi it all came to nothing. Except he was not allowed to accept nothing. He must keep breathing, and keep going through the days. For what? His thoughts were not merely confused, they were self-destructive. What kind of God would take such a beautiful young mother away? Sandi had so much to offer, she was one of those rare personalities who would give more to the world than she would ever take from it. How could the heavens be so cruel? He wondered if despite the emotional pain that was so suffocating, there was an element of spirit, of soul, an immortality of love that could prevail against all the world's grief. He wondered if life with all its warts and blemishes was meant to be lived, not planned for. He was bitter toward God, he was angry with Sandi for leaving him, for giving him another life to be responsible for. It would have been a reprieve to fling himself into numbing nothingness, but now he had Eddi to hide his grief from.

He lifted his head and stood, and as his emotions gave way to rage he cried out, a tortured, animal scream. He seized a garden spade from the floor of the gazebo and flung it violently against the brick carport wall. Then he stood trembling, his head hung. Something about the air, the scents and the sounds, reminded him of some old memory he could not quite bring to mind. It was like forgetting a loved one's face. He hated this wallowing in anger and loneliness, but could not seem to stop it.

He began to walk through the half-illuminated yard. There was a bed for seasonal flowers which Sandi had made, now gone to seed and wasting away. There was the play set the two of them had spent all one Sunday afternoon assembling, consisting of a swing, a seesaw, and a small slide. Beyond a border of fieldstone were young trees Sandi had planted — crepe myrtle, dogwood, crabapple — and all through the garden, little interstices of flowers. For the elevated stone patio, she'd had masons construct a brick wall around a twenty-four-inch hickory. Upon this tree hung a bird feeder which attracted a community of house finches, jays, cardinals, doves, and woodpeckers and wrens. Everywhere the touch of her hand could be seen.

He stole around the yard, finding little reminders of her and realizing how much he missed her in both trivial and significant ways. On the stone wall, iridescent sienna and charcoal blue in the semi-dark night, he found a pair of cotton garden gloves. Not far away were a small spade and half a package of seed, forgotten by a gardener who'd been called away in a critical moment. He missed Sandi's love, her lovemaking, her support, and found memories of her haunting and disorienting. He saw her behind the wheel of her car. He saw her damp footprints in the carpet beside their tub. In a dark-haired girl wearing jeans and a lavender shirt guiding a stroller steadily through the park, he saw her, her sunglasses large ovals in white, gold-trimmed frames. In many respects, he realized she would never completely leave him.

Friends came by to bring food and tears. "Neal, we're so sorry about Sandi. What can we do?"

They didn't know what to say, and he didn't know how to relieve their tension.

Tia was doing her best to manage the office, and the loyal men pitched in wherever they could. Neal went back and forth, half-hearted about his business but knowing that now that he had a daughter to care for it would be self-destructive to let all these years of work and struggle go.

After a couple of months he finally brought himself to go through Sandi's things. He boxed and stored articles he thought Eddi might want some day, the rest he tried to donate to some good cause. He was startled to realize how many small details Sandi had taken care of. From the first he'd known how much she depended on him now, he saw how much he had depended on her. He wished he could tell her how special she was to him, and tried to convince himself that she'd always known. She worried about leaving him alone to raise their daughter, but he was pretty certain she had found peace in the belief that Eddi was the truest gift she could give him of herself.

He made sandwiches and took Eddi out to picnic in the gazebo, the place where they'd shared many happy times. Never did he stop talking to her. He saw no reason to think she would forget her mother.

"We have a pretty garden, don't we, Eddi? So nice and secure. Your mother loved flowers."

"I love them, too."

"I know you do. She would be so proud of you."

Eddi was two now. Sometimes she would go for days seemingly content. At other times she cried dramatically, almost hysterically, "Mommy! I want Mommy!" She resisted his arms, furious without knowing why. Perhaps more pathetic were the times she crawled quietly into his lap and sat still, as though her fierce little heart was broken.

Occasionally, he found a little space of his own. He jogged around the park, his head bent. Other joggers hammered by, echoes of their feet fading like a memory. Sandi, in sun visor and shorts, had been his jogging partner for so long. Passing a girl walking at a fast clip, swinging tiny, one-pound dumbbells, he inhaled her trailing perfume, strangely familiar, disturbingly stirring. Such impressions assumed a particular, biting clarity, a poignant consciousness, as though he saw everything from both his old perspective and a new one.

He often walked into the nursery to check on his sleeping daughter. Her face was half on the pillow, one hand pulled up under her chin. She was beautiful, he thought, a beautiful prism. He adjusted the covers, pushed back a lock of her hair. She was so innocent, so dependent. A tight fist closed on his stomach. He was all she had.

In his own bed, the sheets felt cold and strange. He tried scrunching a pillow up against his back, but it was so unnatural, he kicked it off onto the floor. He remembered a book Sandi had given him for a birthday, a book by Spencer Johnson. "Pain is simply the difference between what is and what I want it to be." She had always tried to tell him one could not go through life yearning for some other life. Happiness was circumstantial; true joy should not rely on circumstances at all.

During these first months he tried everything he could think of with Eddi. He gave her all the time he could, let her sleep with him, rocked and loved her, changed her diet, conferred with Sandi's mother. Some of the hardest times were taking Eddi to the doctor. He tried to break the news gently. Tears welled up in her eyes, she looked at him pathetically. "No, Daddy!"

"Eddi, I wish I could have these shots for you. I wish I could take away all our pain, but I can't."

She set her little jaw and narrowed her eyes, reminding him just how like Sandi she was.

He wondered what went through her mind, what she dreamed, what her deepest fears were. He wondered how much of her mother she remembered. He left things around to remind her — pictures, sunglasses, Sandi's guitar. Even before she was born, Sandi had sung to her. He doubted his ability to give her all she needed. Love had been torn from him, and he was ashamed of his uncertainty about her.

Then one afternoon he established her in a play area on the patio, surrounded by a wooden pull train, a cardboard playhouse, and two or three dolls. He was slumped in a patio chair writing in longhand when a big truck descended a nearby hill. Downshifting, it backfired, tearing the peaceful air with a violent explosion. He glanced up to see that the noise had terrified Eddi. She sprang to her feet, and arms raised, eyes fixed upon his face, she blundered toward him as fast as her little legs could carry her. Her expression was contorted with fear, but stronger than fear was the certainty that could she just reach him, her father and protector, she'd be safe.

He threw the pad aside, swept her into his arms. "It's all right, darling. I'll never let anything harm you."

She pressed herself hard against him, making certain he held her tight. In her wide blue eyes, in the small twist of her lips, he saw something he could hardly bear. He saw Sandi. And in that heartbreaking moment, he knew Eddi would be all right. He saw Sandi — not her face or features, but her disposition, her bravery, her forgiveness, her tender feelings, her determination to find happy lightning in bitter things. He remembered that Sandi herself had said as long as he had Eddi he'd never forget her.

In that moment he knew she was right. He would not forget what she meant to him. He would love and tend and protect their daughter. But he was determined never to expose his heart to that kind of pain again.

Chapter Sixteen

I t was five-thirty a.m. Neal threw off the covers, dropped his feet to
the floor. It had been a restless night. Bed wasn't friendly to him.
How often he found himself reaching for his absent lover. He went into
the bathroom, dressed quickly. His habit had always been to dress as
soon as he woke. He slipped down the hall, looked in on Eddi, then in
the kitchen made himself a cup of coffee. He went to his home office
hoping to write a while. By starting early and working late, when Eddi
was asleep, he'd finally been able to hammer out a few more chapters of
Samson's Revenge. He wasn't happy with them, but sent them off to Sam
Harris anyway. Sam's response was lukewarm. "Tell less, show more,"
wrote Sam. "Readers nowadays demand suspense, action."

Neal wrote back, "I remember my original passion which seems
now to surround me like paintings of bright dreams, but paintings
still, somehow devoid of life." Almost defensively he wrote about the
demands of running a business and trying to raise a daughter alone. And
in a pensive voice he reflected on how quickly life can be changed by one
fateful incident, one unexpected twist of events.

Sam answered, "Why don't you write about these things then, Neal?
I get the feeling you're holding back."

But he wasn't ready to write about his own life. At this point he
felt incapable of expressing all the conflicts steaming within. The sheer
pressure of time bore heavily on him. The irony was that *Samson's Revenge*
was about the twists and turns that so disrupt one's carefully crafted
world, and this was such a mystery to him he was not even certain of
a satisfactory conclusion. He knew his agent believed in him and really
wanted to help him break in. But Sam was tough — he had to be. There
was just so much time he could devote to an unknown author when his
first obligation was to pitch those who had a track record and who might

make a little money. Neal never knew when he opened a letter from Sam if he'd find words of sympathy and encouragement or the blunt realism of rejection. His writing life was an isolated, solitary one, and he wondered if success might make his work feel and sound more at ease.

He discovered an odd thing about his writing. Whenever he felt he'd written something worthwhile, he was happy, though more often than not almost every sentence, every paragraph seemed torn loose with hammer and claw. But when he read over what he'd written days or weeks earlier, the work he had felt was most fluent sounded no better or worse than those pages he'd thought a failure. His prose neither suffered nor benefitted from his mood during any particular phase.

He remembered Sandi saying, "I know you never wanted to live an ordinary life, Neal, but why you believe that in the absence of an extraordinary one you've failed, I don't understand." Though Sandi had never felt herself a part of his writing, he yearned every day for her vivid bursts of wisdom.

He sat at his desk sipping coffee and trying to get the juices flowing. Sometimes he retyped the last paragraph he'd written the day before. Sometimes he read a page or two aloud, though he hardly ever found this stimulating. Sometimes he merely sat haunted by the spirits of his original and almost forgotten self, aware of an aloneness, of a thirst for flight, for romance, for mysterious places. How much time had he wasted weaving intricate details about his success, his fame, his fortune, of the legacy he'd leave, the contributions he would make that would live on after his death. He realized this thirst for purely a creative life was just another part of himself seeking one world while he lived in another.

When he heard Eddi stirring he broke off and went to her room. He had decided never to let her awaken thinking she was alone. "Hello, darling, how are you today?" Sometimes he'd find her talking and playing in her bed. Sometimes he found her standing, holding onto the bed rails, looking straight at him. He took her into the kitchen, sat her in the highchair, then as he made breakfast he kept up a cheerful monologue, hoping to set the stage for her day. Sometimes when he simply didn't feel like talking he found her looking at him wonderingly.

He shaved and dressed, then he took her to one of her grandparents' or to a daycare center. Occasionally he was able to stay at home late and conduct business over the phone. By the time he dropped Eddi off the morning was well underway, and the minute he walked into the office Tia came to him with some item of business long past due. "We have to make a decision about this insurance, Neal. I've had these quotes for weeks."

On the days Eddi was sick or needed to be taken to the doctor, everything was thrown off. He always tried to do this himself, but from time to time had to call one of her grandmothers. Also, he had to learn quickly about clothes and hygiene, about medicines and leg cramps, what to do for nausea and headaches. He learned to cook a little. She liked ravioli and macaroni which made it easier.

One evening when he was adjusting a loose door latch he caught Eddi fiddling with his screwdriver. He took it from her and slipped it into his pocket. "Gone, gone," he said, a lamentation used often.

She peered at him with grave eyes. "Mommy's gone, gone."

It stopped him cold. He reached and crushed her into his arms. "But Daddy's here, honey." He knew it would never be quite enough.

Another time she noticed a scratch on his arm. "You hurt yourself?"

"It's all right. Nothing at all."

She drew his arm up and held it against her cheek, as if she wanted to mother *him*. In some way she must have sensed his loneliness.

He read to her then put her to bed with her music, wondering whether he should buy her dresses or jeans, if he were feeding her right, how to help her cultivate friends to invite over. He thought of the unfinished page in his typewriter and a feeling of urgency flared up. He looked in on Eddi, laid out her clothes for the next morning, then inevitably thought about how much she needed a mother. This pretty much was his typical day.

One Sunday afternoon about a year after Sandi died, he drove Eddi out to the cemetery. It was a pretty setting, a grassy hillside dotted with hardwood and pine trees. They walked up an ascending curved walkway until they came to Sandi's marker. He held Eddi's hand, and they stood side by side looking down at the bronze plaque with the upturned bronze urn in which were flowers he paid a fee to have replaced on a regular basis.

"Mommy's here?" asked Eddi.

"This is where your mother was laid to rest, Eddi. But she lives in our hearts. She'll always be there."

He told her some stories about Sandi. "One day when she took you shopping, you were in a stroller. Although she always kept you with her, when she got back to the car and took you out of the stroller, she found about a dozen pairs of little panties under you. You'd been fascinated with the colors and one by one collected them and sat on them. She had no idea. She hurried back into the store. 'Look what my baby did!' They laughed it off, but she worried that you were about to get her arrested. You remember that, Eddi?"

She shook her head.

"You might remember someday, when you're older. Your mother always wanted a baby, and even before you were born she knew you'd be a girl."

"I wish she didn't die," she said.

"So do I, Eddi." He turned quickly from her.

She began to investigate, walking here and there, careful of the flowers strung across the hillside. Slowly she drifted from one to the other, smelling to see which ones had scent, which ones were real. He hoped this would act as some kind of closure for her. There was a bench nearby and he sat down as she amused herself. At the bottom of the slope was a small reflecting pool with ducks and water lilies. He was fighting a collapse into melancholy when he noticed that abruptly Eddi had stopped walking. She became still and sat down on the edge of the grass. Her expression became melancholy and troubled. She was just two and a half now, but the sorrows of her young life often made her pensive and sad. Something about her demeanor reminded him of Sandi. It caught him unexpectedly, and try as he might he could not keep the tears from his eyes. He pulled out his handkerchief. Eddi looked up at him then with a sensitivity beyond her years, came over and put both her hands on his cheeks. "It's all right, Daddy. Mommy's in heaven waiting for us." He drew her into his arms and they sat quietly until it was time to leave.

Eddi's moments of sadness touched Neal more than her obstinacy ever could; and she could be stubborn, especially when she was confused and hurting. Sometimes she refused to let him dress her. About the time he'd get one arm into her shirt, she tore loose and scrambled away. "Eddi," he said, "don't give me a hard time. This is what you're wearing today."

"No! Don't want to!"

"It's a pretty outfit. Your grandmother gave it to you."

As he pulled her back, she stiffened her arms and legs tightly, making them impossible to manipulate.

"Eddi . . ."

"No! I want Mommy!"

"Your mother isn't here, Eddi. It's you and me and no one else."

He hated losing patience with her, but sometimes it was inevitable. When he finally got her dressed, she pulled away, sat on the floor, and began some silent game known only to herself. She was a determined little thing. Unable to achieve some task, she'd become angry, her face turning red, her lower lip drawn tightly. She struck the floor with her tiny fist, and sometimes with her head. "Eddi," he said, "this is not the way we act."

Secretly, he admired her determination. She was an outgoing, sweet child, but the losses she'd suffered manifested themselves in her uncertainties and anxieties, and occasionally in her stubborn defiance.

It seemed when he was tired, when he especially needed a few minutes of quiet time, was when she was most likely to come, take his hand, and draw him into her room. There on the floor she had established a circle of building blocks or boxes, with an opening for a door and one or two baby chairs. "We have party, Daddy."

"That's sweet, Eddi, but could we wait a little while?"

"No. Sit. I bring you tea."

Hard as it was, for half an hour he'd chat and pretend to drink from her elfin cups. How many parents were compelled to indulge in these games at the most inopportune times he could only imagine. Fortunately, a little while was all that was required to satisfy her. She had pretty much learned to play alone, and when he said, "May I be excused?" she was content to let him go.

The best thing he had going was a woman who'd worked for Sandi's mother off and on for years. Her name was Charlotte Insley, and she was a treasure. At first she declined to come because all her days were taken. He tried to convince her she could find time somehow. "Charlotte, you knew Sandi all her life. This is her baby."

Charlotte finally managed to rearrange her schedule and on two afternoons a week she came, put the house in order, washed and ironed, prepared meals, and spent some time with Eddi.

"You can't always feed this child packaged stuff," Charlotte said one evening. "She needs real food."

"Believe it or not, I'm learning to cook a little. Before now, all I could do was scramble eggs and make toast."

"Well, it's a good thing to know. A lot of men are helpless in the kitchen."

After finishing her work, Charlotte took Eddi for a walk around the neighborhood, introducing her to the dogs, the cats, the odors and sounds, and the flowers and voices in her environment. "That child had rather be out in the sun more than anybody I know."

"I'm not surprised," said Neal. "Sandi and I both loved the outdoors." His own moods seemed to be tempered by light and darkness, and it was seldom too bright or too warm for him. He liked the sun to blaze down, but he remembered how Sandi had always preferred sunless, overcast days.

Eddi had a vital, healthy complexion and a suggestion of dimples in her round cheeks, and he thought her black hair, blue eyes and sweet smile made her a pretty child by anyone's standards. "You're such a doll," he'd tell her or, "You're so smart . . ." — anything to build her sense of well-being.

As often as possible, Neal took Eddi to visit her grandparents and her cousins. Attached to Eddi in a special way, Mrs. Steele restrained herself from acting the doting, overly solicitous grandmother.

"I hope you'll bring her over as much as you like, Neal."

"It's a comfort to know you're here, but we don't want to impose."

"We'll get through this together," said Mrs. Steele. "All Sandi ever really wanted was a home and family. That's why she was so good with those special children, I think."

Despite her constant pain she clapped her hands together, smiled in her old way and put her own feelings aside to support him and Eddi. Neal wondered if a parent ever got over the premature death of a child or only absorbed it as enduring, ineffable pain.

One day he was sitting at his desk at NEA Courier, swamped, when Tia put through a call from Eddi's teacher at the daycare center. "Eddi's not feeling well and wants to come home."

"What's the matter?"

"She has no fever, but says she doesn't feel like playing."

He thought through his alternatives, all he had to do, what he could put off. There were no simple answers. As he hesitated, the teacher asked, "Would you like her to stay anyway?"

"No, it's better that I come for her. Tell her it won't be long."

He ran through a hasty recap for Tia, then jumped into his car and drove over to the daycare center. It was a converted frame house in a quiet neighborhood, somehow more personalized and intimate than the big centers. As he pulled up to the curb, he could hear and see children running and playing in the fenced side yard, while Eddi sat in a small chair on the porch, alone, waiting for him. His first response was one of irritation. Evidently she wasn't ill and neither did it seem to bother her that the other children were laughing and playing. He felt that even at this young age she must learn there would be moments of discontent.

But he remembered that as a child he, too, had sometimes felt miserably isolated without knowing why.

Without rising from her chair Eddi, with a smile that was like ribbons of sunlight, asked, "Daddy, do you like yourself?"

"Well, pretty much, yes," he said. "Why do you ask?"

"Because your hair looks terrible."

He laughed, thinking there was more to this than artless observation. He wondered if in this moment Eddi had seen the need to relieve tension, hers for having felt so dependent on him when the other children were having a good time, his because he was afraid that perhaps she unconsciously suspected he would be impatient with her. Or it might be that she had already developed a sense of humor. As he took her hand and walked down the steps, he wondered what the missing element was which seemed to hold her apart in a way that confused and frightened her. He wished he could take her into his arms and explain about the world, but he had neither the wisdom nor the conviction to tell her that things would all work out, that someday everything would be as she dreamed they would be.

At home, he put together a light lunch, then while they ate, he asked her why she was unhappy. "Did anything upset you, Eddi?"

"No. My teacher's nice."

"One of the children said or did something?"

"No, Daddy. I don't know why I wanted to come home."

"You just had a bad feeling, is that it? I've felt that way before. It's hard to explain."

She looked up at him and a tear formed in her eye. "I was homesick," she said. "I'm sorry."

"Eddi, why would you be sorry?"

"That you had to come for me."

"Darling, when you have these feelings I want you to tell me. I want to do everything I can to help you feel better. Do you understand?"

She nodded. "Are you going to stay here today?"

"I could take you to Grandmama's."

Her spirits seemed to flag again. "If I have to."

He remembered all the work piling up, and finally asked, "What do you want me to do?"

"Stay and play with me."

"All right, I will."

As they walked out to the gazebo, he saw that whatever had troubled her had disappeared. She giggled and chatted and then suddenly cried, "Chase me, Daddy!" and darted through the yard. He ran after her. As she squealed and tried to get away, he swung her high, put her down, and pursued her again. Then something happened. He suddenly remembered chasing Sandi exactly this way, through these same trees. It seemed to cripple him for a moment, and he fought valiantly not to let Eddi see this. As she tired of the game and ran to her swing set, he gave in, walked over to a big pine, leaned his head against the rough bark, and stood trembling and crying. After a while he was able to sit down in the gazebo and watch Eddi playing and humming to herself.

He wished he knew how it all seemed to Eddi. The heart of another is a dark forest, no matter how close to one it is. He wondered if she understood about his loneliness, his frustrations. He'd brought her into the world, now he had to help her make sense of it. His ambitions and desires must be placed on the shelf with the tatters of prose and sketches filling folders and boxes like research papers on his own life.

From time to time he caught Eddi looking at him in a special way, her lips pursed, her eyes unblinking, her hands quiet in her lap, and wondered what she was thinking. One day as he sat typing she said, "Write me a story, Daddy."

Surprised, he answered after a moment, "Well, maybe I will."

All afternoon he stayed with her, grabbed the phone when she decided to take a nap, then took her with him to the office in the late afternoon. It was a juggling act quite different from anything he'd ever prepared for.

Chapter Seventeen

S am Harris managed to place a story with a new magazine which so far had limited circulation but significant promise. Neal read Sam's letter with excitement and dismay. "This is a breakthrough, Neal, but follow-up is very important. Try to move on with more of these."

God only knew what with time he might be capable of, Neal thought, but for the opportunity to occur now became in a way more painful than miserable failure. Probably he and Eddi could get along, but to pull away from his business after all these years would just about guarantee an uncertain economic future. And prosperity was a kind of snare, too, that was hard to escape. The better his business, the more irresistible it became to expand more and grow more and make more. Even if he succeeded with his fiction, the kind of fiction he wanted to write wasn't likely to produce more than a modest income. Still, if he had only himself to think of, if he hadn't married, had no child to raise . . . . For days he was out of sorts. He wanted to be here, he wanted to be far away — he hated being in the skin of two men, each somehow distant from the other.

He wrote Sam thanking him for his confidence and appealing to him not to lose patience with a client who promised little in monetary reward. "If you'd just let me reimburse for the time you spend on these things . . ."

Sam wrote back, "Nonsense. Even if no one ever buys your books I'll be a loyal reader."

Such words from a highly qualified agent were bracing. Still, in a subtle way Sam seemed to be confirming that the kind of fiction he wrote had limited chance of appeal to the contemporary publisher. He hungered for more time to read, to adjust, and to compose, but felt he could not turn his back for a minute on his business or bringing up a bright, sensitive, needful child.

Neal wondered how Sandi might have advised him if he'd been able to ask her. Hardly a day went by that he didn't think of her, especially when he tried to make decisions about their daughter. He wanted Eddi to remember her, too, and left pictures and mementos around to remind her. Once she ran her fingers over Sandi's guitar where it stood against the fireplace. "Did Mommy have a pretty voice?"

"She had a sweet, soft voice. Like wind in the leaves."

"She singed to me?"

"She sang to you before you were born and every day after."

"I'll sing to my babies, too."

There were times when she asked about planting flowers or recalled things they'd done together as a family. He wanted her mother to be as vivid and real to Eddi as she was to him.

After church one Sunday, he asked Eddi what she'd like to do.

"Let's go to the park."

"Oh, no, not the park again."

"Yes! We go there!"

Neal had hoped he might grab an hour or two at his typewriter, but Eddi's request gave him a moment of restrained regret. He hid his sigh and went dutifully in to make lunch. She joined in, setting the table and carefully arranging silver and napkins as he had clumsily shown her how to do. Then they changed clothes and drove down to the park — the same park where he and Sandi had jogged together, where he had proposed marriage.

A warm spring sun tempered by a gentle breeze brought out children of all ages. Sweaters were flung aside and lay in patches of grass like the shed skins of transmuting animals. Here and there daffodils poked their heads around brick barbecue grills. From the courts close by could be heard the rhythmic plop, plop of tennis balls. There were at least fifty children playing around on monkey bars, slides, and spinning machines, while parents sat on the grass or on benches nearby. Several charcoal grills were smoking, and music came from a couple of jam boxes.

Neal followed Eddi to a swing set, wondering if she were conscious of all the children with their mothers, and if she felt an absence. Probably she could never transfer all her love and dependency to him, but would always feel that there was something missing. He helped her climb onto a swing and they chatted as he swung her. After a time she dropped off and stood looking around, sizing things up before deciding to plunge further onto the playground.

"I'll sit over there," he offered. "Or do you want me to go with you?"

"Sit there."

She drifted out amongst the other children and he took a position on a hard wood bench, hooked his arm across the back seat, and followed her with his gaze. He saw she wasn't entirely confident of her place among strange children, and looked toward him often or walked over and braced herself with her hands on his knees. Eddi had an open, innocent appeal and a willingness to befriend almost anyone, and it tugged at his heart to see that from friends and strangers alike she sought the face of affirmation or kindness or love.

She was almost five now, in kindergarten. It hardly seemed possible that Sandi had been gone nearly three years. Nearly every day he weighed what he thought Sandi would do, how she would respond to any situation or challenge. Sometimes he came to conclusions he believed would be more hers than his own. He wondered if death didn't extinguish love but somehow made it stronger and more supporting and if this were not a kind of immortality.

Neal sat up straight when he noticed an interaction between Eddi and a small boy out on the playground. The child looked about three. Eddi was standing near the slide when he came down and hit the sand at an awkward angle. He sat half crying, rubbing his knees and making no effort to pull himself up. Watching him for a moment, Eddi walked over, helped him to his feet, and put her arms around him.

Neal thought how sensitive his daughter was, how her little heart went out to the lonely and confused, and how like her mother she was. He hoped she'd never lose this quality, not even under the most trying circumstances. As he leaned back, he became conscious of a young woman looking his way and he sat up straight again when a moment later she walked over.

"You her daddy? The little girl?"

"I am," he said.

"Thought so. Same hands, same features."

"People do say that."

"That was about the sweetest thing I ever saw, the way she mothered that little boy."

"Thank you."

"Children reduce things to their simplest form, don't you think?" She turned her cool eyes fully on him. "Nice you let it play itself out."

He drew his arm down from the back of the bench and shifted toward one end. "Won't you sit down?"

She hesitated, then assumed a position on the edge of the slats. She wore jeans, sneakers, a blue and white striped shirt with sleeves rolled up to her elbows, and a cap over short, light brown hair. She had a tilted nose and a bold mouth. Her tone was cool and casual, evidently as uninhibited as Eddi with strangers. He sensed the quality of a bird in flight, an elusiveness, as though she were prepared for escape at any moment.

She extended her hand suddenly. "I'm Kara Frost. At first I thought I'd seen you here before, then I was uncertain."

"Neal Austin." He took her hand. "Yes, we come to the park often."

"I bring my nephew sometimes. Play tennis on these courts." She gestured toward a little boy in fatigues with deep pockets, high-top sneakers and a red shirt. "My sister's child over there. I'm babysitting. His parents have split and his father's in and out of the picture — unlike you, apparently." She glanced at him briefly, then turned toward the children again. "Every time they pass their child from one to the other, he has to listen to their incessant squabbling."

"Well, to put your mind at rest, my wife and I don't argue." He explained how he'd become a single parent.

"It's really sad about your wife. Trying to raise a child without her mother. If you're like my sister, you spend a lot of time juggling."

He laughed. "I was just thinking that. How'd you know?"

"When you have to be so much for everyone else, it takes over your life."

How often did this happen? he wondered. Often, probably, but it wasn't always such a bad thing. For three years he'd struggled with the logistics, the complex balancing of the practical, the expedient, and the whimsical, and found it both exhausting and intriguing. But he really wished he had more energy left to be creative.

Kara Frost sat forward and presented him with her striking profile. She then turned suddenly and looked at him with startlingly honest eyes. "Don't mind me saying this. I've had some experience with my sister. Don't forget to think about yourself, too."

"I know what you mean."

She stood suddenly and held out her hand again. "Well, glad to meet you, Mr. Austin. Hope I didn't intrude."

"My name's Neal. Perhaps we'll see each other again."

"Yeah." It was the first time she smiled. "Perhaps."

As she walked jauntily away, leaving the sweet scent of her perfume, he watched the evocative sway of her hips, and something cracked through him. It was like a thunderbolt, an awakening, a resurrection of feelings that had been buried for three years. It wasn't that he was looking for romance, but just knowing the responses were there, knowing they could be aroused — his heart gave a leap at last. Hello, happy lightning!

Chapter Eighteen

Kara Frost reminded Neal of a poster he'd seen somewhere — an old World War II poster maybe, or a Norman Rockwell cover from decades past. It was of a trim girl in pants and shirt, her hair in a scarf, carrying a lunch pail to her factory. She was slender and efficient in work clothes, and in evening dress for Friday night's dance transformed into all loveliness and femininity. Her wit was sharp, her observations caustic, at the same time she could be shy. Much as Sandi had done, she would cock her head and fix him with a still blue stare.

Kara had a talent for mimicry. She could replicate practically any quirk of speech or idiosyncrasy and charm her victims in the process. Her short hair, her full mouth, and expressions and movements gave her an impish appeal. She would pantomime someone they both knew, employing a barely disguised habit of speech or nervous gesture, then finish with a sly laugh. Eddi giggled most when Kara twisted her mouth into a stubborn line, balled her fists and tried to pound her shoelaces into correct knots. And Neal laughed most when she pretended to be him, with tightened lips and an exaggerated serious expression in her eyes.

After they ran into each other in the park a second and third time, they agreed it must be fate and Neal asked her out. It was the first real date he'd had in over three years. They went to dinner and he found out a good deal about her before the evening was over. She was employed with New Concepts Lithograph, where she was an expert in color and quite talented with pen and ink. Occasionally one of her sketches appeared on local calendars or in art programs. After they began to see each other she did several renderings of their gazebo and two or three profiles of Eddi. Of Neal she said, "No, this isn't right. You're too difficult. There's something about your eyes . . ."

She was relatively happy in her work. "There are some fantastic things happening in printing and color," she said, "and whole new possibilities with computers. I guess I can go about as far as I want."

This was to let him know she could hold her own, he thought, both economically and in the business world.

Often enough when Neal called her for a date Kara would suggest, "Let's bring Eddi with us."

He didn't always agree. "Much as I love her, sometimes it's good to get away."

Although she was always happy to be included, Eddi occasionally declined on her own. "No, you go on, Daddy. Bring me a prize." She somehow sensed that he needed to be on his own. He dropped her off at his parents or the Steeles, and sometimes Charlotte Insley babysat. If he forgot to pick up some toy or stuffed animal for her, Kara reminded him, "Gotta get Eddi something. She counts on us bringing her a present."

One night Kara drove over, bringing with her several boxes. "I got these for Eddi. It's all right?"

"You don't need to do this, Kara. I hate to see you spend your money."

"What better use do I have for it? Anyway, what d'you know about dressing a little girl?"

She went to find Eddi and a while later they made their grand entrance, Eddi twirling and strutting.

"How pretty you look!" said Neal. "That's exactly the right color for you!"

"A little large, maybe." Kara turned her around. "But that's okay. She's growing fast."

Sometimes the two girls flopped onto the floor and Kara suggested over her shoulder, "Go do your work, Neal. Eddi and I have fish to fry."

As they embarked into some creative effort or a game of Old Maid, he slipped away to his desk. It was a treat to steal an hour without having to monitor every movement, every sound from the house.

They had been dating more than a year when Neal asked Kara if she'd like to take a holiday with them.

"Thanks, but no," she said.

"Why not?"

"Too serious."

"It's only a vacation."

"You ready for more?"

"Why, I don't know."

"Then wait till you know."

Kara often shot him her opinions and observations in cryptic little bullets much as Sandi had. It was amazing how similar their personalities were, and this frightened him a little. She had burst onto the scene with spirit and imagination, but he was uncertain about weaving a fabric in which he wasn't prepared to be enmeshed. Never would he want to repeat his history with Sandi, who until the end had felt left out of part of his life. He knew Kara had reservations of her own, too. She had no wish to get deeply involved with a man who made no solid promises.

One evening the three of them went over to the Palmers for a cookout. Eddi liked the two Palmer girls, who were older and fought over her. As Nan escorted Kara in to change, Pat and Neal put on their trunks and walked down to the pool. Rob Fuller had the grill going.

Kara and Nan came out, crossed the patio, and strolled over to the pool. Kara was wearing a black two-piece bathing suit and she looked maddening. Pat said, "Wow!" and gave Neal a jab with his elbow. She glanced toward them with a cool, detached air.

Eddi and the girls ran out, threw themselves into the pool, and engaged in a game of "Marco Polo." Then, wrapped in shirts and towels, they all sat in patio chairs and Rob told one of his usual outlandish jokes. This set Kara off and, unable to resist, she stood, swept back her hair, and demanded in a mimicking voice, "Hey, have ya'll heard the one about the pole sitter in Bavaria?"

In two minutes, they were all broken up with laughter. She followed with a John Wayne, a couple of people they all knew, then with her best by far — Henry Kissinger: "I like girls. Girls are very much like third world countries. You cannot always depend upon diplomacy. With girls, there are some regions we have yet to explore . . ."

About the time she had them all hysterical, she broke off as though suddenly self-conscious, glanced at Neal with a faint look of embarrassment, and sat down quickly.

A while later, Neal went up to the kitchen for a bucket of ice and Nan came along for some sauces and spices. "What are you waiting for, Neal? Why don't you marry Kara?"

It caught him by surprise. "But what makes you think she'd have me?"

"You know she would. Her feelings for you are written all over." She turned, folded her arms, and leaned against the counter. "Much as you — much as we all — loved Sandi, it isn't good for you and Eddi to live alone. Free as it may seem, it's really a kind of prison. People tend to crawl into themselves and get set in their habits. The further you grow from companionship, the harder adjustments become."

"My priority right now, though, is Eddi."

"You aren't afraid of some disloyalty to Sandi, are you?"

"No. Sandi expected me to remarry. She knew Eddi would need a mother. And Kara is devoted to her."

"You have to take chances," said Nan. "Eddi's growing up fast."

"But I can't marry just to give her a mother."

After dinner they swam again. Neal and Kara climbed onto floats and engaged in a battle to upend one another. Her arms were strong, her legs shapely and athletic. When they fell off and went under, he planted his lips firmly against hers. She kissed back just as hard, but when they surfaced, she swam fast to get away.

Later, as Eddi fell asleep on the back seat he drove Kara home. "I see why they're your friends," she said. "What smashing people." Her tone became uncharacteristically nostalgic. "It's the American dream, I guess, to have a nice home and family like that."

"I guess so."

"Remember that day we first met in the park and talked about juggling time for yourself? All these ideal conditions you hope for aren't nearly so exciting as just having lived your life as it is." This struck him a blow. It was exactly the sort of thing Sandi would say. Kara looked steadily at him. "Our relationship isn't exactly going that great, is it?"

"What do you mean?"

"You know what I mean, Neal. We seem to be drifting."

He didn't answer but as he walked her to the door, he said. "Maybe we could talk about this tomorrow night."

"Can't," said Kara. "Got a date."

"Oh."

"Yes. Oh."

"Well." He heard irony in his voice. "Have fun."

He hadn't thought much about her dating other men, but when he did he was surprised by the jealousy that whipped through him.

Chapter Nineteen

When they celebrated Eddi's seventh birthday, it surprised Neal, though not Kara, to realize it was the second birthday they'd shared.

"You know how many times I've dated someone for nearly two years?" She looked at him with blazing eyes, one hand on her hip as though hiding a dagger. "Never, before now."

"I'm flattered," he said.

"When do you think people begin taking things for granted?"

"I never assume anything, Kara."

"So you say, but probably it's inevitable. What sort of decorations you using?"

"What? You mean for the party? Why, I don't know."

"I might as well give it a shot, then, if you don't mind."

"Please. Be my guest."

On Friday, when he picked up Eddi late from the Steeles, they arrived home to a riot of color. Their trees, fences and lattice brick walls were all strung with crepe paper, ribbons, and balloons. The gazebo was interwoven with tinsel and *papier-mâché* parrots, parakeets, and macaws perched on the rails and eaves. It reminded Neal of his and Sandi's honeymoon hotel in San Juan. Kara must have spent the entire afternoon here. This was a birthday Eddi was bound to remember. She ran to the phone and he heard her exclaiming, "Thank you, Kara, oh, thank you!"

Saturday morning Kara brought over a bright red bicycle, with a big ribbon and a card which said, "To Eddi, with love."

"Wanted to get the edge on your father," she explained. "I knew he'd be thinking of a bike soon, and thought it'd be neat if I gave you your first one."

"Oh, I love it, Kara! Can I try it now?"

"Better wait and let your dad help."

"This is too much," said Neal.

"Not at all. Thought about it all month."

Kara left to go get ready and a couple of hours later the children began to arrive — about thirty altogether. Spellbound by the decorations, they rushed about the yard like wild Indians. The big surprise came a while later when Kara returned dressed as Raggedy Ann, her brightly painted face set off by a large white blob of a nose, and her hair pulled up under a red plaid cap. The children rushed over to them as Eddi introduced her boldly. "This is my Kara!"

"I didn't think you could look so fetching," Neal laughed.

"Y'think this an improvement?"

"Maybe with a little brighter nose."

As the radioactive pair rushed off together, it occurred to him that under Kara's influence Eddi was becoming more and more outgoing, with a sparkling personality really. The two swept through the yard like scraps of confetti, while the children moiled and laughed. He began to feel guilty for allowing her to contribute so much when he promised so little.

His sister Lori and her children came, and he noticed that Lori and Kara found intervals to stand together and talk.

Mrs. Steele drove over, clapped her hands together and said, "What a wonderful time! Your yard looks fantastic!"

His parents came and his mother mused, "I can't believe Eddi's seven already. She's getting to be quite a little lady."

"It's been a challenge. You think I've done all right with her?"

"I don't see how any man could have done better."

Mr. Austin, always wanting to make himself useful, asked, "What can I do?"

"Help me serve," said Kara. "And, Neal, you need to make sure the kids find places to sit."

They all pitched in, using the gazebo for the refreshment center. Kara had this all planned, he realized. He hadn't even thought about party gifts, but she had brought over a box of baskets full of treasures and tied with red ribbons, one for each child. As he stayed busy with supervision, drinks, and directions to the bathroom, he saw her acting out some skit before a fascinated audience, mimicking various Disney characters, and the birthday girl herself. He was sure that with this party, Eddi was going to be elevated in the eyes of her peers, with Kara to thank for it. All the adults seemed to enjoy this celebration as much as the children. He was surprised, however, when after the cake and ice cream was served, Kara came over to him. "Beautiful party, Neal. Thanks for including me. I'm going now."

"What? You can't leave! I thought we'd go out to dinner."

"You didn't say anything. I have other plans."

"Plans? What plans?"

"You think you have the right to ask that?"

"I'm sorry, I guess not. But I wish you'd warned me."

"Why should I? Think about it."

He wanted to argue but saw she was right. "I guess I assumed . . ."

"Sorry. Thought maybe you planned something with Eddi. You want to see me, you better say so."

He felt a stitch of disappointment, the certainty of a long and empty evening stretching before him. He seized her hands. "You can't do this!"

She jerked away. "I'm going, Neal. I'm sorry if that hurts you, but next time you'd better pay more attention!"

The argument drained out of him as he realized he had no right to protest. "This has been Eddi's best birthday, and I owe it all to you."

"I enjoyed it," said Kara. "I'd do anything for Eddi."

He wanted to sweep her into his arms, kiss away her resistance and insist she cancel her other plans. Why he didn't he couldn't say. He knew Kara would be good for Eddi, he knew she could make his life easier. He was determined never to hold back any part of himself as Sandi felt he had. But maybe there was more than that. If he were in love with Kara would those old faults and inconsistencies matter? For the moment his heart wasn't in it and he knew Kara saw this, too. Neither of them wanted to let go, yet the imminent threat of separation hung over them, as palpably as the stenciled shadows of the big trees.

She put her arms around him in a brief hug, then turned and ran out to her car, leaving behind the faint odor of ice cream and the cheerful aura of Raggedy Ann.

Chapter Twenty

Eddi made friends easily and would go up to perfect strangers, adult and child alike, and initiate a conversation. She was a bright child with a spirited outlook and a sense of humor. As soon as she arrived home from school she sat down to do her homework; she wanted nothing hanging over her. She was neat, too, and kept her room orderly and precisely arranged. Unlike Neal, little things excited her, and as far as he could tell she was relatively contented at this age.

But he felt that something about her little heart reached out — she needed others, she wanted to be surrounded by friends, she desired earnestly to be liked. But children can be cruel, and the closest of allies won't hesitate to betray a trust when another choice is more attractive. One day she learned she hadn't been invited to a birthday party of a boy who had attended her own party. Neal felt certain this was an oversight, but Eddi made up her mind that it was a deliberate rejection.

"I'm sure they didn't mean to leave you out, Eddi, especially since he came to your party."

"I think they don't like me."

"Nonsense. I've never known a child with more friends."

Tears came into her eyes and no amount of reasoning persuaded her.

"Eddi," he said, "what do you expect me to do?"

She thought a moment. "We have a party."

"You mean just us?"

She nodded.

"But I have to work. Don't you understand?"

Her eyes began to well with tears again.

He took a deep, long breath. Nothing would satisfy her but for him to break off from work the afternoon of the party and have a little celebration of their own. Day by day NEA Couriers presented its own problems, and at the most crucial times men took sick leaves, vehicles went down, collections were slow and carelessness or poor judgment on the part of the drivers always ended up in time-consuming patch work. He felt cornered, but left the office early to take Eddi for a pizza and to a movie, and her good friend Lisa chose to skip the birthday party and go with them.

Neal, too, was having a particularly hard time with his writing. Most of the stories he managed to finish were making the rounds unsuccessfully, and work on his novel, in which he held out most hope, was agonizingly slow. At night he walked out under the sky's glittering stars and sat in the gazebo, desire and urgency lying on his chest like a heavy stone. The drama was there, the passionate love and equally passionate resentment was there, but despite continuous revisions it seemed every version he wrote fell short. He knew he would probably be better off to write as fast as he could, get the thought and mood on paper, then go back to honing and shaping. But his fatal inclination was to get things as right as possible as he went, to return to the previous day's work with painstaking revisions. The rewards of perfectivity struck a counterforce of frustration with painfully labored progress. His days were so hectic that sometimes just a paragraph or two of *Samson's Revenge* was all he could muster:

He'd worked energetically preparing the yard and house all through the day, but as he brushed down cobwebs on the patio cornices he sighed suddenly and sat down, staring out across the yard. The energy drained from his face, though his eyes were still alive with urgency and suspense. He kept tapping his chin with his knuckles as if trying to unravel something. The cover of clouds crept over and the brightness of afternoon became a somber shroud of a false evening. He sat motionless before his hands moved from his chin to his knees, drumming absently, as though he were holding himself away from something, his childhood, his brother, even the wife and children who were the only real life he'd known for these three decades — holding himself from everything save those moments of light which drew him from the world and placed him on the couch of warm memories like a basket of beautiful treasures . . .

Was this drama, Neal wondered. Suspense? Or just rumination. Flaubert was a master of not interfering with his characters, staying out of their heads, all emotion communicated by speech, glance, gesture. Hemingway, too, on a much-scrubbed level. But he, Neal Austin, spoke in a melancholic voice that only the most tenderhearted would seek. . . . A soft breeze fanned the limbs overhead, a cricket sang near the gazebo, and he stood with his head against a wood post, his arms tense, his mouth open, a young man whose restlessness betrayed all his ambitions to do one significant thing.

He was surprised one day when Tia showed Lori into his office. The only other time his sister had been here was when he first opened the new facility, not long before he and Sandi met. She wore a silver spruce pant suit and matching earrings, and he noticed she had put on a little weight. Her blue eyes were made bluer by tinted contacts. Today they were uncertain and anxious. He knew she was reaching out to him with reluctance. She held her right wrist with her left hand as though steadying herself. Her fingers were long like his, a musician's fingers, her nails neatly painted. She spent the first few minutes looking around the room where he spent too much time — at the gemstone world globe, the framed map of old Columbus with its fiber mills and linen factories, the wood bird decoys, and a bookcase full of leather-bound classics and business journals.

Lori picked up a picture of Sandi. "I still miss her. We were getting really close."

"She loved all our family," said Neal.

"I know she did. After she stopped teaching, we spent hours on the phone together. She was so full of love — for everybody, really."

"And she always had a bright outlook. I wish I were better at that. I think Eddi inherited that from her at least."

"You've done so well with her, Neal." Lori smiled. "You've had good practice. You used to ride me on your bike and have little picnics in the backyard, and once when I wandered off, you ran up and down the streets yelling until you found me."

"I think of that from time to time, but I'm surprised you remember. You were so little."

"And at my parties you made sure my friends had fun. They all adored you." Her look was at once whimsical and remote.

"Why don't we sit down, Lori?"

As she slipped into a chair, he noticed that she'd cut her hair shorter and her cheeks were fuller, with more color. She sat with her feet flat on the floor, her purse, a large baggy pouch with long straps, in her lap.

"Aren't you about ready to make an important announcement, Neal?"

He knew what she meant, but answered evasively, "Should I be?"

"It's been nearly three years now since you introduced us to Kara. Aren't you still seeing her?"

"Yes. Not quite so much these days, though."

"Don't you think Sandi would approve?"

"Sandi expected me to remarry. I know her prayer was that the woman who helped raise her child would love her."

"She trusted you. She knew when and if you married it'd be to someone who'd cherish Eddi. And Kara really does, doesn't she?"

"I think so."

"Then what are you waiting for? Sandi loved you and I don't think she'd want you to be alone. She knew she was your first love." With one slender finger, Lori traced the pewter trim on her purse. "It's still hard for you, though, isn't it, Neal? To fall in love, I mean."

"I don't know. I guess so."

"I wish you'd open your heart again and make room for someone."

"I hope it is open, Lori. I confess that when Sandi died I told myself I'd never expose my heart to that kind of pain again. But for now I have to guard against is being unfair to Kara, too. Not that I haven't thought about marriage."

"I know you must have. She's a sweet girl, and so in love with you. You know that, don't you?"

He'd heard this before but he could only shake his head.

"Any woman can see it. Besides, she admitted it to me."

"When did you talk to Kara?"

"Oh, we've run into each other a couple of times. Think about this. What if she decided to drop out of your lives? What would you do then?"

He really couldn't answer. He'd already had a conversation like this with Nan Palmer. "Lori," he said, "you remember that all my life anything I've done I've thrown my whole heart into it. I've just always believed anything worth doing is worth doing well. Right now I don't think I should involve Kara in a relationship when I can't promise her everything she deserves. Eddi'll grow up some day. I can't let this be a factor . . ." He hesitated, then asked suddenly, "Is this what you came to talk about, Lori? Are your kids all right? What about Cloud?"

After a moment she said, "Cloud's determined to start his own business, Neal, and I want to know what you think."

"What sort of business?"

"Storm windows, aluminum siding. The things he's always done. But he'll have to borrow against our home, use all our savings."

"A start-up business is a huge risk, although people do take these kinds of chances."

"We may not have any income for a year. That really worries me."

"My advice would be to make sure you can survive at least a year. It takes time to build a business."

"I don't know how much he can borrow. But he's determined, and every time I discourage him, he becomes impossible to live with."

"What do you want me to do?"

"I don't know. Advise, I guess. I told him I was coming to see you."

"I think Cloud has an unrealistic perception of things. Running a business doesn't automatically mean lots of money or free time. On the contrary, I'm sure he'll be surprised at how much he'll have to put into it."

"Will you talk to him, Neal? I'm really nervous about this."

"I guess I can if he wants to."

Neal walked his sister to the door. Lori was a kind-hearted person who'd never had the sort of marriage she'd dreamed of, though Cloud was good-hearted and personable and always willing to help out. Neal remembered something he'd heard about Cloud which was supposed to have occurred before their marriage. A group of students visiting some wildlife kingdom in Florida were looking across a moat at a Chimpanzee Island. Through some fluke a baby Chimp fell or was flung from a tree branch into the moat. As Chimpanzees are skittish of water, the adults of the tribe rushed in panic to the bank and initiated a cacophony of screams and arm-waving as the hapless baby struggled for life. Cloud, who was a better than average athlete and had lifesaving training, went in after the baby. Somehow he managed to push and propel it across the moat to the far bank, at considerable danger to himself. The excited Chimpanzees could have taken his arm off. He escaped to safety, the baby was saved and he was the recipient of riotous applause. Had this been all, Cloud would have been hero enough, but he couldn't resist the opportunity to milk his adventure. Making sure his feat was communicated to every news outlet that would listen, he yuked it up and milked the adventure until it wore thin.

Afraid this kind of characteristic bravado might lead Cloud into a misadventure in business, Neal was afraid his thirst for success and money was far greater than were his talents and his capabilities. He had no wish to be drawn into Cloud's schemes, which he judged to be about seventy-five percent delusion and twenty-five percent willingness to work, but when he saw the appeal in Lori's eyes he couldn't refuse. He'd always helped her and it was really too late to stop now.

"It's hard to offer advice on something like this, Lori. But tell Cloud the first thing he'll need is to develop a business plan."

She looked down at her big purse. "I didn't know whether to come to you or not. I know it's an imposition and I hate to get you involved in anything else." She smiled suddenly and hugged him. "I hope you can be happy someday, Neal."

She went out. He watched her leave, then with a deep breath he turned back to his desk.

Chapter Twenty-One

N eal was dead asleep when he heard Eddi cry out, "Daddy!"
He jumped out of bed and rushed into her room. She'd been sick,
the covers were soiled, and she was curled up in a ball.

"I'm sorry, Daddy."

He took her into his arms and carried her to his bed. He located a
thermometer and found her temperature to be a hundred and four. He
went to the medicine cabinet and brought back Tylenol and a small cup
of water. "Take this, Eddi."

"I can't, Daddy, . . . my stomach."

"Just a little sip."

Obediently, she took the Tylenol. He had the bedpan ready and
within seconds she had to use it. "Well, I guess that did no good at all."

He went to get a damp cloth and for an hour sat sponging her face
and arms with cool water. Still, the fever didn't come down. A hundred
and four could be dangerous, he knew. Eddi lay on her back, her head
on his pillow, and drifted off, then jerked awake as though some invisible
hand shook her. Her cheeks and arms were fiery hot, her eyes drawn and
weak.

He looked at the clock on the night table. It was three a.m.

He wondered if Lori, his mother or Mrs. Steele could tell him what
to do, but was reluctant to call any of them at three a.m. He'd read that
a hundred and four for a long period of time could cause brain damage.
"Eddi, we have to get this fever down. I think we'd better put you into a
tub of cold water. I'm sorry. It'll be pretty terrible."

"It's all right, Daddy."

In the tub he turned on the cold tap. Even to his hand it was cold, and
he knew what a shock it would be to her. But he felt he had no choice.
He carried her over to the tub. "I wish we didn't have to do this, darling."

As he let her down, slowly at first, then all the way, she gasped and her little body stiffened. He hated it, and wished he could substitute himself for her suffering. But she tensed her jaw and didn't complain. She was such a brave little spirit. She held her lips tightly and closed her fingers into a fist, lying motionless. After a few minutes he lifted her out, wrapped a bath towel around her, and dried her face and feet. He shook down the thermometer and checked again. Her temperature had dropped below a hundred.

"I think we succeeded, Eddi. I'll let you sleep with me the rest of the night."

He lay beside her but couldn't fall asleep. From time to time she shivered but at last settled down and lay still. He listened to her quiet breathing, his eyes wide open, staring at shapes and shadows on the half-illuminated ceiling. The house was empty, silent, solitary.

He slipped out of bed, touched his cheek to Eddi's, found it not hot, and left her sleeping. In the kitchen he made coffee, poured a cup, and walked into the den. He sat in the darkness, his eyes closed. How fickle life is! he thought. No matter what grand plans one has for the future, a single twist of circumstances can derail everything. All the fame, fortune and power in the world meant nothing when tragedy struck, when that one fateful moment against which there was no preparation drove its staggering blow. Yet human nature was to want it all, to plant one foot in the world and one in heaven. The pure simple splendor of love was not enough. Sandi believed that where one is at his time in his place is precisely as it is meant to be. And why not? Under any circumstance peace with self is preferable to interminable conflict. At times like this Sandi would know what to do. If she were here the house wouldn't feel so big and cold. But she would never be here again.

In the darkness, sipping coffee, he began to wonder how he might have fared had he never met Sandi, how different his life would have been. He remembered the great aspirations of his youth which had never left him. He was now almost forty, and he couldn't see that he had made one significant contribution to the world. Things would be infinitely easier if he asked Kara to marry him. He didn't love her in the same way he'd loved Sandi, but he realized people can love in many different ways. His time to write was so precious, he hardly felt capable of taking on another emotional commitment. He could never marry Kara or any woman just to be a mother for his daughter. He loved Kara enough not to ask her to marry a man with such divided loyalties. But he knew their lives wouldn't be the same without her, and this made him sad.

He heard little feet padding down the hall, and a moment later Eddi walked into the den.

"Whatcha doing in the dark, Daddy?"

"Waiting for you to get up. How you feeling?"

"I'm hungry."

"I'd say that's a good sign."

"Can I have something to eat?"

"Actually, I don't think so. At least not until we see the doctor."

"When we going?"

"I'll call as soon as they open."

At nine o'clock he phoned the pediatrician's office. All they would promise was to work them in. Eddi looked wrung out and hollow, but she was steady on her feet. He let her sip a little Coke but didn't trust solids. He telephoned the office and as he had countless times in the past few years dumped everything on Tia. "Just cover for me as best you can. I'll be in touch as soon as I see how the day's going." He helped Eddi dress, brushed her hair, then put his arm around her shoulder as they walked out to the car.

They found the doctor's waiting room jammed. Parents sat chatting or thumbing through magazines, children were playing at the game tables or on the carpeted floor. The only chair available was in the section for little children and they took that. Still not feeling well and not happy about visiting the doctor either, Eddi sat in his lap. On the floor before them was a five-year-old boy meticulously arranging a carpet puzzle according to shape and color. He was becoming frustrated because he couldn't get the shapes right. After watching a while, Eddi, characteristically, got down and, without a word passing between them, proceeded to help him. This diversion seemed to make her feel better and it certainly energized the little boy. His face fell with disappointment when Eddi was called in. In the small examining room the nurse took her temperature, pulse and blood pressure, and fifteen minutes later the doctor came in. Neal explained about the fever and how he'd dealt with it.

"The cold water wasn't really necessary," Dr. Rembert said. "With children, a hundred four isn't that critical."

"You mean I put her through that for nothing?"

"Probably."

"Well, I guess I should have known better. But I've read so much about dreadful diseases which aren't caught in time."

"Don't be too hard on yourself, Neal. Single parenting is a hard job."

"So what's the best thing now?"

"I'd suggest you keep her home a couple of days. Give her only liquids for the next twenty-four hours."

"Is Jello okay?"

"Jello, Gatorade, chicken broth is always good."

As they finally drove home, Eddi asked, "What're we going to do, Daddy?"

"Is it all right if I call Charlotte? I don't know if she can arrange her schedule."

"Today, too?"

"Oh, I don't know. The morning's gone. Maybe I'll stay with you the rest of today."

"Good. I'll have Charlotte tomorrow."

With the help of Tia and the phone, he was able to remain home to keep a close eye on Eddi. From time to time the nausea came back and she had to lie down. He felt that they had dodged a bullet. Whatever she had could have turned out much worse than a twenty-four-hour virus. As she dozed off he paced the floor, thinking of a thousand things he needed to do. When she got up he hid his restlessness from her, knowing that the hours they spent together were her happiest times. But he could see a growing element of independence in her, too.

Two days later she was able to go back to school and they resumed their routine. As often as possible he took her and picked her up, though the times they carpooled to school or one of her grandmothers brought her home provided him a few precious extra hours. Eddi was smart, learned easily, and was diligent in her homework. This, too, made things easier for him. As she ran out of school one day her gestures were expressive and she informed him authoritatively, "Did you know of the millions and millions, no two snowflakes are alike?"

"Now who can say that? Has anybody ever looked at every snowflake?"

"You're being silly, Daddy. Only God knows for absolute certain. But that's what the scientists say."

"Ah, that makes a difference. Who would question a scientist?"

Smart and sharp as Eddi was, her motor skills weren't that great. Kara had given her her first bike months ago but frightened of falling she had been reluctant to learn. Many of her friends had been riding for a year or more and her fear was a source of displeasure to her. She took dancing lessons and her grace and poise on the dance floor failed to translate to assured balance on wheels. She was, nevertheless, determined. "I want to go to the park today, Daddy, and ride my bicycle."

"All right, we'll do it. You're sure?"

"I'm sure."

They loaded up and drove down to Weracoba Park. As they brought the bike down the hill to the grassed center field he saw from Eddi's expression that she was both excited and reluctant. She kept biting her lip, but her jaw was set with purpose. The afternoon was mild and balmy, and throughout Weracoba people were jogging, throwing Frisbees, and playing basketball. They could smell the crushed grass of Columbus High's practice field, and over to one side was a heavy orange and blue scrimmaging dummy.

Out on the field Eddi took a jaundiced look. "I think this bike's too big for me."

"No, it isn't, Eddi. We have the seat adjusted exactly right. Come on now, climb on."

As she swung herself on he held the bike steady, then began to propel her with one hand on the seat. "Don't let go, Daddy," she commanded.

She pedaled tentatively, as he ran alongside, then she began to gain confidence and to throw her body into it. As she became more aggressive he encouraged her. "Don't hold back, Eddi. The faster you go, the easier it is to balance."

"But don't let go, Daddy!"

She began to get the feel of it and pedaled harder, with increasing confidence. Looking back, she warned, "Don't let go!"

"Keep your eyes straight ahead, Eddi, or you'll lose your balance."

After a time he did let go, and she rode on without his help. Wobbling suddenly, she took a spill, fell on her side and lay unmoving. Then she sprang to her feet, pushed her palms down flat on her hips and gave him one swift glance of dark accusation. "I told you not to let go!"

He laughed and shrugged. She set her mouth and jerked the bike into a riding position. "Come on, Daddy, and really don't let go this time."

An hour later, she was riding on her own, catching herself as she started to fall and beaming with the kind of joyous relief her mother had always expressed when something turned out exactly as she expected.

The riding days became some of their most treasured times. Neal dug out his own seven-speed, and they rode through quiet neighborhood streets or the parks where riding was allowed. Eddi's best friend was Lisa Grantham, a pretty girl with delicate features and coal black hair, and occasionally they all rode together. Sometimes they'd tether their bikes against a pine or oak, and sit down in the grass. This was when the girls ganged up on him. One day, before he knew it, they were jumping on his back. "Hey! Two against one!" They tumbled and rolled and leaped on him and pinned his arms down.

"What's this! Who's jumping on my back?"

"It's me, Daddy!"

"That is not you, Eddi. That's Lisa!"

"No, it's not! Here's Lisa!" And down would come more weight.

Afterward, hot, sweaty, their clothes stained with grass, they rode home and as the girls went in to take baths, he prepared a light meal. Eddi was such a joy, Lisa was a joy, to live, to breathe, to play, to have others in one's life was a joy. Had Sandi died before Eddi came he didn't know what twists and turns his life might have taken. Perhaps he would have chucked business and buried himself in the art of prose, the hermit writer with a beard, a pipe, a frayed, scuffed coat. He laughed at himself. Prior to his daughter's birth he had said to his wife that children change things. The extent of this truth he'd hardly fathomed. He would never give Eddi up, yet that first heat, that original love would not let him totally alone. It wasn't reasonable that he couldn't be a regular father, lover, breadwinner and write, too. What was his roadblock, then? Perhaps not the work at all but the vision of some nebulous glamour, insubstantial as a puff of thistledown. He was glad he hadn't entirely forgotten how good it was to be carefree, but when a couple of days later his brother-in-law came to see him he wondered if anyone who had a family was ever really free.

He was in his office, toiling as usual, trying to do the work of two men, when Cloud at Lori's insistence came to call on him. The reluctance and disgust was written all over Cloud's face as he let himself down into one of the chairs in front of Neal's desk. Neal felt no less constrained but for his sister's sake he tried to relieve the tension. "Well, how are you, Cloud? You look good. The outdoors is kind to you."

"I need to be out right now. Plenty of stuff to do." Cloud wiped imaginary sweat off his brow. His movements were jerky, his shoulders tense. Still, underneath was a glint of excitement, a sort of buoyancy smoothing out the radial lines in his sun-splashed forehead. They talked about his new business.

"I don't know why I didn't do this years ago. I was stuck in that old job because Lori hates change."

"Just be careful," said Neal. "I understand you've pretty much mortgaged everything you own."

"With the way these jobs are rolling I'll have those paid off in a year."

"Why are they rolling in? Aren't you competing with your former employer?"

"I'm beating the socks off him with pricing." Cloud assumed his old jock-on-campus bravado. "I can sell. One thing I know how to do is sell. Selling's everything." His versatility of expression was limited. "I had to get me a secretary to handle the calls."

"Do you know that for over a year I managed this company without office help? Don't you think that kind of overhead might be premature?"

"I've got to have some time off," said Cloud. "That's the beauty of owning your own company."

Neal began to get frustrated. "My experience in owning your own company is working twenty-four seven with no time off. What sort of business plan are you working under?"

"What d'ya mean?"

"You must have some kind of projections, Cloud. How much business you can do with available capital. How much manpower, how much equipment, overhead. What's your schedule for repayment for personal expenses."

"I ain't making it all that complicated," Cloud said. "I sell, I do the jobs and collect. Now I can afford some things for my family."

"Can you really? What about paying your debts? My advice is to decide on a budget you can live on and don't take out another penny until you pay off your loans."

"That will all come sooner or later."

"I see. Well, Cloud, what is it you'd like from me?"

"I don't know there's anything you can tell me right now." He smiled his affable, good-natured smile. "Mostly, I came to get Lori off my back."

"I appreciate your honesty. Sometimes our wives see things we don't see. I wouldn't be too quick to shrug her off."

Overall, the interview was pointless. As Tia came into the office Neal shook his head.

"Another wayward dependant?" said Tia.

"I'd like to believe Cloud and Lori could become fabulously wealthy, but . . ."

"But you think he's setting his family up for failure."

"How'd you know?"

"I've worked for you long enough to know how you read people. Maybe he'll surprise you."

"I suppose he has the capability if he just weren't so haphazard . . ."

"I just hope," said Tia, "he's not digging another pit for you."

Chapter Twenty-Two

Eddi's idiosyncrasies were amusing, self-organized and obstinate. She wanted her food hot — frequently made him return to the microwave after they'd already sat down. The bows of her shoelaces had to be exactly the same length. She couldn't stand anything askew; an upended salt shaker violated her strict sense of order. When she became excited, she tended toward queasiness, her cheeks reddening, her stomach distressed. She loved photos, insisted on a camera of her own from about age three. At times she could happily occupy herself, at others she couldn't seem to let him out of her sight. As much as possible, they had Lisa and other children over. They spent time with the Palmers and Fullers and their kids. Still, Neal could see that they needed to break their routine before they both fell into an ennui of stagnation.

They had enjoyed few real holidays together since Sandi died. In Eddi's seventh winter, he resolved that they should take a vacation, and he decided to introduce her to ski country.

He made a big production of it. He drove her to Atlanta for outfits, then sat down to show her schedules and maps. "Here's where we live. Here's where we're going."

As they made preparations, she asked over and over, "How much longer, Daddy?"

"Another week. What we'll do first is enroll in ski school. Then we'll have a couple of days to practice our skills."

"Could we go sledding, too?"

"I don't see why not."

A single father packing for a small daughter is no little thing, he thought. He noticed that the item Eddi put in her suitcase first was her beloved teddy bear. At seven she still wasn't ready to give up this loyal friend. When bedtime came she took it out of her suitcase and returned it to her pillow.

"Don't worry, darling, you can pack Teddy last thing before we leave. We won't forget."

As Eddi grew up he wanted them to travel, he wanted her to see how other people lived. He heard her on the phone eagerly explaining to Kara all the details. "Oh, I *wish* you'd come with us!"

This was an offer Kara had already declined. "No," she'd told him, "I won't go. That would just be nice and easy for you, wouldn't it, Neal? But I want you to remember me when you go out to dinner or climb into a cold bed."

His relations with Kara were strained. From a strictly self-serving point of view, nothing would make life easier than to bring her into his house, to allow her to mother Eddi as she was eager to do. He excused himself on the rationale that he could not do Kara the injustice of divided loyalties as he had Sandi. She deserved better. But how rational was that? Kara loved him, she would marry him in a minute, be his helpmate, companion, lover, mother of his child. It really made no sense that he couldn't work, write, enjoy a certain element of freedom, and be a husband, too. He was anything but the literary genius whose burning passion for his work necessitated giving up a normal, healthy life. Kara was real. He wondered if what he expected to contribute and receive from his writing was delusional, or perhaps he simply feared the other face of marriage — to be a good husband he must give a good deal of himself, his time, his devotion, perhaps there would be other children . . .

The evening before their departure, Kara phoned to offer words of caution. "Keep a close eye on Eddi. There're plenty of weirdos around. I know you'd like some time on your own. You'd be a lot freer if you weren't alone."

"But I asked you — "

"I've never believed in letting a man have it both ways." Before hanging up, she said with biting insincerity, "Have fun."

He put down the phone thinking he was about to blow a good thing.

In the morning, Eddi hopped from bed wide awake. "Is it today, really?"

"It sure is. We'll get everything in the car, then have breakfast."

About the time they sat down to oatmeal, toast and orange juice something happened. Eddi's cheeks became deeply flushed and she could hardly touch her breakfast. Neal went over, placed his face against her forehead and found it hot. "What's the matter, darling? Don't tell me you're sick."

"No, no!"

Still, she couldn't eat and her face became redder, her mouth tense with anxiety.

"Eddi, I'm afraid you're getting sick. Maybe we'd better not go."

"I'll be all right, I promise!"

There was little time, certainly not enough to put her to bed, though he was pretty sure she had a slight fever. He could think of nothing worse than flying off to Colorado with a sick child. The more he paced with uncertainty, the more anxious she looked.

"I'll be all right, Daddy. I promise!"

He could imagine trying to nurse a sick child in a hotel bed, trying to reach a doctor. On the other hand, if there were nothing to this, their holiday would have been ruined for nothing. Finally he said, "All right, we'll take a chance. I hope this isn't a mistake."

They locked the house and drove to the airport. He wished for the thousandth time that he didn't have to make such decisions alone. It was still dark, but there was a cheerful glow in the east. They fetched their bags from the car and crossed the cold parking lot. As they walked through the glass entrance doors, a pleasant blast of heat hit them, but in a few minutes they had to strip off their coats. Lines had formed at the counters, the coffee shop was doing a brisk business, and up and down the brightly lit corridors car rental windows and news stands were wide open. All around them people were hugging and shouting goodbyes.

Neal monitored Eddi's expressions. She was intrigued by all the hustle and bustle, but her eyes were anxious. As their flight was called and they lined up to creep through the gate, she whispered, "So many people. . . ." Her movements were nervous, her glance distracted. He hardly knew what to do. In five minutes it would be too late to turn back. All his energy had gone into preparations for this trip, he wanted her to have a good time and he needed the break, too. Now it looked as if it was all doomed. With tense uncertainty he led her up the steps into the crowded plane, noisy with passengers looking for their seats. "Where're we sitting, Daddy?" Eddi whispered.

"We'll have a seat, darling. Don't worry."

Minutes later they were buckled in, and Eddi sat rigidly peering through the window. Then, as they rose into the clouds, a strange thing occurred. A healthy color returned to her cheeks and she became happy and animated. She brought out her books and began to hum and sing. Neal wondered what had happened. Apparently the anticipation had been so great it must have made her physically ill. Her stomach had become upset and he believed she actually ran a fever. But once she settled down, she was well again, and by the time they arrived in Colorado, she had read, slept, eaten, and was back to normal. It seemed to him her personality was expanding and growing, but she was touched in ways he was discovering almost day by day.

In the baggage claim area they retrieved their luggage, then caught a shuttle to the village. Pressed tight amongst strangers, Eddi said little, but finally, peering out the windows, she whispered, "It's beautiful! Look at the Christmas trees! Let's get one for our yard!"

"I'm afraid our winters are too mild. But remind me and I'll look into it."

They passed through mounds of snow piled high, and were dropped off at the lodge, which was three stories, with cedar siding and rough-hewn beams. Snow was banked against the windows and cleared from the walkways. Aspen and blue-green spruce stood half submerged, casting pale shadows against the blinding white. In the lobby was a large stone fireplace with a blazing fire, oiled wood floors, and a wide interior stairway.

"Oh," said Eddi, "logs so big."

"That fireplace must be eight feet wide. Takes strong shoulders to lay a fire, don't you think?" They checked in at the desk, then climbed one flight of stairs and entered their room, where there were two beds, a chest of drawers, and a couple of chairs.

"You take the lower drawers, Eddi, and I'll take the upper ones."

"Okay."

As they put their clothes away he noticed that characteristically Eddi arranged her drawers in a deliberately orderly fashion — underthings on one side, socks on the other, jeans and shirts grouped together. It seemed to him that her desire for order in her life manifested itself in an almost regimental neatness — the death of her mother as an infant brought chaos but she restored order through pictures, through regimental arrangement and all that was familiar and known.

From the front window, they had a good view of the ski lifts and village, and from the side, a scattering of aspen and birches, all covered in snow.

"I want to put on my ski clothes," said Eddi.

"Well, it's too late to do much outside."

"Just for a little while."

He helped her dress and they went out. She flung herself into the fluff, making snow angels. They then walked through the village along heated sidewalks, and in a shop that sold carvings, sculptures and porcelains he chose gifts for his mother, Mrs. Steele, and Kara, including Eddi in his decisions. "What do you think, Eddi? Think Kara would like this hand-carved owl?"

"Yes! I want to get her something, too."

"Just from you. Good idea. Find something you think will make her happy."

Later they came across an outfitter and decided to go ahead and rent boots and skis. These he lugged back to the lodge, where there were stacking racks in the lobby. They walked to a restaurant about a block away, which presented walls of windows looking out on the mountain peaks, glowing with the last shafts of sun.

"Are you hungry? You only had a light lunch on the plane."

"Spaghetti," said Eddi.

"Oh, no, you can have that at home."

"Spaghetti, please," she laughed.

"All right, then, spaghetti it is."

In this alpine restaurant, the waitresses were dressed in short skirts, and one striking young woman with long golden hair, well-shaped legs and a seductive smile caught his eye. He let his imagination play a moment, letting lust become a healthy ski-village emotion, then forced it aside, glad that his erotic responses were as sure and swift as they had been years ago when a glimpse or a suggestion, or sometimes even the mere beat of music stirred his blood.

As the restaurant began to grow crowded, Eddi chattered spiritedly, but the service was slow and her eyes grew heavy, she began to nod, and by the time the food arrived she was half asleep with her head leaning against his shoulder. She woke enough to eat a little and then they headed back to their room. He was able to keep her awake long enough to get her teeth brushed and put on pajamas, and then just before she gathered her teddy into her arms and fell asleep she asked, "What'll we do tomorrow?"

"Sign up for lessons, I think."

"Can we go high in one of those chairs?"

"Probably we'll stay on the beginners' slopes, but we'll see."

Eddi fell asleep at once, but all night he tossed and turned. The sheets felt cold and cheerless, the room silent and solitary. As he lay awake he thought of what was happening to him now. On this holiday with a beautiful, trusting daughter and spectacular scenery, he wondered what sort of brighter light might have been thrown on everything, even these moments of joy, had he accomplished just one of the things he'd set out to do. Only by the sheer force of will had he resisted moods of depression and, worse, the anguish of unrealized dreams. Eddi was growing up quickly, he had published not one piece of significant fiction, and he got no pleasure out of bachelorhood. The young woman in the restaurant invaded his thoughts, and he fought to extricate her, too, before she became walled up in him.

He thought of Kara. He knew he was out of his mind, he knew his actions were greedy and selfish. He could keep her in their lives only by forcing aside that part of her life which led her day by day away from them. He could imagine her eclecticism, her creativity, her working girl resources with money, food, clothes, and holidays, and he could imagine the men touching or passing through her life who found irresistible her good looks, her sharp wit and evocative sensuality. In moments like this he felt not the favored but the obstructionist, the selfish man who held this lovely, willing young woman in suspension. Despite spasms of jealousy, he could only hope that Kara's life not touched by him was as she chose it to be. But he knew even now, even this day as she went to work, paid homage to her graphic art, had lunch with girlfriends or office staff, even now there was a lump in her chest no lighter than the one in his own. His sleep was restless and sporadic.

It was Eddi who first awakened. He felt her hands pressed gently on his cheeks. "Look, Daddy, it's snowing!"

He roused himself and looked out. Great soft flakes fell on the windows and the trees and slopes below.

"Will we be able to go anyway?"

"We'll ride over to the school and find out."

They dressed and went downstairs. The small dining room was crowded, but a continental breakfast came with the room and they were able to find a table. As they went together through the line Neal said, "I want you to eat a good breakfast and have plenty of energy."

"I will. You too, Daddy."

He laughed. "I intend to."

After breakfast they went back upstairs to get ready. Through the windows he saw that the sky had cleared and the sun was victoriously shining.

"Do you see what I see, Eddi?"

"Yes! Sunshine. Hooray!"

Eddi brought out her new ski outfit and he helped her into her boots. They went downstairs to catch an early shuttle out in front of the lodge. The spectacular rolling hills were blanketed by layer upon layer of icy white, the aspen and birch and dark spruce holding spatulas of snow, and he sucked in an energetic clarity like a man starving for breath. Queues of brightly dressed people were boarding and a look of apprehension came over Eddi again. She held tightly to his hand and turned her face up to him. The bus was packed, but everyone pressed in anyway, unwilling to wait for another shuttle. Eddi stood crushed against his legs, and he kept his hands on her shoulder. There was much laughter and talking, and people trying to squeeze together so others could board. He wanted to pick Eddi up, but had no room to bend. In the tightness of her arms wrapped around his legs he detected anxiety. When she tilted her head up to say something, she was drowned out by the din of loud voices, and she gave up.

The shuttle crept along through banks of new snow, through gates opened by the driver with remote controls, past skiers traipsing along toward the lifts, past lodges and bungalows from whose chimneys lazy smoke curled, and after a short and boisterous ride they disembarked in front of a big ski lodge at the foot of a high slope.

As they got off the bus, he took Eddi's hand. "Here's the ski school, honey. We'll arrange lessons and gear up."

"Lots of people," she muttered. Her lips were tight with uncertainty.

"It'll be fun, though. There'll be plenty of beginners like us."

It was a crisp, clear day, not too cold, the picture-postcard mountains etched onto a cobalt blue sky as though with an artist's knife, the trees between the slopes silent, strong, magisterial. From the restaurant at one end of the lodge came the odors of breakfast, and there were people sitting out on the snow-piled deck drinking coffee. In the stone fireplaces six-foot-long logs burned, stoked occasionally by an attendant, cinders hissing and glowing. Off the lobby was the ski school where people were signing in.

"Sit here, Eddi, and I'll go enroll us."

As he walked up to the counter, he glanced back to see her perched stiffly on a bench. An attractive girl with cheeks rosy from wind and sun took down the information while he kept an eye on Eddi, whose hands were clasped tightly in her lap. He signed various papers and releases and was introduced to her instructor, a young man of about twenty who held out his hand. "I'm Brantley. Looks like we'll have about a dozen kids in the class. She ever taken lessons before?"

"No. Neither have I."

"Well, I'm sure she'll be fine. We'll get started in about half an hour."

Neal walked back to the bench, took Eddi's hand and guided her out onto the snow again, where skiers were snapping on boots, fixing goggles and drinking from steaming Styrofoam cups. The sun was flinging yellow sparkles across the eastern peaks and amber morning light splashed down through the breaks. At a distant altitude, the ski chairs became tiny specks, ejecting their passengers, who grew larger and larger as they skied down. The beginners' lifts were slower and wider spaced, clipping off pairs of skiers at a patient rate.

He bent to adjust Eddi's thick hair under the brick-red cap. "You'll take lessons with children your age, Eddi. Then I'll pick you up and we'll have lunch together."

She scrunched up her lips anxiously. "But I don't know them."

"The other children? Well, that's true, but you'll make friends quickly. You always do."

Why she'd fallen into this mood again, he didn't know. He wished she could understand how much he needed her to be responsive and content. He would give anything if he'd had the opportunity to master this skill at her age. The sun, reflected off the slopes, was dazzling, and the brightly colored figures swooping down off the hill appeared vigorous, young, happily buoyant, the girls with tight pants over slim hips and curved buttocks, the men healthily strong and electric with energy. Cold blasts of air were invigorating to him, and he wanted Eddi to feel this too. As he watched, enjoying the spectacle before him, he felt himself slipping into melancholy, lonely and deprived. He shook it off, but sensed some of the things Eddi might be feeling, this likeminded replica of himself. Her instructor came out, barked names from a handwritten list, and began to collect children around him.

"That's your group, Eddi. Now don't worry, he'll take time and make sure you understand everything."

"Where you going?"

"I have my own class right over there. I won't be far."

She gave him one last glance, then fixed her gaze on the other children. It was disappointing that she wasn't able to join right in and enjoy the experience. The other kids appeared excited enough, and God knew he needed some time to do his own thing.

He hugged and kissed her, then left her as the instructor began. He joined his own group, a mix of ten or so men and women, and listened to the preliminary basics of maneuvering. He was ready to begin the sidestepping up the incline when at the last moment he decided he'd better go and check on Eddi. Walking back, he found the class beginning to trudge one way while the instructor appeared quite oblivious of the little girl who declined to follow. There Eddi was, standing alone well away from the others, her back to them, her chin pulled down into her chest, frozen in a look of utter aloneness. It crashed down on him. Walking up behind her, he said gently, "Eddi."

"What!" She refused to turn, but as he knelt beside her, she looked at him defiantly.

"It'll be all right," he said.

"I don't *care!*"

"Don't you want to learn to ski?"

She blinked hard, "If you want me to . . ."

Her fear and uncertainty caught him in such an unguarded way he wanted to crush her in his arms. I love you. I love you. There were tears in her eyes. She fought them; nevertheless, they streamed down her cheeks.

Stopped cold by her fear, he said gently. "It's all right, honey. Lessons can come later."

She bit her lip. "But what will we do?"

"Whatever you want. I just want you to be happy."

He held her, realizing that many fathers would growl, "Go learn to ski. Someday you'll be glad." But feeling the tension all through her body, he remembered his own childhood sensitivity, when almost nothing anyone could say or do would relieve his unhappiness.

He drew her closer. If only he could shield her from all the world's dark threats. "Tell you what," he said, "we'll get a rain check on the lessons and just mess around today. Maybe I can give you a few pointers. Then if you decide you want to learn . . ."

"You aren't mad at me, Daddy?"

"Of course not. We'll work through this together."

He hid his disappointment and made every effort to pick up the pieces of these shattered expectations. They put away their ski equipment, changed into regular snow boots, and took shuttles everywhere. In big inflated tubes, they flashed down a hard-pack hill; they ski-bobbed down an incredibly beautiful mountain, Eddi riding with the guide, he with the wind in his face; they laughed and threw up their arms, the sounds of Eddi's joy sweeping back to him like angels' wings, and with all his heart, he wished her mother could see her. In the afternoon, they took up their skis again and practiced on the gentle bumps at the bottom of the beginners' run. Eddi's motor reflexes, he was reminded, weren't as nimble as they might have been, but she began to venture further and further up the slope.

"You're doing wonderfully, darling!"

It intrigued him to see her determination. A couple of times she became angry and struck her gloved fists together.

"I don't think that helps, Eddi. You just have to keep trying."

"I know, Daddy."

It was a spectacle to watch her. One moment she giggled, the next flung herself down in frustration. God only knew what went through her mind. Then she jumped up and started again. They remained on the slopes long after the last rays of sun faded and most skiers had called it a day.

"I think it's about time we headed back, Eddi. Did you enjoy today?"

"Yes! I want to do everything again!"

They caught the bus back, tired and satisfied. Eddi climbed into a hot tub, while Neal phoned home to receive messages from his office, his parents, and the Steeles. He tried to call Kara, too, but got no answer. He wondered where she was, or more crucially, whom she was with. He took a hot shower and then they went out to dinner, walking along heated sidewalks which still held puddles of slippery ice. In brightly lit shop windows skis and clothes, leather goods, paintings and art work, porcelain and jewelry and flowers were displayed. The air held the scents of candles and spice shops, of pastries, of steam rising from beneath their feet. A group of about six young girls, smelling of cologne, burst from a lingerie shop like a flight of excited birds, and something in his heart flew after them.

From one of the shops he obtained a village map.

"All right, Eddi, think we can navigate through these turns and twists?"

"You can, Daddy."

"So. You trust me not to get us lost."

"If we get lost you'll find our way again."

They emerged into a court full of music and backlit spruce trees. There were patrons drinking beer from mugs and hot tea from demitasse cups, and eating pretzels, sausages, and popcorn shrimp. Big outdoor heaters looking like rockets blew warm waves across the court. The restaurant was configured with many kinds and shapes of wood — heavy overhead beams, board walls, hardwood floors, and thick wood tables. From high on the walls the mounts of various animals kept guard, and over the huge stone fireplace the wood wings of a beautiful bald eagle soared as if alive.

They went up to the maitre d'. "We're the Austins. We have reservations."

"Yes, sir. Right over here."

She led them to their table. It was early for most diners and their server took their order right away.

"I'm hungry," said Eddi.

"Good. Maybe you'll stay awake this time."

As they ate their soup a family — father, mother and two boys — were seated next to them. The boys looked a little older than Eddi. Neal noticed her and the boys exchanging glances, and when one of them dropped his spoon she quickly slipped from her chair to hand it to him.

The mother smiled, "How nice," and smiled. "Tell her thank you, Dan."

"Thank you."

The father introduced himself to Neal. They were from Phoenix. "We've just come," he said. "Our plane was delayed. We were hoping to get outfitted tonight, but I guess it's too late."

"Probably not." Neal told them about the rentals where they'd gotten their boots and skis. "You can sign on for lessons there, too, if you need them."

"We need them, all right. The boys haven't skied before and we're both beginners."

He wasn't surprised when Eddi seized the opportunity. "It's a *nice* school. They have this machine that helps you go up." She then launched into an excited pitch, evidently forgetting her earlier misery.

The mother, looking over the three kids, said, "Maybe tomorrow you could come along with the boys."

"What about it, Eddi," said Neal. "Want to take lessons with them?"

"Yes! I already can do *some* things."

He appreciated this insightful mother coming to his rescue.

With someone to talk to and a little band playing, and Eddi excited by the boys, the evening passed quickly. They decided which dessert to choose and what time to meet in the morning, then said goodbye. At the condo Eddi fell asleep at once, but Neal was restless and discontent. He felt he'd hardly fallen asleep when he felt little hands on his cheeks. "We have to meet the boys, Daddy!"

"I know, I know. There's time enough."

After breakfast, they went back up to their rooms to get ready. "Don't forget to brush your teeth."

"I won't, Daddy."

So what are we going to do today?"

"You know, we ski."

"You want to, really?"

"Oh, yes. I learned to ride a bike, didn't I?"

He laughed. "So you did."

They caught the shuttle over to the ski school where after about fifteen minutes they found and reintroduced themselves to their new acquaintances from Phoenix. Eddi joined the boys — she took command of them — and led them happily off for a fresh start with their instructor. Neal joined the adults but kept a watchful eye on her. Buoyed up by these reinforcements, she set her mind on learning to ski and he was amused by how much better she did. Finally they all hit the beginner slopes, Eddi waving to the boys but no longer dependent on their reassurance. The next couple of days flew by as they skied, tubed and snowmobiled.

"How do you like this sport, Eddi?"

"I love it!"

"So do I. It may be a little late for me but I believe if you persist it'll be a pleasure you can enjoy for a lifetime."

On their last night he said, "We have to go home tomorrow, Eddi."

"Oh, must we?"

"Afraid so. Have you really had a good time?"

"Yes! Except I wish Kara could have come with us!"

In the morning, they both were quiet as they ate, rode to the airport, checked their luggage, and boarded the plane to Atlanta. He hoped Eddi wouldn't fall into a mood, and as they soared above the clouds he was relieved to see that her face was rosy with the healthy bloom of wind and snow. "That was the most fun I've ever had!" she said. "When can we come again?"

"Well, maybe next year."

She fell asleep, curled to one side with her cheek resting on her arm.

Neal wondered what it was that made her so timid on the one hand and so outgoing on the other. The initial fear and loneliness of her first day had been put completely out of her mind, and it seemed to him that her personality was growing more and more like Sandi's. In the face of hurt and disappointment, she seized upon something that would excite her, something that would bring joy into her day, exactly as her mother had done.

Chapter Twenty-Three

Weracoba was the park where he and Sandi had jogged together and where Neal had taught Eddi to ride. There was a regulation four hundred forty yard cinder track, tennis courts, ball fields, band shell, and picnic tables. For Neal the most treasured assets were the oaks and dogwoods and bald cypresses which sentineled the park, the bridges over Weracoba Creek with its breaks and freshets, and the grassed infields. A Girl Scout cabin anchored one end, a children's playground the other. A variety of birds found the eighty-year-old oaks favorable to communal congregations. There was one especially, a cardinal, he thought, which achieved a clear-throated warble nearly every time he and Kara came.

"He's always waiting for us, isn't he?" she said. "You think he has a name?"

"Of course."

"You'd probably know it, too. Is he always happy, or does he just pretend to please us?" She tilted her head, assumed a birdlike posture of her shoulders and arms, and raised her voice to a pitch close to the bird's.

"Not bad," Neal said. "He's getting tired of it now, though. There he goes."

As the bird flew away, they walked on down past the picnic tables, the series of rectangular flowerbeds, and the band shell where with Eddi they'd attended outdoor concerts and magic shows.

He had told her about their ski trip. She said, "I'm glad this was a good time for you, Neal." Her tone was sincere, but cool.

"We could have had a good time together," he said.

"Yes. But think how I would feel when you brought me back to my apartment." She was quiet a moment. "I don't know how you can be so intelligent, yet so blind."

"You think I'm blind?"

"Are you kidding? Excuse me for casting a dark shadow over your happy experience, but I doubt that you'll ever get your little soldiers in a row."

"Meaning what?"

"Make your business a success. Make money. Get Eddi grown. Write something spectacular. Then when you're about ninety think about love and companionship and living life."

"Now that's a poison arrow if I've ever received one."

"Yeah? Well, here's another one. You're too blind even to value what you've found. Specifically, me. I guess I'm the one who must be crazy."

That was the night they returned from Colorado. Now as they walked in Weracoba she said, "Y'know, Neal, when we first met here and I saw you with your daughter I knew even then that you'd decide against me."

"What are you talking about?"

"It's funny, isn't it, how we have an instinct for such things. Anyway, I gave it my best shot."

"Kara, what on earth do you mean, decide against you?"

"Do I have to spell it out for you? Your work, your writing, your ambition is all you need in life. I've just been a too-available convenience."

"None of that's true. Not a word."

"It's been three years, Neal. I may be dense, but not that dense. It's just that I wanted something so badly I kept hanging on."

They walked silently a moment. "I hope you don't think I ever intended to deceive you," he said.

"Oh, no, you're too honest. I just thought you didn't know what you wanted and someday you would."

"Three years isn't that long."

"Ha! In some ways they've flown by, in others it seems forever. Why do you think I've kept waiting?"

"I don't know."

"Yes, you do. It wasn't just you, though. It was Eddi, too. The screwy thing is that's what you're doing — waiting."

"And what is it you think I'm waiting for?"

"To get your little soldiers in a row. I've never known anyone who could plan life so sequentially. It won't work, Neal. Too many variables and coincidences."

He said gravely, "I never intended for you to wait on me to 'plan life.'"

"I know you didn't. It's a burden, isn't it, having someone feel for you in a way you can't return?" She folded her hands behind her and walked with her head down. "I know you're scared of getting hurt again or of giving only half yourself. Wish you'd take some chances, though."

"I take enough chances. Not with other people's lives, though."

"I admit we've had some good times together, but they haven't done much to move you off center." She gave a little shrug. "You've heard that before, haven't you? What, about ten years ago?"

"I guess I deserve that."

"Somehow Sandi and I were caught in the same net. Except she won."

They crossed the bridge where he'd asked Sandi to marry him and walked a little way up the creek. There was a single bench there and light from a silvery lamp slithered down across the hillside.

They sat down. Miserable, he realized that this was bound to happen, but the thought of their relations ending was more painful than he expected.

"Much as I love you, I tried to think of a way not to be such a problem for you," Kara said. "I know you can't stand to hurt anybody. That's too bad, Neal. I just hate to see life slip away because you've postponed yourself."

"Now *that's* something I've heard before."

"You have this damn preconceived notion. Don't you know the life we're given isn't just for practice? It's all we have, and it doesn't last forever. In no time, Eddi'll be grown."

"But until then I have to do everything I can to make her safe and responsible, and maybe even happy."

"You still don't know, though, what you may face — alone. I admit you've gotten her off to a good start." Her look was whimsical. "Eddi's so full of life, one can't help but love her. And she loves you with a special closeness. That's a real accomplishment, I'd say."

"She's taken a lot from you, too, Kara. You make her think of her mother, I guess."

"I know you say that to be kind, but it frightens me. I'm me, Neal. I'm vulnerable, but I know that nothing stays the same and there's a danger of investing every bit of ourselves in someone or some thing. Sandi and I are different in that way."

"Well, you're right. I don't blame you."

"But that's what *you're* doing, you see."

"I've made every effort not to suffocate Eddi. I want her to develop a free spirit."

"That doesn't mean you don't have a great deal to give others, too. I don't think you'll ever turn loose again, if you ever did."

He knew there were tears in Kara's heart and she deserved better, this energetic girl, slim in sneakers and jeans, lovely in an evening dress, with an easy laugh and a delightful sense of the absurd. For a long time he had been afraid he was standing in the way of her finding a more settled life, but guilty as he felt holding on to her, the probability of letting her go sent waves of regret through him.

They sat quietly, listening to the crunch of joggers on the gravel track nearby. "In my work we deal with dyes and colors," she said. "Some will not mix. They'll separate and you'll get millions of little spots. Others stain, while still others are easily washed out. But you know what's more interesting? You can have two absolutely beautiful colors, both true on their own. Mixed together, they don't lose their value, but become even more enchanting. It's intriguing, really, and quite challenging." She leaned back against the bench as though the analogy had failed. "Anyway, I thought you should understand how mixing two distinctive dyes can create something even more beautiful."

"I understand what you're saying."

"I wish you could give in a little and allow for other possibilities. You wouldn't really have to compromise anything."

Neal thought of every defense, but he knew she'd see through anything he said to protect these moments together without deceiving her.

"You have so much to give," Kara said, "to some lucky girl someday, if you ever find her. I see it's not me — not now, at least. It's better to face it now."

"I wish I could explain," he mumbled.

"Nothing to explain, really. I understand about giving up one's life for someone else. I'm not that brave, but I understand."

She stood and walked away, becoming a silhouette against a descending night sky. Then she came back and sat beside him again. "It's strange how circumstances change priorities. When I was little, I thought I would grow up to be a surgeon or a doctor. Everything about medicine fascinated me. Now I'm squeamish at the sight of blood. What'd you think you'd be?"

"I don't know. An architect or a builder, maybe."

"That's reasonable. Fits your personality."

"Then I found out I had to write. At any rate, I never dreamed of what I'm doing now."

"You feel cheated in a way? I suspect lots of people do."

He leaned forward, his hands on his knees. "I don't know if very many people really enjoy what they find themselves doing. But children change everything."

"Still, I wonder — is Eddi always going to be enough?"

"I don't know. Sometimes it's frustrating and scary. But it seems to me that love becomes a light that's never extinguished. Still, I wish you could see it has nothing to do with us."

"I wish I could, too," said Kara. "But I can't. I could share Eddi with you, but something else keeps us apart. Why can't you see that your light doesn't have to be for her only?"

"I do see that. It's just that . . ."

"That you don't love me. Isn't that it? At least not enough."

"I do love you."

"Oh, don't say that! I don't know if any woman can ever take the place of whatever it is you're after." A sudden toughness came into her eyes. "I know you enjoy my company. I know it's nice and comfortable for you to be with me when you want me. But I'm insane to just keep waiting!"

Darkness fell quickly, as though without warning a solid curtain was pulled across the sky. He tried to think what he could say to Kara. After these three years, he realized that now a curtain had dropped between them, too.

Chapter Twenty-Four

The day Kara broke with him completely Neal thought he had a taste of how it was between two people who, married for years, split not because they ceased to love one another but because their "irreconcilable differences" simply ceased to be worth the courage. He was miserable and realized that he alone was to blame. They sat out on her small patio, where Carolina jasmine cascaded down the fence in budding vines. With her feet propped on a chair and her legs crossed, she said in her straightforward way, "You've never asked me not to date anyone else, Neal. That was to keep *you* free, I guess. For some months now I've been seeing someone. Got to know him pretty well."

He was astonished. "You don't mean it's serious?"

"Beginning to look like it."

"But why didn't you tell me?"

"I'm telling you now." She bit her lower lip and recrossed her legs. "He's in the same line of work as me, in Atlanta."

He sat stunned. He couldn't believe things had gone this far without his knowledge. "How can you date a man from Atlanta?"

"I guess he thinks I'm worth the drive. He's like you that way — persistent. His name's Paul. I thought it was time I should let you know." She uncrossed her legs, and kept her tone flat and unemotional. "He's managed an attractive job offer for me up there. It means I'll be leaving soon."

"What! You can't go!"

"You've never really given me a reason to stay." Her voice fell a little. "It's been a hard decision. I had the offer months ago."

He leaned forward, his chest tight. Flashing before him were the empty days ahead.

"You'll miss me," said Kara. "I've been good for you. That's where I made my mistake, I guess. You've always assumed I'd be here."

"But, Kara, it takes time to get to know someone."

"Oh, damn, Neal! Did you really say that?"

"No, no, that's crazy."

"It *is* crazy. Three years! How long had you known Sandi?"

"I don't know. A year."

"Triple that! You just can't fit me into your equation, and that's not my fault. I can't blame myself for that."

"Of course it's not your fault." He leaned forward and pressed his hand against his forehead.

"You love Eddi and you're so determined about your work. But there's only one thing that keeps you from including me in your life. You don't love me."

"I do love you."

"Not enough that you can't live without me. Not as if we merge like two dyes." Her chair scrapped as she dropped her legs down. "Anyway, I just wanted to tell you I've accepted this job."

"What about your family? Your sister?"

"They think I'm crazy for waiting for you this long. They want me to be happy with a man who'll love me and marry me."

"But how do you know this is the man?"

"I mean the world to him. Or he thinks I do."

His stomach was churning. He tasted something unpleasant on the back of his tongue. There was so much to accomplish, so much to think about. He felt the pain, too, of hurting and being hurt. With failing voice he said, "I don't want you to go. Can't you just delay this decision a while?"

"Please don't even ask, Neal. That would just take the pressure off, then you'd fall right back into the same pattern."

"But it's your life, too, Kara, that I'm thinking about."

"Don't say it. I can't trust anything when I know you're terrified of losing me. And I won't treat Paul that way, either."

He stood and drifted around the small patio. He was ready to fight but he knew trying to hold onto her was little and treacherous. He said glumly, "This will make Eddi very unhappy. I dread telling her."

"I'll tell her, then." Tears came into her eyes, and she tried to blink them away. "This is so unnecessary. I hate you for what you're doing to me! But I love you, too. I love Eddi. Oh, what a waste . . . what a waste . . ."

"It's not as if we can't stay in touch."

She wiped her lashes. "Well, I'll have to think about that. Time goes by so fast, Neal. Life offers so many possibilities, but I try not to allow one single thing to become overwhelming. That very first day I met you in the park, I knew something was going to change for me, but I was afraid, too. Now here we are, three years later, and nothing's really changed at all except . . . except we're older — and I can't make you love me."

"This makes my heart ache," he said.

"I know it does, but you'll survive. Someday maybe you'll have regrets. I hope you do. But you can't make yourself fall in love."

She dropped her dark lashes again, and this time a tear crept down her cheek. "I wish you could have loved me that way but I don't know anything else I could've done. It makes me furious, though. Three years!"

He tried to take her into his arms. She turned away.

"It's no use, Neal. The only thing left to do now is for me to tell Eddi. I do want to see her again."

"You make this sound so final."

"It is final. Has to be. Why drag out the pain?"

"But when — how?"

"We'll take her out one last time. She's always loved that."

They agreed on Friday and it came all too soon. Eddi was excited but seemed to suspect something too. They picked Kara up and as they drove to the restaurant she was more animated than usual, as though her chatter and enthusiasm would make everything all right. Throughout dinner the girls bantered as Neal sat quietly, knots in his stomach. Following dinner they drove back to Kara's apartment. After ten minutes of settling in she said, "Come with me, Eddi. I have something to tell you."

They went into the bedroom as Neal paced miserably. Everything here was familiar to him now — the pictures, the glass candy jars, the sketch book on the coffee table, the portfolio of some of Kara's striking lithograph work. It would all be gone, he thought, moved out, devoid of life and expectation. He had been this dejected and confused only one other time in his life.

Half an hour later they walked out of the bedroom. He searched their expressions and found both with a brave face across cheeks that were red and tear-stained. Eddi gave him one searching, defiant look, and clamped her mouth shut.

As though determined the evening would end on a cheerful note, even a false one, Kara said, "C'mon, I have a new board game. Let's play."

She brought it out and insisted that they join her, Eddi on the left, Neal on the right. For about an hour there were some clever moves and manipulations, then Eddi, as if she had pretended long enough, stood up, put her arms around Kara, and said quietly, "I'm ready to go home, Daddy." It seemed to Neal that she had sadly learned about the inevitability of painful departures. But there was something in her face and in the severe line of her mouth that alarmed him, that made him feel selfish and treacherous.

This time Kara let him kiss her goodbye. All the way home neither he nor Eddi said a word. Then the minute they entered the house she turned on him accusingly.

"Why did you do that, Daddy! It was so *mean*!" She stood stiffly, her lips trembling. "Now I'll never see Kara again!"

"We don't know that."

"You're making her go away."

"You don't understand," he said. "She's found another job."

"All you had to do was ask her to stay."

"What'd she tell you?"

"She told me it hasn't worked out between you." She started to speak, closed her mouth, then whispered, "Kara loves us."

"Yes, I know."

"But you don't love her."

"I do love her."

"She could have been my mother! She wanted to!"

"It's not that simple, Eddi. There's a lot to consider."

Tears streamed down her cheeks. "I wish you didn't let her go, Daddy."

"Eddi, listen. My heart hurts, too. Just like yours and hers. Calm down and I'll try to explain."

"No! I don't care! I just thought someday Kara would be my mother!"

She jerked away from him and ran to her room.

Chapter Twenty-Five

For a year Neal heard nothing from Kara Frost — no card, no phone call, no contact of any sort. Then one day he ran into her sister at a field meet for grade schools. Claire's son, the little boy Kara had been taking care of the day they met in the park, was a little older than Eddi. After a few moments of casual exchanges Claire said, "Kara has announced the date of her wedding."

For a moment Neal stood silent, then mumbled, "Has she? I hadn't expected it so soon."

"Once she moved to Atlanta, Paul wanted to marry right away, but Kara chose to give it a little more time."

"Is she happy?"

"Oh, who knows? Happiness is relative, Neal. I wouldn't say this marriage is everything in the world to her."

He was about to question this when a gang of athletic kids swept her away and they were unable to talk further. He felt cheated and left drifting, realizing how much he missed Kara — her wit, her devotion to Eddi, her generous nature. She'd never taken Sandi's place but had commanded a place of her own. He could not defend his selfish in-looking or the rationale that kept him from marrying her. He knew he'd been blessed with the love of two women. For over three years, Kara had opened her heart to him, and a note, a phone call from her now would have been a relief. He deserved neither. There was no reason to expect she would ever open her thoughts or her life to him again.

Occasionally, Eddi said with disgust, "Kara could show me what to do," or "I wish Kara were here to help me."

When he told her about the wedding, she said tersely, "You could have married her, Daddy."

"Eddi, it just wasn't right at the time."

"Well, what *is* the right time?"

"Why, I don't know."

"She loved us." Eddi said nothing more but he knew she held it against him and was relieved when finally he thought she'd forgiven him.

Three years later he heard that Kara was still working at her job in Atlanta and that they were thinking of building a house. He considered contacting her, but decided against it. He wondered what her husband Paul was like, and if he appreciated Kara's sharp and sensitive mind, her forthrightness, her sense of the absurd, and if he was good to her.

Eddi, twelve now, swept him into a constant rush of activities. "Don't forget, Daddy, I have to go to cheerleading today," or "Daddy, do you think you can get my ballet shoes dyed? They have to match my costume." She'd learned early to keep tabs on her own activities, and impressed Neal with her penchant for efficiency. "A card came in the mail from the dentist reminding us of my appointment."

He found it remarkable the way she pitched in to handle her share of managing the house. Seldom did she leave things on the floor, forget to put away her clothes, or expect him to straighten up after her. Her devotion to orderliness, which surfaced at an early age, became more pronounced as she grew older. If he or Charlotte happened to move a picture or a vase from the dresser to the chest of drawers, she cried, "Why does somebody keep rearranging my room? I want my things where I left them!"

He realized how much like himself Eddi was. How such peculiarities were passed down, he didn't know. As a child, he'd claimed a small space behind an overstuffed chair in their cramped living room, where he neatly stacked his boxes, his cowboy and Superman outfits, his games and books and puzzles. And now he saw that Eddi had the same predilection for neatness and order.

One evening he came home to find an entire meal prepared and a beautiful table set, including Sandi's fine silver and dinner dishes, and a bowl of cut flowers for a centerpiece. "What's this! I didn't know your grandmothers were coming over."

"They didn't. I did this myself!"

"I can't believe it!"

"Come and see. This pan was for the fried corn. Mashed potatoes in this pot. And the ham's here. It was precooked, though. I only had to heat it up."

"I had no idea you could do this," he said.

"Oh, yes, I've been taking lessons from two grandmothers. I wanted to surprise you."

"And now that I know you can cook, I won't ever have to worry about another meal."

"Wrong. This just happens once in a while."

"And what's expected of me?"

"You have to clean up," she laughed. "I hate that part."

Despite all the daily pressures, Eddi's energetic optimism and heightened outlook brought joy into the house. As she became increasingly bold and independent, he remembered the times he'd given up something he wanted to do to take her somewhere, to play games, or watch a movie with her. There were whole weeks gobbled up as he transported her from one activity to another. Still, he realized that soon Eddi would be grown and so many of the things he'd wanted to do would no longer matter. He thought this was sad in a way. Which was worse — to finally give up on dreams, or to expend every last tittle of hope and expectation on an unrealized cause?

One Saturday morning he received a disturbing phone call from his mother. There had been a fire out in the shop and his father was struggling to right things. "Was anyone hurt?" Neal demanded.

"Your daddy grabbed the garden hose and finally put it out. He burned his hand some."

"You think he'd better get over to the emergency room?"

"Oh, you know he'd never do that."

Fortunately, Eddi was spending the day with her friend Lisa. Neal dressed immediately and drove over to his parents'. So much for a morning on his own. When he pulled up he found his mother standing in the driveway, her arms folded across her chest, gravely watching his father struggling in and out of the smoldering shop as though unable to decide what to do. Neal put his arms around her. "Looks like you need another cup of coffee, Mama. Why don't you go on in and we'll take care of things."

"We're sorry to spoil your morning, Neal. He didn't want me to call."

"Nonsense. I would've been hurt of you hadn't."

After he persuaded her to go in he turned to his father, who was sweating, his shirt drenched, and the bandage wrapped loosely around his wrist providing practically no protection. "What happened?"

"I don't know exactly. I was heating some tubing with the torch and something caught fire."

"Well, don't you think you'd better go in and take care of that hand?"

His father shook his head. "It's not that bad."

Neal looked the situation over. The shop was flooded, water draining through the open door, and the walls scorched, but at first glance nothing appeared burned beyond hope and the flames had not reached the roof structure. Tools, machinery, and articles for repair would all have to be removed one by one, set out in the yard, cleaned, inspected, and put back. The building would have to be stripped, perhaps the smoke-smelling walls painted. It was a daunting task and he hardly knew how he'd make a dent in the course of the day, with an impending rain moving in.

Then Cloud and Lori showed up — her mother had phoned her. Neal was relieved and surprised. Behind them was a truck with two of Cloud's men. With an athlete's springing touch Cloud hit the ground, leaving the van door open.

"Why, Cloud, thanks for coming," said Neal. "You've brought help?"

"Yeah. Why don't you try to get your father to go on in? We got this covered."

"I've tried. I guess he's the one who'll have to tell us what to do with this. Quite a challenge."

"Aw, it's no biggie." Cloud's half-bald dome shown with excitement, his movements quickened with stimulation. He was at his best when in rescue, making most of the heroics. But Neal was grateful — amused and shocked, but grateful.

The two men hurried over to pitch in and as his brother-in-law barked disjointed orders Neal quietly organized the group to remove, clean, arrange — hand tools here, power equipment there, customers' repair work over on the driveway where they'd receive most care. At intervals, observing the men, Neal said, "Thanks for bringing the help, Cloud. They seem willing enough."

"We got two crews," said Cloud. "Thinking about adding another."

"Well, be careful. Don't try to grow too fast."

The day was successfully concluded and Neal thanked the men, shook their hands and gave each of them a twenty dollar tip. He thanked Cloud, too, said goodbye to his parents and Lori, and drove home thinking he really could not get a firm fix on his brother-in-law. Cloud was all but a dual personality, the one convivial, excited to help, personable, and back-slapping, the other boisterous, overzealous, overindulged, and overambitious. Despite his debits Neal gave him credits, with two lines under it, for plunging in on a day which without him could have ended in disaster. And he was deeply pleased to see Cloud and Lori doing so well. Yet, he couldn't escape a certain element of misgiving. One day after the Saturday fire he happened to run into a wholesale distributor of aluminum products whom he'd known several years. The man asked about Cloud.

"You're related, aren't you?"

"He's married to my sister," said Neal.

"Just wondered." The dealer seemed thoughtful, reluctant to go on, but finally said, "I think Cloud's okay. Seems to know the business pretty well. I'm a little concerned about his accounts."

"You mean he's slow paying?"

"I wouldn't mention this except my company has a pretty strict credit policy and I'm not sure where he'll turn if his line's closed."

Neal had pretty much kept Cloud and his business venture off his mind, but this conversation with the aluminum distributor reminded him that during this first year of business Cloud and Lori were living it up. They had invited Neal and Eddi out to a nice restaurant one evening and as they sat down Lori billowed over the table and held out her hand. "Look, Neal and Eddi, what Cloud gave me." It was a good-sized diamond. "To replace the tiny little one when we got engaged."

"Oh, how pretty," exclaimed Eddi. "It's elegant, Lori."

Neal all but asked what creditor's money was used on this lavish gift, but instead he said, "You're apparently doing well, Cloud. Still getting plenty of work?"

"About all we can do."

"Save some of your money. Rainy days are sure to come."

"Aw, we gotta get *something* out of this."

Neal said nothing more that would take away Lori's pleasure, but it seemed strange to him that Cloud thought an extravagant salary was justified by the sheer volume of money that passed through his hands. He knew nothing he said would carry much weight, and remembering what an austere lifestyle he'd lived since opening NEA Couriers, he wondered if his own struggles growing up had made him overly cautious.

Whenever Eddi happened to be spending the night away or off with her friends, Neal took advantage of this free time to work. But not always did work come. He sat in his home office or walked out to the gazebo with feelings of melancholy or loneliness, occasionally satisfied with what he had accomplished, mostly with feelings of discontent and lostness. He wondered if his original ideals and aspirations were never realized, would this mean that he'd slowly let them erode and die, or was there some kind of reprieve to see the energy of these dreams dulled by frustration? Or had they meant something in some private way? He didn't know. He felt it would be a relief to just give it all up, simply to let the days come as they might, with no great hopes of making a difference. He was half inclined to destroy everything he'd ever written and half compelled to forge on if only because it was the one way he could extricate himself from whatever it was he had always been looking for. He remembered an observation old Mr. Steele had made: all life is just moving a little — no matter where a man finds himself, even against a wall, his only hope is to move an inch or two.

One afternoon he was out at Fort Benning, finalizing a contract with the Army to transport electronics. He always enjoyed driving through the shady streets with their thick canopied oaks, the marching platoons, then the mess halls and barracks, and especially the handsome white stucco officers' quarters. He was passing a large field when he happened to look up and see a small object fall from an airplane. Startled, he pulled over. The object appeared no larger than a suitcase, but as it came down he was shocked to see it was a man falling from almost out of sight. In fascinated anguish, he watched him plunge earthward, toward inevitable death, then with great relief he saw a parachute open and realized it was a jumper freefalling, followed by another and another. Together they soared, turning and circling like eagles, and it arrested him in a moment of reflection: whatever earthbound moods and miseries these young paratroopers might suffer, it must be deliciously liberating to enjoy three minutes of such utter freedom.

About his only reprieve from work usually came in the form of canoeing or trail bike riding with Rob Fuller and Pat Palmer. Eddi always encouraged him to go. "I'll be fine, Daddy. You don't have to watch over me every second."

"It could be late when I get back."

"That's all right. I'll ask Lisa to come over and keep me company."

Her growing independence was something of a relief, but it saddened him to see that she was weaning away. She was growing up too fast. She had begun to insist on makeup, on choosing most of her own clothes, on having her own private telephone. And, much as they loved each other, the older she became, the more friction developed between them. It seemed to him that, her hormones raging, her flare-ups were unreasonable, swift as a flame and sharp as a whip.

One night they were in a dispute over the clothes she intended to wear shopping with a friend. "Can't you find something a little nicer, Eddi? You have so many pretty outfits."

"I'm fine. This is what everybody wears."

"I don't have to look at everybody."

"You don't have to look at me, either." Her color deepened and her eyes narrowed defiantly. "Why are you always criticizing me?"

"Criticizing you?"

"I can never do anything right!"

"Eddi, what are you talking about? I never criticize you."

"No matter what I put on, you have some complaint!"

Stunned, he retorted, "That's totally untrue! I'm always complimenting you. It's my responsibility to tell you when some outfit's inappropriate."

"Because you think I'm incapable of deciding for myself!"

"Why are you twisting this around? You know I give you every liberty."

"Well, maybe I'm just never going to measure up!"

Exasperated, he stalked out. "Sometimes I wonder if children are worth it!"

He expected a harsh rejoinder, or at the least the slamming of drawers. Instead, there was no sound behind him. Hesitating, he turned back and peered through her door. Eddi was sitting on her bed, tears streaming down her cheeks. Feelings of regret swept through him. Every parent, he thought, must at times feel their offspring driving them to say such things. But at the sight of her silent and unexpected pain, all his anger melted away and he went and sat on the bed beside her.

She didn't look up. "Did you mean that? That I'm not worth it?"

"You know why I said that, Eddi. You were being quite unreasonable."

"Even so, you can't say things like that to me."

He almost laughed. Evidently it was all right for her to say whatever came into her head, but not him. "Okay, but you can't accuse me of something that isn't true."

She looked at him with wide, wet eyes. "You really do think I'm worth it, don't you?"

"You know how much I love you, Eddi."

"I love you, too, Daddy. I'm sorry I'm so unreasonable sometimes."

Their disagreements usually ended with her getting over them more swiftly than he. She was better at putting things behind her, at forgiveness, like her mother, while he tended to anguish over their disputes for days.

Chapter Twenty-Six

The peal of sirens interrupted Neal's work for the second time since early morning. Tornado watches had been in effect all day. This time he paid little attention, knowing that the warning network covered such a large area, a dangerous system might occur so far away the leaves outside the office would scarcely move.

Tia stuck her head in the door. "Should we get under our desks?"

"It's probably another false alarm."

"You did hear the sirens, though."

"Yes."

"Look at that sky. It's really threatening."

As Tia left, he walked to the window. Great heaps of black clouds boiled and twisted, tumbling over and over. Whirling, angry pillars were lit by an eerie backlight while beneath, flashes of silver and red lashed the distant skyline. This was the making of a lightning storm, he thought, not a tornado. He was fascinated, though, by the power and energy of the sky, the whipped-up caldron steaming black and gray as far as the eye could see. At two o'clock, it was a dark night, a peculiar darkness which sent static electricity through building walls.

Feeling excited, he returned to his desk, but for the moment he'd lost his concentration. The lights flickered and the moisture in the air pricked his skin, energizing the tiny hairs along his wrists and forearms. Huge masses of cold and warm air were colliding, spinning off erratic whirlwinds. This wasn't unlike his own nature, he thought, forces warring against one another. It seemed that every moment of his waking hours had become a clash of expectations and disappointment. The lure of success was addictive, but what he really wanted was another kind of life.

As a false night pressed against the windows, he sat trying to work, considering the possibility of expanding his company to include highway trucking operations. His projections and decisions must be made within the next day or two. Every time the phone interrupted him, or Tia called through the open door, he felt a tightening along the muscles of his shoulders.

As she returned with a cup of hot apple cider, she asked challengingly, "Do we really need more business, Neal? You work too hard now."

"I don't know. You're probably right."

"I'd give it more thought, if I were you."

As she left, a great clash of thunder slammed the windows like an exclamation point. He was working hard when she came to the door again, and with a frown said, "We've had a tornado."

"What? It seemed to me things were dying down."

"I was trying to find out more before telling you. It hit the Stonewood area. Eddi goes to Stonewood School, doesn't she?"

"Yes."

"Well, don't worry until we know more about it."

Tia's logic wasn't calming. He knew how things could be exaggerated, how uprooted trees and dislodged shingles might sound like something much worse. But as he tried to concentrate and wait for Tia to make calls, his hands became taut and clammy.

When she returned, he could see by the look on her face that the news wasn't good. "I'm told Stonewood School was hit."

"How bad?"

"I'm not sure. Some walls fell in."

Eddi, he thought. "Were there any injuries?"

"I can't tell you, Neal. I only know that the streets are blocked and lines are down."

He jumped up and without so much as a windbreaker, ran out to his car. A tornado! Here around the office there was no evidence, not so much as a traffic signal out of order. But as he sped toward Stonewood, everything changed. It was amazing how dramatic the destruction suddenly appeared, as though a line had been drawn across the landscape. Power poles and wires were down everywhere. Great trees had been uprooted. Street signs, traffic lights, garbage pails, aluminum awnings, trash containers, bicycles, and vehicles were strewn to and fro. Cautiously, homeowners were beginning to creep out of their houses.

A couple of blocks from the school, police cruisers with flashing lights blocked the street. He wasn't the only one flagged down. A caravan of cars, unable to approach, were fanning onto side streets. Utility crews were working to restore downed power lines, the whine of chainsaws everywhere like raging beasts. Getting parents to their children was the first priority, but police were moving people back. Half-broken poles, dangling, hissing wires, and tops of trees barricaded entire streets and yards. Adding to the congestion were frantic men and women, unable to get to the school. Two fathers had jumped in to assist the policemen in trying to restore order.

When finally he could see the school, his heart nearly stopped. A deceivingly blue sky filled the space that was once roof line. Part of the school had been turned into a tangle of steel, masonry, and glass. It was impossible to drive closer. He jumped the curb and wheeled his car around. As he did so, a huge oak hung up in the gable of a house about fifty yards away slipped and crashed with a great explosion of shattering branches.

He jumped out of the car and stumbled and ran across soggy yards, through the tops of trees and downed wires. Quite suddenly, nothing he'd left behind mattered anymore. His ambitions and expectations vanished. All that counted now was Eddi. To his left, a child's red wagon was perched on a swaying oak branch. A small car rested with its front end straight up against a brick wall. With every discovery, his panic increased. The world — his world — had turned upside down.

When at last he came to the school grounds, he ran into a mass of confusion. A large portion of the front wall of one wing had caved in, and mortar, plaster, desks, paper and chalkboards and books were strewn everywhere. Windows were blown out where walls remained. He knew how deadly flying glass could be. He ran up the circular driveway where pupils, teachers, parents, and emergency workers either rushed about or stood still, strangely subdued. Everywhere, children were crying, clinging to each other, looking for their parents.

Neal ran up to one group of children, then another. "Do you know Eddi Austin? Have you seen Eddi?"

Dazed faces greeted him. Finally, he found a teacher surrounded by frightened children. "Eddi Austin. Have you seen her?"

"Eddi? She must be here . . ."

He ran toward another group of pupils and teachers. Then he saw people digging into a pile of rubble. Men were throwing debris aside, trying to reach someone trapped there!

He cried, "Eddi!" With his bare hands, he began to fling hunks of metal, jagged sections of wall aside. A shard of glass sliced into his palm but he scarcely noticed. An emergency crew worker caught his arm.

"Take it easy, man, or you'll be a casualty yourself!"

"Who is it?"

"We don't know. Someone said they heard a cry . . ."

Frantically, he clawed at the rubble. It took a full second for him to realize that someone was tugging on his arm, shouting at him. "Daddy! Daddy!" Eddi clutched at his shoulder and burst into tears. "I'm here, Daddy!"

"Oh, Eddi, my God, I thought it might be you . . . !"

"No one's under there! We all got out!"

He swept her into his arms and held her so tightly she gasped. "You're sure?"

"Yes! The teachers got us all out. We were in the hall when it hit."

He finally came to his senses, relaxed his hold on her.

"I couldn't call," Eddi said. "They won't let us have phones. What about our house?"

"I don't know. As long as you're safe, what does it matter?"

She pulled his arm up. "You've cut your hand!"

"It's nothing."

"We'd better go get you stitches, Daddy."

There was blood on his clothes, dripping off his fingers. He wrapped his handkerchief around his hand and she tied it tightly. Then she scrubbed away her tears and they gathered her things. "It's pretty treacherous going back to the car, Eddi. You wait and I'll try to drive around."

"I'm coming with you, Daddy."

"You'll be safer if you wait."

"You can't leave me!"

"All right, then, walk close to me."

He took a firm grip on her hand and they trudged back toward the car, negotiating fallen trees and dangling power lines. They came to a tangle of wires humming and spitting against the wet earth and Eddi pulled back. Blue sparks flew and wires sprang and coiled like some live thing. Stopping dead in her tracks, she gripped his hand desperately.

"I'm afraid, Daddy!"

"Step exactly where I step and you'll be all right."

"I can't!"

He bent to pull her up onto his back. "Hold fast and I'll carry you."

She clung to him and they picked a path through the maze of debris back to the car.

As he put her down, tears streamed down her cheeks again. "I love you, Daddy!"

"I love you, too, darling."

"Don't ever let anything happen to you! Don't ever go away!"

By the time they reached home, she had become calm and brave again. They cleaned and bandaged his wound, deciding he wouldn't need the emergency treatment.

It was one of the worst tornadoes the town had seen, but by a miracle there were no fatalities. The funnel had touched down, skipped, and touched down again fifteen miles north. The school had received the hardest blow, deflecting the main force of the wind. Within weeks, the children were talking about the catastrophe with great animation, but he knew Eddi suffered uneasy dreams. He had dreams, too, of a terrifying hour when everything about his life stood naked in one fateful moment, of opportunities dangled before him like a tempter's charm, and a fleeting glimpse of how fragile they all were.

Chapter Twenty-Seven

By middle school Eddi had become involved in drama camp, cheerleading, gymnastics, dancing, chorale and others. She had a pure, sweet voice like her mother's, and often enough was selected to carry the solo lead in various school productions.

In eighth grade she decided to go to summer camp. This would be her first time away from home for more than one or two nights. "The cabins have sides," she explained to Neal, "but they're half-screened with flaps that drop down. It'll be like camping out."

"How many girls to a cabin?"

"Eight. Four bunk beds to each side. At least three of my friends are going."

"And you'll choose a place to arrange all your things in a neat little stack."

As the time approached, she began to get cold feet. "When we get to camp, no matter what I say, you have to leave me."

"Of course," said Neal. "We wouldn't want to make that long drive then change our minds."

"You know they won't even let us call for three days."

"You'll be too busy to call."

"I can write, though. And you'll write me?"

He laughed. "It'll be time for you to come home by the time you get a letter."

"Write before I leave, then, and I'll get it while I'm there." She said anxiously, "I know some girls who were awfully homesick the whole week."

"Homesickness can be painful,' he said, "but I'm sure you'll make new friends and want to stay forever."

Following her request, he wrote several letters and mailed them during the week before her departure. That would assure her of mail nearly every day. On Saturday they loaded her sleeping bag and duffel bag and made the forty-mile trip north into Harris County. He noticed that Eddi kept biting her lip and changing stations on the radio. Despite her increasing independence, she had decided not to accept a ride with any of her friends. She wanted him to take her. They twisted up a long dirt road heavy with dust and cooled by tall pines, and passed through a gate of fieldstone columns with a trace chain curled to one side. Here they found a dozen or more cottages perched on a wooded slope above a six-acre lake. The main lodge and dining facility were a short walk away. On the big covered porch, tables with light refreshments had been set up, and there they met counselors and staff.

A young woman wearing shorts, sneakers and a baseball cap came over to him. "Hi, I'm Jill, Eddi's group leader. Were going to have a blast."

"You'll take good care of her, then?"

"You bet. This is my third year."

Eddi gave a tug on his arm. "You have to help me find where I'm living, Daddy. It's number seven."

"All right, let's go on up."

He threw her sleeping bag and duffle bag over his shoulders while she carried her small suitcase. They left the reception area and made their way down, then up a gentle slope covered with white oak seedlings, crossed a small stream on a bridge shaped like an eyebrow, and followed a bark-lined path up toward cottage seven. It was a rustic wood cabin constructed on reclaimed power poles. Entering through a screen door, they inhaled the odors of wood, ammonia and insect repellent, and she identified the bunk assigned her.

"I'm glad I'm on the bottom. And look, I can put my things here in the corner."

"So I thought," he said.

He checked out the bunk beds, which were built of sturdy four-by-four posts. At the foot of each bed was a rolled military blanket and a pillow. Almost at once Eddi unrolled her sleeping bag and fitted it neatly over the mattress. She'd brought a pillow, too. The floors were of clear pine, the sides half-screened, with a good view of the lake and the little skiffs bobbing on a mild breeze. About the time they settled her in, several other girls arrived, flighty as birds. Two of them were friends from school, the third a tall, dark-haired girl to whom they all introduced themselves.

"We got lost. How'd you get here so early?"

"I don't know," said Eddi. "I just leave it all to my daddy."

From nearby cottages, other girls came hurtling over and he saw that his daughter was one they all wanted to befriend.

"Hi! I'm Sandra . . ."

"I'm Laurie . . ."

"I'm Eddi Austin . . . my dad . . ."

In a few minutes it seemed she had all but forgotten him. "This is my first year," said Eddi, "but I want to learn how to paddle a canoe. Has anybody done that?"

"I have. It's not hard if you learn to turn together."

"I want to hike," said another. "I love to explore!"

Already Eddi had found her niche, Neal thought. Half an hour later, however, when he said, "It's time for me to leave, Eddi," he saw her expression cloud over.

"Why don't you stay and have dinner with us? Parents are allowed."

"Most don't, though. And I don't think they encourage it."

"Well, I'll walk you to the car." She glanced at her friends. "I'll be back! Don't anybody leave."

As they strolled down the hillside to the dusty parking area, he could see anxiety on her face. "You'll be fine, darling. Be careful. Have a wonderful time, but don't let anything happen to you."

"You either. Whatcha gonna do for a whole week?"

"I have big plans," he laughed. "Freedom at last!"

She hooked her hands into her pockets and muttered solemnly, "Well, I guess I'll stay then."

He thought it was her way of asking him to tell her she didn't have to. "Why don't you go ahead and join your friends? After you're settled in, I'll take off."

"No, I think I'll just hang around here until you go." She came close and hugged him hard. "Bye, Daddy."

Her words went through him like a spear. Only with a great effort was he able to conceal his emotions. The very last thing Sandi had said to him was "Bye, Neal." Quickly, he turned away and got into the car.

She'd be fine, he knew. Within an hour, her nostalgia would be replaced by a flood of activity. But he wished he hadn't, at the last moment, looked into his rearview mirror. The last image he had was of Eddi standing in the road, one hip thrown out, her long hair catching a sparkle of sunlight, a lonely figure watching him drive away. He blinked hard as he turned a curve, slicing into the dust of oncoming arrivals.

On the way home he stopped for a take-out pizza. He simply didn't think he could go in and make dinner. All evening he kept listening for the sound of Eddi's music, her bath, her chattering on the phone. Nothing was the same without her. His ear was attuned to many voices and sounds, but without the music of her laughter, her conversation — even the slamming of doors and her funny sneezes — without these he could hardly believe he'd be able to function in a normal manner.

But he knew he couldn't allow such feelings to encumber Eddi in any way. She was growing into a young woman, and the emergence of her free-hearted personality had been his objective all along. He thought of the time their house would be truly silent, when she would no longer be there. He wondered what thread he might gather up then, what embers of those original fires might be relit.

After his pizza he tried to write, but somehow this late evening work was becoming more and more difficult. A compelling desire came over him to telephone Kara, but of course that part of his life was long over, and since Kara there had been no woman who really appealed to him. He phoned his mother, Mrs. Steele and Lori and finally it was late enough to go to bed.

Sunday morning, he found a card in his shaver drawer, handmade, with hearts and kisses, and words that said, "I love you, Daddy. I miss you. Buckle your seatbelt." It was just like Eddi to think of him this way. He walked into her room and was impressed by its neatness, its loving arrangements, her teddy bear, her books, her mementos, her tapes, her bed made and towels hanging at precise levels on the towel bars.

Unexplainably, a sense of freedom came over him. He walked out to the gazebo and observed a redheaded woodpecker on a pilgrimage from the bird feeder to a large elm near the patio. From a neighbor's yard, the perfume of tea olive and sweet gardenias wafted across the summer breeze, like beautiful maidens wandering down from the hills. And on the playhouse he'd built for Eddi, he noticed a splintered and decaying board which needed repair. He felt like a liberated bachelor.

He went back to his home office and brought the manuscript of *Samson's Revenge* out to the gazebo. He always attacked revisions in longhand. He settled down onto a bench and manuscript and pencil in hand he read:

When he heard about his brother's tumor he fell apart. Outside, walking among the trees, away from everyone, he wept softly, his breath torn out of him from moment to moment in guttural snatches. He pressed his hands against his eyes and stood waiting for the wretchedness to pass. He'd never imagined his brother, that hulk of man, sick, but of all the illnesses which might have befallen him disease of the brain must, he thought, be the worst. One might lose limbs, lose mobility and physical functions, but to lose words and thought and reason, and realize they had been lost, must be the most treacherous, sustained torment of all. Still, in some peculiar way, that vile mass on the periphery of his brother's brain let in a glint of hope — no defenseless enemy can be without an element of compassion. He wiped away the tears and began to think of what he must do to reach out — to reach out beyond pride and resentment and jealousy which suddenly became so useless and petty and destructive . . .

Neal put the script aside on the bench. This was not a passage he should attempt to revise today. His mood was too pensive and melancholy. He scratched back in memory to evoke those earlier writings which were more scintillant, heightened by a confident optimism. But like his black hair those days were turning gray. The times when he was inspired by an idea, by an occurrence or glimpse of some dramatic scene, and rushed to his desk to write furiously into the night, or cram in half an hour at lunch, were becoming fewer and further between. Fragmented and evidencing signs of distraction, the scribblings of paragraphs and phrases lay on the desk or floor like the scattered shavings of some reclusive carver's agonized sculptures. Passages which began as swift crystals of inspiration died from too-long delay.

He remembered those evenings years ago when he was writing his best, hearing Sandi's movements and Eddi's infant squeals from the kitchen. The most important pattern of someone's personal history, he thought, was interwoven with impressions, with aromas and memories and small experiences. Despite this, he had never gotten over the feeling that his creative ambitions held him slightly apart in some way.

He was now in his forties. In no time Eddi would be in high school, then college. Years had vanished almost before he'd gotten a hold on them. He'd envisioned himself living some sort of extraordinary life, now he wondered if it were merely a feeling he was looking for, some idea of what a writer's life should look like. He saw himself as two personalities — one making an ordinary place in the world, the other standing silently by, waiting for the first to move out of the way. He pushed the thick, dog-eared, overworked manuscript of *Samson's Revenge* aside, but he wasn't yet willing to give up the idea that he could accomplish some special thing.

About midweek, the house became cruelly empty again. For a few days freedom had been invigorating, but he realized that the real quest of the heart is loving commitment. He became more poignantly aware of reminders of Sandi, her guitar, pictures on walls and tables, decorative dishes her children had made at The Learning Room. Love is still love, he thought, in different form. He couldn't see Sandi's sweet smile or chase her through the trees or bring her lime ice milk, but the memory of her assumed a kind of immortality of its own. Memory became his lamp, his bedfellow, and he took courage from it all.

Then he began to wonder about Kara again, how she was faring, if she missed him. He wondered if he would ever see her again. He went into the house and ate a solitary lunch.

At the end of the long week he drove up to the camp. Out of a big crowd of parents and campers, Eddi saw him and came running. "Hi, Daddy!" She threw her arms around him. Her face and arms were tanned, her cheeks rosy.

"Well, how was it?"

"I had a wonderful time!"

They hugged, then tossed her bags into the car. There was much hubbub, dozens of girls squealing and embracing, parents gathering up pillows and sleeping bags, finding lost tennis rackets. "Just give me a minute, Daddy." He stood waiting for her to exchange addresses and phone numbers with new friends. "Bye!" "I'll see you next year!" "Write me!" Finally they were ready to leave. As they pulled out and drove down the pastel dirt road, she plunged into a nonstop recapitulation of her day by active day. "You got my letters, I suppose?" he said.

"Yes, but I didn't open them."

"Why not?"

"I was afraid they'd make me homesick."

What a sensitive little creature, he thought — objective, practical, square-dealing, and touched by the simplest things. In Eddi, he found better things than he had ever expected in the world.

Chapter Twenty-Eight

C loud continued to live it up — boxes of lobsters imported from Maine, a beautiful purebred Collie puppy for Brandi, more jewels for Lori. Neal instinctively felt that something didn't ring true. He knew Cloud's sales were strong but his brother-in-law was so unaccustomed to handling so much cash he treated it like a windfall.

"Big receivables don't necessarily mean big profits, Cloud," Neal warned. "I assume you're keeping accurate records." Cloud shrugged and frowned.

Lori was happy during this time. "I knew once he settled into something everything would be fine. He's on top of the world!"

"I'm glad for you, Lori. Someone's helping with the books — payroll reports, F.I.C.A. returns, unemployment insurance — the red tape?"

"Oh, I'm sure Cloud's taking care of everything. Hard as he works, he says we're entitled to *something*!"

Well into the second year disaster struck. Neal wasn't surprised. The economy slowed down, sales tapered off, there was no more drawing against new jobs to carry the shortfalls, Cloud's bookkeeping was so sloppy he'd never really known whether he was turning a profit or not. Desperately trying to hold things together, he began to cut corners and invited the wrath of angry customers and creditors.

Neal didn't know all this until one evening while they were having dinner at their parents. He noticed Lori looking so downcast he pressed her for an explanation. Finally she blurted, "We have no money! They're about to take our house!"

"But Cloud's been living like you're rolling in cash."

"I don't know what happened!"

He knew, though. Mismanagement and extravagance had caught up with them. This wasn't even the worst of it. For several months Cloud had failed to deposit payroll taxes, and the Internal Revenue Service was threatening criminal charges.

When Neal saw Cloud he demanded, "My God, do you think you can withhold payroll taxes and get away with it?"

"It's these banks," Cloud swore. "Damn if they'll let up a minute!"

"Yes. They do expect loans to be repaid."

Neal decided to distance himself from it. Cloud's checks were bouncing and he was running on and off jobs trying to dodge the tax man. Their troubles began to seep like a bitter poison through the family. Mrs. Austin was so concerned for Lori that she began to suffer anxiety attacks. Finally, disgusted with it all, he went to see Cloud's banker, a man named Walden.

"Nothing we've tried to work out for him has materialized, Neal. Frankly, he hasn't met a single commitment."

"Well, I understand he's strapped."

"No doubt. A lot depends on how sincere he is about working things out."

Personable as Cloud was, he'd evidently become belligerent and defensive with Walden, a fatal mistake. Until he learned to admit his failures, no banker could be expected to give him much slack.

"I can imagine the position you're in, Neal," said Walden. "She's your sister and I know you've always felt responsible for her. We'll do what we can."

Neal's mother lamented, "I suppose if they lose their home they might move in with us. I'm not sure where we'd put Brandi, though."

"That would be a terrible mistake," Neal said. "You don't need another family to raise."

One by one, Cloud had to let his men go and throw himself into trying to finish his jobs. Lack of personal supervision had been one of his downfalls from the beginning. His new truck was attached and every day he and Lori squabbled over who most needed transportation. As collections drifted in, he either skimmed off the top to keep his home life from collapsing or rushed to stave off some crippling threat.

Neal waited until the last minute and then when foreclosure on their home was imminent, he called Cloud to his office. "Bring me a list of all your assets and liabilities. Don't screw this up, Cloud. I want an accurate picture."

When Cloud came back with the numbers, Neal looked them over with undisguised disgust. "How on earth did you dig a hole this deep in such a short time?"

Cloud scowled.

"Probably the best thing for you is to get thrown out of your house," said Neal. "Or do time for tax fraud. For Lori's sake, I'm going to bail you out. This is the last time, Cloud."

"I ain't asking you to do anything."

"If it weren't for Lori and Brandi I'd let them nail you. This is probably the most irresponsible abuse of other people's money I've seen in a long time."

They went to the bank. Neal paid off a sizable chunk of the debt and worked out a payment plan with Warden that Cloud could reasonably meet. It was all such an unnecessary and pointless waste, and gouged another hole in Neal's escape to independence. His anger was so intense he wanted to stay away from Cloud for as long as possible. As they left the bank he let him have it. "You've acted the fool, Cloud. Do you realize just what a rotten mess you've made of everything?"

Cloud clamped his jaw shut.

"Every man isn't cut out for business. Maybe you've got that through your head now."

"If they'd left me alone, I could've — "

"You could have dug yourself deeper. You're never going to straighten out your life if you refuse to acknowledge your mistakes."

A tinge of remorse flickered across Cloud's forehead.

"It's okay to try something and fail," said Neal, "if you give it your best. But the way you threw money away was just damn stupid."

Cloud nodded. "I know I screwed up."

"All these years Lori has stuck with you. If you don't focus on your wife and children now, you're an utter fool."

Cloud lifted his head, and Neal thought he saw both angry denial and a glimmer of contriteness. "I know they deserve better than me."

"So what are you going to do about it?"

"First I gotta try to get my old job back. Then maybe someday I'll have another chance."

Only with his hat in his hand did Cloud talk his old boss into rehiring him. Even so Cloud never ceased to blame all the malicious forces which caused his failure. The only positive thing that came out of the disaster was that Lori seemed enlightened at last. "I'm sorry you had to do this, but I'm grateful. You're a kind and generous man. I've told Cloud I'm sick of his schemes and bitterness. If he can't learn how to take care of his family he should get out."

Neal decided not to tell Lori how much this fiasco cost him.

Chapter Twenty-Nine

After three or four revisions Neal felt that *Samson's Revenge* was about as good as he could do for now and he sent it off to his agent. He'd labored over the novel off and on for a decade, starting and abandoning others in between, and he wasn't confident about the final result. Some of the writing was good, he knew, but he acknowledged that there was a gap between his vision and his execution. He waited in anticipation for Sam's response and hoped that a crucial side of himself was about to emerge at last. The agent reserved telephone calls to his clients for special news only, and each time the phone rang Neal's pulse leaped. But it never turned out to be Sam Harris.

Business became a necessary drag, and he wondered how it was that day by day he lived this life of commerce and entrepreneurship when his heart had always been in something else. Probably, it was a sad fact of life for many people. With his family, with Tia and the men, with his business associates, even with his daughter he engaged in a reasonable and relatively productive life while another part of himself remained separate and unrealized. Sometimes he thought he must write a novel called *Half a Life*. But all along he realized the something missing was his own mind and thoughts, his own self-destructive yearning.

Then from Sam Harris he received not a congratulatory call but a doleful letter. While praising the prose, Sam wrote, "I'm sorry, Neal, but I don't see how we could market this. I'm afraid it falls through the cracks." The agent offered no suggestions about how revisions might make *Samson's Revenge* resonate with an editor, but with a small spark of encouragement suggested, "You've worked long and hard on this. Perhaps you should take a break and then have another look."

Neal read the letter over and over, seeking some glimmer of hope. All these long years! How might he have used those hundreds of grueling hours, not for some imagined contribution but for simple pleasure! For days he didn't want to talk to anyone, didn't want to work, and keeping up the same old front was goading. By sheer force of his will, for the sake of Eddi and others around him, he avoided signs of abject morbidity. He knew how sour moods and depression dampened the spirits of everybody they touched.

But he wanted to believe he had accomplished something, too, if only that by working hard and with intense foresight he had saved himself and his family from the financial straits they would otherwise have suffered. He remembered his father forcing himself out of bed on cold mornings, lighting the little gas space heater to warm the house before the rest of the family rose, shaving in the cloudy mirror of a tiny medicine cabinet over the lavatory and then at night coming home dead tired, only to eat a quick meal and go off again to do some work which would provide extra income. Even so, he had little to show for it, little to fall back on, and little security in old age, except for the help Neal was able to give them.

And this, of course, was why the acquisition of wealth held him in its spiteful grip. He knew he couldn't let up for a moment. He'd planted the field, now it must be continuously cultivated.

Eddi was now at such a vulnerable age, it was a time in her life when all he had taught her and all she had learned growing up would be either embraced or rejected, and her view of the world would be entrenched. He had scarcely begun to recover his equilibrium and accept the inevitable concerning his literary fate when she said one night, in a rather offhand manner, "Mrs. Potts said what we were doing today was cheating."

"Cheating?" He was stunned. "What were you doing?"

"Helping each other with our homework. We all looked up a question and shared the answers."

"What's wrong with that?"

"I don't know. We stopped as soon as she told us."

"So you're not allowed to do homework together?"

"I guess not."

The last thing he needed in his present frame of mind was

confrontation, but since Eddi didn't appear particularly concerned, he allowed his thoughts to struggle back to his ill-fated *Samson's Revenge.* Then the following evening Eddi met him in tears. "Mrs. Potts registered a complaint against us. We have to go before student council!"

"What!" Nothing could so jolt him back to reality as an attack on his daughter. "You mean she's really accusing you of cheating?"

"Yes. It'll go on our records and everything!"

"Did you explain to her you thought it was okay to work together?"

"We all did. I don't know how you can cheat if you don't understand something's wrong."

"I think I'd better speak to Mrs. Potts."

"Oh, no, Daddy, it'll just make matters worse!"

"It's ridiculous. You may have made a mistake, but if I've taught you anything, it's to be honest and truthful."

She pleaded, "Well, just don't do anything until we have our hearing."

"What precisely does that mean?"

"A committee of upper classmen and teachers hear cases, then decide if there's an infraction."

"And how often do you suppose they find against a teacher?"

"I don't know. Not very often, probably."

"Not very often is my guess, too."

She said earnestly, "I didn't mean to be cheating, Daddy!"

He had little hope for a student council heavily influenced by a teacher. And as he expected, when they met on Friday the board found in favor of Mrs. Potts. Telling him about this, Eddi was pale and shaken. "There's to be no disciplinary action," she mumbled. "No suspensions or anything."

"How charitable of them."

"The charges will appear on my transcripts, though."

"Well, we'll see about that."

"It can't be helped, Daddy."

She was too upset for him to argue with her, but he saw this as no petty injustice. If Eddi had been guilty, he wouldn't blindly defend her.

But to be accused falsely was an affront to the principles she'd learned to believe in.

On Monday he telephoned Mrs. Potts and explained that the girls hadn't intentionally broken any rules. She offered no response. "They didn't understand working together to be an infraction." Still she did not answer. Irritated by her silence, he demanded, "If I had helped Eddi at home, would that have been cheating?"

"That would be acceptable," she replied curtly.

"Oh, I see. You're saying it's all right for a parent to help a student look up answers, but not for friends to work together. I'm afraid that distinction is lost on me, Mrs. Potts."

She remained silent and in exasperation he gave up. He telephoned the main office and spoke to the middle school headmaster to arrange a meeting. It was agreed on for the following Monday. He said nothing to Eddi about the meeting.

On Monday he drove to the school, walked straight into the office, and was escorted into a small conference room where Mrs. Potts and Mr. Frank, the headmaster, joined him. A substantial woman with brownish hair, cool narrow eyes, and a compressed, fishlike mouth, Mrs. Potts looked like a person who'd forgotten how to smile. Wearing a black dress, a few dull pieces of costume jewelry, and a detached expression, she carried a stack of papers, suggesting that no small inconveniences were going to distract her from her professional duties.

Mr. Frank was a well-dressed, not unhandsome man distanced by the guarded look of someone in the middle of a controversy. His chin was strong and square, with the hint of a dimple. Neal felt that had they not been adversaries, he could like the man. But right away he saw that the headmaster didn't take challenges to his teachers lightly.

Neal recapped the event to date, and insisted, "These girls had no intention of cheating. They saw nothing wrong in doing homework together."

"My rules are quite specific." Mrs. Potts was unmoved. "Research is a major tool in learning."

"You're teaching research, then? I thought it was history."

"I'm a history teacher. They get the answers only by reading the entire text."

"But was that clear to the girls?"

The headmaster spoke in a cultured, modulated tone. "These girls are intelligent enough to understand our rules, Mr. Austin. We believe our students should be responsible for their actions."

"Are you suggesting Eddi's irresponsible?"

"In this case her actions appear so."

"Eddi understands responsibility, but she's totally confused by the distortions of your viewpoint." He shifted his chair to look more directly at Mr. Frank, who sat at his side. "If I were in school here, or anywhere else, I'd think nothing of sitting down to do homework with other boys."

"Doing work together and taking answers from someone isn't the same," said Mrs. Potts.

"Please explain the difference to me."

"They can look up answers together. They cannot avoid studying by trading answers to the material."

"The point is, they didn't comprehend this. A simple warning would have been sufficient."

"This is a warning," said Mrs. Potts.

"I beg your pardon. These are accusations brought before your council."

"The students agreed with Mrs. Potts," allowed Mr. Frank.

"And do any of them happen to be in Mrs. Potts's class?"

After a brief hesitation, she answered, "Two of them are in my third period."

He let the fractional silence carry the weight of these implications.

Mr. Frank insisted, "Our student council members are serious young men and women, Mr. Austin. They've been taught to think for themselves."

"And have they been taught the principles of integrity?"

"The student body elects them. We would hope they use discretion."

Neal struggled to keep his manner restrained, fixing his gaze upon the man whose decision now meant everything. "Look, these are serious charges. I can't speak for the other girls . . ."

"Some of the parents have contacted us," said the headmaster.

"And do they endorse Mrs. Potts's procedures?"

"Not necessarily." Frank reached into his coat pocket and asked portentously, "Have you seen this letter, Mr. Austin? It's from Eddi. She agrees with us that she did cheat." He handed over the neatly composed letter.

As he read through his daughter's uniform, carefully arranged script, he saw that, true to her nature, Eddi was so concerned with the attack on Mrs. Potts that she pleaded in behalf of her accuser. That was like Eddi, he thought, so sympathetic her own defenses crumbled under the weight of someone else's pain.

Tossing the paper back, he said with disgust, "Do you see what she's doing here? I admire her for it."

"Yes?" said Mr. Frank.

"Listen to what she says. 'I understand now why this is cheating.' You call that a confession? She's agreeing because she feels sorry for the trouble she's caused. It merely proves her innocence."

The headmaster wasn't convinced. "I'm afraid we're making too much of this."

"To some of the families it may be a small issue. To us, it isn't. At least Mrs. Potts should have discussed it with the girls before bringing it before council."

"I agree with that," replied Mr. Frank.

"Why didn't she, then?"

The stoic teacher lost a small degree of her composure. Neal felt there was an element of vindictiveness in her personality, but remembered that professionally she was known to be a capable and respected instructor.

"So much for the way this school treats its students," Neal said. "I'd be most concerned if these charges were to appear on Eddi's transcript."

"We'll take that under consideration," said Mr. Frank.

"Perhaps you misunderstood me. I will not allow this distortion to show up on the girls' records. Who is the school's lawyer, Mr. Frank?"

A chink then appeared in the headmaster's armor. "I don't believe we'll have to make this a legal issue."

"I hope not. But if these ridiculous accusations show up in Eddi's records, it will be a very expensive mistake for the school."

He stood and walked out, feeling the battle half won. What those people thought was of little consequence to him, but the damage to Eddi's self-esteem and to her record was significant. At the least, he believed they understood now that there was one parent who'd fight for his child, and he doubted that they would be so swift to pass judgment in the future.

He'd felt it unnecessary to inform Eddi about his conference until he learned the results. But as news always travels fast, she'd heard all about it, and when she came home from school she flew at him. "Why did you go and see Mrs. Potts and Mr. Frank when I asked you not to!"

"You asked me to wait until the student council met, Eddi. They ruled against you, as we predicted they would."

"I didn't *want* you to go. Now everybody knows!"

"You don't think they didn't already know?"

"About the hearing, yes. Not about my daddy seeing Mr. Frank!"

"Don't let that embarrass you. Most kids wish their parents *would* get involved."

The flush of anger in her fair cheeks and the tightening of the skin around her eyes confused him. This confusion forced a toughening of his own resistance.

"As you probably know, Eddi," he said, "we can't expect any apologies."

"Because they proved us wrong."

"Wrong? Mrs. Potts doesn't recognize the difference between indiscretion and moral failure. I'm sorry you felt compelled to write an apology."

"Mrs. Potts is a good person and she was getting in trouble for the way she handled things."

"Rescuing her by admitting to cheating didn't do much for your own position. I appreciate your charity, though."

"It didn't change one thing!" she cried. "What you did didn't change anything, either! I'll never get in any college if they think I'm a cheater."

"That isn't going to happen."

"I could've sorted this all out myself!" she insisted. "None of the other girls' parents did anything!"

"Too bad for them. My purpose is to protect you. I'll always do that whether or not you ask."

She fought against her tears. "I'm so *ashamed*!"

"Ashamed! You mean you're embarrassed that I defended you?"

"About . . . about everything!"

Disgusted beyond further discussion, he stalked into his office and stayed there. When it came time for dinner, Eddi didn't emerge and he put food on the table then sat alone, refusing to go to her. He spent the evening alone, then went to bed without kissing her goodnight.

He was lying awake in the darkness when he sensed Eddi enter the bedroom. A moment later, he felt her sit down on the bed at his side. "I'm sorry, Daddy," she whispered.

He didn't answer for a moment. "That's all right."

"I don't know what makes me act like this. Something just comes over me. I pray and pray that God will help me be better."

"Sometimes you just have to stay silent, Eddi," he said. "You can't say everything that comes into your mind."

"I didn't even mean what I said. I'm so proud that you stood up for me. None of the other parents even bothered. All the kids envy me. I'll always be glad that you're willing to fight for me."

'Why were you angry then?"

"I don't *know*. Because I was hurt inside and took it out on you. I'm sorry. Nothing anybody says or thinks is as important as you. You aren't mad, are you? Don't be mad. I can't stand that."

"No. And even if I were, it'd make no difference."

She sat silent a moment, then leaned down and pressed her cheek against his. "Okay. Maybe I can sleep now. I was going to be awake all night."

"Me, too."

"Good night. I love you, Daddy."

"I love you, too, Eddi."

He watched her pass through the brief slant of moonlight, her head bowed but her shoulders straight, and he felt a great relief of tension. She was just a child still, but it was amazing how healing the poultice of a few kind words could be. Growing up was such a struggle, he knew. Parenting was hard, too. Attitudes, words, actions could explode in ways totally contrary to one's true feelings. He suspected in the morning she would emerge bright as day, as though nothing had happened. That was one thing about Eddi. As quickly as her temper flared, she forgave, and forgave herself. She put all unpleasantness behind her, even her own failures, her own disappointments.

An hour or so later, he slipped into her room to look in on her. She was sleeping peacefully, her teddy bear hooked protectively under her arm. He leaned down and kissed her cheek. She smiled, and he knew in her subconscious she sensed his presence.

Chapter Thirty

Neal heard that Kara's marriage wasn't going that well, and he was sorry. He felt that she deserved happiness. He thought of her often and knew Eddi did, too. That time and opportunity in his life were gone, but he hoped she would find contentment in some way. She was a brave and loving young woman, willing to risk an experiment in courage. From time to time when he thought of her he felt jealousy and regret, too.

Then out of the blue one day he picked up the phone and heard her say, "Neal? How are you?"

It took him a moment to realize who it was. "Kara! Gosh, it's good to hear from you."

"I'm just here for one day and felt the urge to call you."

"I'm glad you did. What brings you down? No bad news, I hope."

"Just some old business."

"It's great to hear from you. You sound wonderful."

"It's hard to believe we haven't talked in so many years. I've wondered what's going on in your lives."

"I said we'd stay in touch," he reminded her. "But you didn't want to."

"I knew a clean break was about the only way I could get over you and Eddi."

"Well, look, I'd like to see you. Can we get together somewhere?"

"No. I have to go back."

"You must be able to spare an hour."

"I don't know, Neal."

"One hour," he insisted.

"Well, maybe just one hour — in the park."

He dropped everything, drove straight to Weracoba, and found her car near the band shell. Kara had walked a little way down the hill and had her head slightly tilted as though listening. She looked exactly as he remembered her. She wore gray slacks, a pale lavender blouse and gray loafers. Her hair was longer and fuller than when he first met her. A rush of emotion swept through him, and he knew if it were the first time he'd ever seen her he would have fallen in love with her. He walked down to her and they hugged.

"I was listening for our bird," she said. "Wonder if he's still sharpening that note? You ever come here?"

"Almost never, except to jog."

"They haven't moved our bench, have they?"

"I doubt it. Why don't we go over and see?"

As they walked side by side, he found it difficult to resist taking her into his arms.

"You don't look a bit different, Neal. I hear you're working harder than ever, but it doesn't seem to age you."

"Where do you hear such things?"

"Oh, from the same grapevine that tells me what a young lady Eddi's becoming. She's all right?"

"She's fine. I know she'd like to see you."

"I'd love to see her, but not this time. Please give her my love, though. I really mean it."

They walked silently, as though having so much to say, they could say nothing. Finally he asked, "And how is marriage treating you?"

She laughed. "I bet you're thinking that if it's treating me well, I wouldn't be walking with you now. We're doing all right. We're getting a new house, in fact."

"A new house? That's exciting."

"It took years for us to decide, and it's more for Paul than me, really. Something he's always wanted."

"Then I guess you'll start a family."

"I don't know. First he wants everything exactly in place — sort of like you, Neal."

"Ouch."

"Not in the same way, of course. Paul's plans are rather mathematical. Yours are more — what should I say — idealistic."

"I hope that experience hasn't spoiled things for you," he said.

"You were the first man I was really in love with. Did you know that, Neal?"

"No . . . but I'm sorry I turned out to be such a poor role model."

"I confess you confused me for a while. Probably I'll never stop thinking about you, but I don't necessarily believe that's bad."

"I felt such responsibility for you, Kara."

"I know you did. To be truthful, that makes you and Paul quite different. You try so hard not to hurt someone."

They turned along the creek toward their favorite bench, which was shadowed by large oaks. Here the silence was broken only by an occasional passing car or a cyclist riding through the park.

"I've always heard that people tend to gravitate toward like personalities," he said.

"Could be. I remember you felt I'm like Sandi."

"In some ways, yes."

"You know what I think, Neal? To make relationships work, people must be willing to give up something of themselves. We don't have to be locked into the way we've always done things."

"And is Paul as innovative and spontaneous as you?"

"Paul isn't much for spontaneity. He's invariably reliable, though."

"Well, that contradicts what I just said, doesn't it? I can't see you marrying a man who isn't just fascinated with your vitality." He glanced over. "I know I have no right to say anything. Maybe it's because I'm a little jealous."

They found their bench, wood slats with wrought iron frame, and an unmowed patch of grass beneath — not a favored spot for the regular walker. As they sat down Kara said, "I guess we shouldn't talk about Paul. I don't know if it's fair to him. Sometimes people who have truly deep feelings are afraid to express themselves."

"I suppose I want to hear only about his shortcomings."

"You really feel a little jealous?"

"Of course I do."

She smiled with her perfect white teeth, and the faint freckling across the top of her nose. "I'll be the same when you find the right woman. I'll search for all her faults, but I'll be happy for you, too — I think."

She folded her hands together and looked down at the grass. "I confess I'm still jealous of you, too. Your life, what you think, what you do. I guess those kinds of feelings never go away. I always had this idea that sooner or later you'd come around." She looked up at him. "I don't regret my time with you and Eddi, though. Not at all. And I don't blame myself. After all, I see that you're still waiting. Anyway, I just had to check on you. You're really all right, then?"

"Yes, we're fine. I sure do want to kiss you, though."

She smiled again and glanced at her watch. "I have to go, Neal."

"You really can't take some time to see Eddi, then?"

"No, maybe next time."

He walked her back up to her car, then reached and took her hand. "I guess I can't, though — kiss you, I mean?"

"No. I'm a married woman, and in a way you're married, too." She brushed her lips to his cheek, got into her car and drove away.

He did not leave the park at once. He sat in his car, door open, feet on the ground. In retrospect, it was hard to reconcile his reasoning for letting Kara go. Or perhaps he wasn't reasoning at all. One of his most staggering emotions when Sandi died was regret. He'd so poured himself into business and writing that Sandi in so many ways had never ceased to feel left out. They could have done so much more together, could have carried on their romance much longer, he could have been a better husband and lover. Why he couldn't have simply lived a regular life and written too he didn't know. He did know that he couldn't bring himself to repeat his failings with Kara. He couldn't bring himself to offer her half a married life.

But now with his feet planted solidly on the earth and his thoughts fleeting he wondered if this had been just more in-looking. He wondered if at that time he'd really been thinking more about what he would feel than about what Kara felt. Still, was this not protecting her, too? Perhaps for some men there was only one great love. But he didn't believe that. More likely he was guilty of selfishness. Had he given more in love, even sacrificed for it, more would it have multiplied to him. Protecting himself from crippling regret was the armor of an ungiving man. Despite his failures he knew this was not the kind of person he had thought himself to be.

For the next couple of weeks he tried to write about his feelings for Kara — the longing and lust — but it fell short and he ended up destroying everything. He really had no creative talent, he decided. At times he hated his writing and the divide between the vision he was trying to evoke and the printed word; but he couldn't bring himself to give up. Perhaps someday Eddi or someone would discover these reams of paper and if not the fiction itself, the ideas would touch a few lives in some way.

When he told Eddi about Kara, she said, "I wish I could've seen her. Sometimes I still pretend she's my mother. I was just a baby when we met her and for all those years I thought surely she'd come and live with us."

"I understand, Eddi. I'm sorry."

"I was truly heartbroken when she left."

"I know."

"But after the initial shock I tried not to make it any harder on you, Daddy. At least I convinced myself it wasn't because of me."

"No, of course it wasn't you."

She smiled lightly. "You know, when I start driving, it'll give you all kinds of freedom."

"I'm not sure I want that kind of freedom."

"It'll be better for you. Then you can get serious about dating again."

"What makes you think I haven't been serious?"

"I know you haven't. Not since Kara. If any lady does look at you twice, you run away."

"It's not your business to notice such things," he laughed.

"I do, though. It's time you thought about your own life, Daddy. I wouldn't be hurt, if that's what scares you."

"No, I believe you'd be understanding about anyone I should date — as you say — seriously."

"Why don't you, then?"

"That's not something you can simply decide to do."

"It's because you work so hard, and because you have me." She looked at him squarely. "What'll happen when I go off to college? Then you won't have anybody."

Just how unsettling it was for him to think of Eddi leaving was something he tried to hide from her. But he wondered sometimes if he would ever be able to resurrect those dreams he'd once had — dreams of doing something which would truly touch the world. If anything, the romantic part of his nature had grown stronger — from sheer loneliness, he supposed. His prose was too sentimental, probably, and his voice too introspective. Still, now and then he felt he succeeded in capturing an original thought, a precise description. His best work succeeded when he could turn loose and express his inner self in his own clumsy way, with little concern about whoever might read it. But that was one of the strangest parts of his life. Expression was a poor substitute for experience. It was as if he had never really given himself over to experiencing life as he'd hoped to live it and to write about it.

Chapter Thirty-One

In her sophomore year, Eddi made the cheerleading squad and was inducted into the Honor Society. Neal celebrated all of her social and scholastic achievements. She was bright, introspective, generally well-liked, and had many friends. He was gratified to see that she sustained her mother's optimistic view of life.

In her junior year she announced that she was having to compete again for cheerleading. "They've decided to have tryouts every year. There're always new people wanting to come in."

"Well, you're one of their star performers."

"It doesn't matter. When politics are involved there's plenty of behind-the-scenes maneuvering."

With her height, her personality, and her easy but somewhat shy smile, Eddi possessed a special appeal, he thought. There was something plucky about her, too, an "I can go it alone" attitude in her quick step and jaunty lifted head. She threw herself into every whirl and jump, making the audience feel she was having a wonderful time.

As the time approached he saw the tension mounting and realized she really was serious about this. "Tryouts today," she said. "Wish me luck."

"I really don't believe they'll find anyone better than you."

"Maybe not, but remember what I said about politics. Probably it works that way in most schools."

All through the day Neal wondered how she was doing, but it wasn't until the evening that he learned anything. She arrived home with a subdued manner which could suggest both reserved excitement and emotion held deep within. He waited for her to break the news, but when she failed to say anything he finally demanded, "Well?"

"Well what?" She gave him one fleeting glance. "I didn't make the cheerleading squad."

"What!"

"They had to cut two girls and I was one."

"And who was reelected?"

"Oh, the in-group, as you might guess. The little darlings who were destined from first grade."

"But what did you do?"

"What did I do? I hugged them and told them how glad I was that they'd be leading our team." After a moment she added, "None of those girls are slackers. But some of the younger ones would have had more chances later on. This was it for me." With a sigh, she said, "I know I'm at least as good as some of them. Oh, well, I did my best."

"Is there nothing you can do?"

"No, of course not."

"Why don't I go speak to them?"

"No, Daddy, absolutely not! The faculty decides and they always suck up to those special mothers."

He saw that she didn't care to discuss it. She chattered about other things, but only pretended to eat her dinner. Following the meal, it seemed to him she made a point not to disappear too quickly, and when she finally did go to her room, he reflected on how well she'd taken this disappointment. But when he passed her closed door a little later, he heard her crying. Her sobs were muffled, probably by bedcovers held to her face. A sharp regret stabbed his heart. Eddi was as good as any of the girls, he believed, and better than several who remained on the squad. He knew this wasn't the last time she'd have to deal with snobbery, but wished he could take the pain from her.

He tapped on her door. "Eddi?" He opened the door quietly.

She sat in the middle of her bed, legs crossed, face buried in the sheets. How many times he must witness such hurt, he couldn't possibly know. As long as they both should live, he imagined.

"Eddi, I'm sorry. I wish there were something I could do."

"It was my last chance," she whispered.

"There'll be other opportunities for things far more significant than this."

"It doesn't seem that way now." She scrubbed her eyes and, dropping the sheets, looked down as though she'd been wrung out. "Some people always have their own way even if they are dorks." These were her first bitter words.

"I agree. But unfairness is something you'll have to struggle with all through life. And hypocrisy, too. But you must never stop being who you are."

"I guess somebody had to lose. If it had been one of them, they'd feel just like I do now."

"Maybe. Maybe not. Sometimes people have different defenses."

"It's so easy for some of them."

"But do you know what I've found? Those who have everything handed to them usually don't amount to very much."

Neal stood beside the bed, wishing he could think of what to say. This was one of those moments of truth for Eddi, he thought. He knew that at school she'd show neither suffering nor ill will. She'd hide her disappointment and disillusion. He was reminded of one summer when she was a little girl. It was one of those rare times he had insisted on having an hour on his own. He was writing while she played outside. She had agreed with the understanding that they would do something together in the afternoon. When he emerged, he discovered her sitting on a stool on the patio with a cold towel in one hand and the wrist of the other puffed up like a little pink balloon. A bee had stung her and she had waited patiently for a kiss and sympathy.

As she dried her tears, a sense of sad resolution seemed to settle the matter. "Oh, well, life goes on. It always does."

"I guess that's the only way to look at things. Sometimes it's hard, though."

"Yes. After all, I have the good fortune to get to go to a good school."

"Try to get some sleep, Eddi."

Next morning Neal woke early, slipped into her room, and stood looking at her with helpless tenderness. It was so important that Eddi think well of herself, that he help her defend herself against people who would discredit her dignity and her self-assurance. It seemed to him that the books and movies and music they saw and heard mostly sabotaged their humanness and self-worth, mostly belittled the value of life and emotion, all for greed and money.

With a cup of coffee he walked out to the gazebo, the place where they'd spent so much of their lives. The sun's first spear caught the top of the pines. Full light emerged softly as on a stage, then came rolling over the trees quickly as a wave breaking. He listened with his senses, while his mind was far away, in another place, another time. It had been seventeen years now since Eddi came into the world. Seventeen years! What would have happened, he wondered, if Sandi had lived? What would have happened had he held onto Kara Frost? How deeply one decision, one movement or response could change one's life forever!

The last time he'd seen Kara was that day in the park when he had felt such an urge to take her into his arms. There had been no further contact between them since. Then one day he'd run into her sister Claire again. "Did you know," said Claire, "that Kara and Paul have split?"

"What?"

"Once they decided, they moved very quickly."

"Claire, I hadn't heard that." He was shocked.

"They're still friends. There were no big battles. Their personalities are just so different, I guess."

"But what — where is she?"

"Atlanta, still, but not in her old job." Claire looked at him reflectively. "It happened to me, too, remember? Divorce. I guess we Frosts just aren't lucky in love."

"The last time I saw Kara they were building a house. What happened to that?"

"Oh, I guess that process was how they finally realized things weren't going to work out. I think Kara was pretty upset that Paul never wanted children."

"Well, maybe she'll have them someday."

Claire gave him an oblique look. "I think it's a little late now. We're all getting older, Neal."

"Don't remind me. It's always a blow to wake up and realize how old you are."

"Life whizzes by. The sad part is we're there before it suddenly hits us."

"Claire, I'm really sorry about this. I want her to be happy."

For days he couldn't get his mind off Kara or of such a sense of waste. Eddi could have been the child she wanted. And he — he'd given most of his life to another kind of marriage, and all that had happened was that they were both older, and he had nothing remarkable to show for it. He wondered if time would ultimately heal the rupture of the heart. He decided it would be appropriate — no, expedient, to contact Kara, and looked in his index for her phone number. But the only number he had was an old one, long since obsolete and probably assigned to someone else. He could get her number from Claire, but the longer he thought about it the more uncertain he became. To Kara it might seem that hearing from him would simply add wound to wound. He let the impulse slip away.

With coffee cup in hand, he sat on a bench in the gazebo and watched the sun break over the yard. Along the low stone terrace wall, the colors changed with the angle of the early rays. Sandi's bird feeder hanging over the well around the big hickory was in disrepair, half its screened bottom rusted out. In the flowerbed where she had meticulously cultivated her annuals, an occasional bloom poked its head, enduring and tenacious. He saw it all with sadness. Sandi was such a loving wife, such a devoted mother. Probably he hadn't seen her kindness and generosity and compassion as clearly as he did now, or basked as deeply as he could have in her tender touch, her loving devotion, her simple and inviolable love. Perhaps things seem more profound in retrospect, but he couldn't help wondering how different life would have been had that virus not attacked her heart. Yet he felt humble, too, that for a while their lives had touched. And that her greatest gift to him was their daughter.

He remembered the year Eddi prepared a special birthday dinner and gave him a card with the verses: "That man is a success . . . who has gained the respect of intelligent men and the love of children; who has filled his niche and accomplished his task; who leaves the world better than he found it . . ." He wished that truly could be said of him. He remembered how Sandi and now Eddi turned small pleasures into happy lightning, and wished his fervent desire to contribute some significant thing to the world hadn't held him apart from love, life's most precious gift.

Chapter Thirty-Two

Eddi had as many dates as she wanted but why she became serious with a young man named Brant Alderman Neal didn't know. He was a tall boy with coal black hair, thick eyebrows, and a faintly aloof air. He seldom smiled or laughed, but his manner was courteous. He was an only child and it was evident that his parents had spared little to spoil him. It seemed to Neal there was about him a sly glance and coiled mouth that suggested a hidden superiority, and a pouting look when anyone crossed him even in jest. Neal could only surmise that Eddi for unknown reasons needed a force in her life that she could neither defend nor explain. He hoped she would see in Brant this strain of possessiveness before it was too late.

Shortly after the cheerleading incident Neal happened to enter through their side gate one evening and surprised Eddi and her boyfriend in the gazebo. She had been in and out of love several times, and usually her boyfriends were decent young men who respected her reservations and her values. Neal had strict rules about her bringing a boy into the house when he was away, conditions she accepted, but not without complaint. "We went to my house and had to sit out in the rain until Daddy came home." In truth she and her friends often preferred the gazebo to indoors whenever weather permitted.

Opening the gate, he inadvertently startled them in a rather intense embrace. The sound of the gate sent them jumping. He, too, having no intention of violating their privacy, hurried up the walkway and into the house. He wasn't crazy about what he saw, and after thinking about it all evening, he asked Eddi to come into the den and talk to him. "I wonder if you realize how little it takes to arouse a boy."

"We weren't doing anything, Daddy."

"I know that something which seems perfectly harmless to a girl might be pretty stimulating to a young man."

"I wasn't born yesterday. You don't have to look over my shoulder."

"I may not have to, but I'll always try to pull you back when I feel you're in danger."

"That may have been necessary when I was a child, but I'm old enough now."

What bothered him, of course, was that she *was* still a child, overwhelmed by adult misinformation. He believed all the sex and violence youth were fed desensitized the natural compassion of a highly intelligent generation, and felt Eddi undefended against the persuasion of an entertainment media which would stop at nothing to turn a profit.

"Brant's good for me," she said. "With the cheerleader thing, he was so supportive. You're independent, Daddy, you don't know how it is to need someone."

"I beg your pardon. I certainly do know."

She went to her room, and again he found himself wandering outside. He'd sat in the gazebo about half an hour when Eddi emerged and, following the same stone path he had used, came to sit beside him.

"I know what I should and shouldn't do, Daddy. I may not understand all there is about boys, but I do know what not to allow." She took a deep breath and added, "I don't plan to do anything until I get married."

"When and why did you make that decision, Eddi?"

"When I was about thirteen. If you have sex with boys what's special about marriage? And I want my marriage to be very special, like yours and Mama's."

"How many girls do you think have made this decision?"

"Not many, but a few."

"Well, I'm glad."

"Someday I hope to fall in love and get married, though."

"I hope you do, too."

"I wish you could've had that, Daddy. You could've, maybe, with Kara."

The old stab of pain rushed through him. "At the time I was afraid I couldn't return Kara's love in the way she deserved."

"It might have been different if you'd given it a chance." She leaned down to rest her chin on her clasped hands. "Has it been terribly hard raising a daughter alone?"

"Maybe sometimes," he said. "But my life would have been empty without you."

"What would you change if you could?"

"Oh, I don't know. If things had been different, you and I wouldn't be the people we are, would we?"

"I guess not."

"Life seldom turns out the way we plan, but the way it does turn out is what pretty much shapes us, I guess."

"But sometimes people have to be better than their circumstances."

"That's true. Kara used to say we can use the pain to become better than we would be."

"Do you think Mama would be glad about the way things have turned out?"

"I know she'd be very proud of you."

"I hardly remember her at all. Just little things from time to time. That scares me."

"It's perfectly natural, though. You can remember her most through the feelings you have now."

"But it worries me that you've been so lonely."

He had no idea Eddi had picked up on this. "Loneliness isn't the worst thing," he muttered.

"I know you've worked hard, but sometimes people bury themselves in work just to hide from their feelings."

"You're awfully young to understand this."

The phone inside rang and she jumped up. "I miss having a mama," she said, "but I have the best daddy in the world!"

He was disappointed to see her go.

A few nights later, it was pouring rain when she brought Brant into the den, close to the office where he sat working. The lights were low, lightning flashed at the windows and thunder clapped and shattered the sky. Several times Eddi drifted in, asked him what he was doing, asked if he were going to watch the news, if he were going to work much longer. He knew she wanted him to make himself scarce, get out of earshot and give them some private space. But despite her earlier reassurance he understood how opportunity can stimulate results, and stubbornly he continued to work at his desk, determined that this would be one time he could emphasize his watchful presence. He knew Eddi wouldn't like this and that her boyfriend was probably making snide remarks. When finally it was time for him to leave, he heard her walk him to the door. A moment later the door slammed and she stormed up to her room.

Neal wasn't sorry he'd interfered but knew Eddi was angry. Too much pressure could have an adverse effect, and he understood how sometimes girls wanted boys to take control. But when he went in to see her, he was surprised to find that she had locked herself in her bathroom. From behind the closed door he could hear a kind of soft moaning, and with a sympathetic heart he called, "Eddi." She didn't answer and he called again.

"Go away!"

"Eddi, open the door."

"No! Leave me alone!"

He rapped harshly. "Eddi, open this door! I need to talk to you."

"Go away! I'm not coming out!"

"Damn the door! I'll break it down!" He meant it and she must have realized this, for as he turned to go and fetch a hammer, she flung the door open.

"I don't know why you can't trust me!" she cried.

"It's that boy I don't trust."

"We've already talked about this! But you don't listen!"

"How exactly would you respond if he tried to make you do something you didn't want to do?"

"He'd never do that! He respects my feelings! You don't know him at all!"

"I know he's not good for you."

"He's not good for *you*! Maybe nobody will ever be!"

"Tell me he's never told you what you could and couldn't do."

"He can do that sometimes."

"Oh, no, he can't. You might think it's sweet to be bossed around a little. But once he knows he can lord it over you, he'll start pushing you around."

"Well, that'll never happen now! I doubt he'll ever come back."

"If he cares about you as much as you think, nothing will keep him away."

Her eyes welled again. "He's so mad at me!"

"Well, I'm not surprised. He didn't get what he wants and he blames you."

"Why do you *hate* him so?"

"I don't hate him," Neal said. "But you've chosen the wrong boy, Eddi, and I'll always defend you from letting yourself be used."

"You're defending me from letting me be myself."

"I think in your heart you know he's bad for you."

"Well, what do you suppose he thinks of me now? That my daddy doesn't trust me? Ever!" She flung herself down on the bed and buried her face in her arms.

He wondered if the time had come when Eddi no longer wanted or needed his protection. He left her room, spent a late hour pacing and thinking, then went to bed disconsolate but unrepentant. He realized that Eddi was probably feeling her own adolescent pain and he sympathized. It was so hard growing up, he thought. It was hard being a father, too. He wondered if, having devoted most of his years to Eddi, there were some other pieces he might yet pick up.

This standoff lasted two or three days, then one afternoon Brant brought Eddi home from some event they'd attended together and they had walked up to the back door when Neal overheard a conversation between them. He didn't mean to eavesdrop, but Eddi had already opened the door with her key and he was sitting not fifteen feet away in his home office off the den. Brant had said something about being in a pickup football game on Friday. "I'll be finished by eight or nine o'clock, and come by here then."

"Oh, but Brant," said Eddi, "Friday's when I'll be at Lisa's overnight party."

"Look, I don't want you going to that frigging party. I want you here. Friday I expect to see you."

"But, Brant — "

"You be here," he said, "or I'll come to Lisa's."

At that point Eddi, afraid her father might hear, closed the door. Neal had a mind to grab the boy by the scruff of the neck and haul him out of the yard. But he didn't make a move, and he didn't have to. Two nights later he heard Eddi talking to Brant on the phone, her door open, making no effort to conceal the conversation. "I'm not your property, Brant," she said. "And I don't like you being mad all the time!" A pause, then, "No, absolutely not. And if you come to Lisa's I'll ask her father to take care of it!"

Neal couldn't restrain a knowing smile, but he was still uncertain about how much of all this she would blame on him. Next morning at breakfast she said, "You were right about Brant, Daddy. He's a spoiled brat. I won't be seeing him anymore."

"You've decided for sure?"

"I've decided. He knows it, too."

It always amused him that she would argue with him to a point, then a week later express his very opinions as though they'd originated with her.

"Well, there'll be other boys," he said.

"Oh, I don't know. I think I'll just hang loose until I hit college."

It seemed to him that one thing never failed Eddi. Like her mother, she could seize the moment and receive pleasure from nearly everything. But she didn't like to be left dangling. She wanted her agenda planned. Her desire for an orderly life utterly contradicted her delight in surprises.

Chapter Thirty-Three

It was a cold, windy afternoon. He was reminded of his younger days as a paperboy when he rode through the darkness, working to put a few dollars in his pocket. Before dressing, he'd wrapped newspapers around his arms and legs for insulation. They crinkled as he pedaled, chafing his knees and elbows. It'd been a hard way to learn a work ethic, but it was how he'd managed a few things his parents couldn't afford.

Today, a raw wind swept down from the north, brittle and cutting. The sun mocked the yellowish freezing earth below. He had just hurried through the swinging doors of the post office when a familiar movement arrested him. At first he was uncertain, she was so bundled in a wool knit cap, her head down in a rush to move out of the wind. When he saw that it was Kara, his pulse leaped, and he literally threw himself in front of her.

"Neal!" she cried. "I'm sorry. Didn't see you."

"Kara! Where are you off to in such a rush?"

"I've finished what I came for, and now I'm getting in out of the weather."

"I had no idea you were in town. Why didn't you call me?"

"But why should I?" She pulled off her cap and shook her hair. Her cheeks were as vibrant as ever, but there was a faintly guarded look in her eyes. "Neal, you have your life, and whenever I bring you into mine, it just complicates things."

"It doesn't have to."

"But it does."

"We can at least talk, can't we, Kara? No matter what, I'd like you to believe we can talk whenever we want to."

She stuffed the cap into her coat pocket and looked at him squarely.

"I've never stopped thinking about you and Eddi, but let's face it — those memories are better left alone."

All around them were people coming and going, their heads ducked against the wind, bundles and packages under their arms. The rat-gray sky seemed to press down into the stiff brown grass, and a vapor of heat from an exhaust vent on top of the post office broke into jagged wedges like shattered glass.

"Come on," he said. "Let's get a cup of coffee."

"I can't, Neal, really. I have to go."

"Then at least sit in my car a minute. Your face is getting all red."

"Well, okay. Five minutes."

They walked together to the car and he opened the door for her, then hurried around and slipped in beside her. "How often have you come to town without letting me know?"

"Not very often, really. Christmas, holidays, when someone in the family is sick."

"I've wanted to know what was going on in your life, Kara, but felt I had no right to contact you."

"It's sweet of you to say that, but really it's better for us just to remember the good times."

"No. It would've been better for me to hear from you."

"Why?"

"Because I love you."

"Oh, Neal."

"Not just the fond memories, either. More and more as Eddi's grown up, I've missed you."

"How is Eddi, really?"

"She's happy, I think, and pretty well adjusted."

"We could have been such great friends. How I've longed to see her!"

"Why haven't you then?"

"Because I knew it'd break my heart."

They sat silent a moment, before he said, "I've heard your marriage broke up. What happened?"

"Oh, I don't know. I guess Paul and I weren't really suited for each other. I wanted children and he didn't. We both kept hoping things could be worked out. I was willing to take the chance — unlike you, I must say. We still care for one another, but it was just better that we not live together." She turned to him suddenly. "I try not to dwell on the negative, Neal. It's been hard and it'll take a while. As I've told you before, we can't let one single thing be everything we have in life."

"Well, now that you're unmarried . . ."

She dropped her head down. "Please don't say it. I'm no longer married, but I know you still are — to those things which always consumed you. Time's passed and we've grown older and wiser. But there are no loose ends with us. I'm moving away — far away. You don't need to know where."

"No, wait, Kara. There's no reason we couldn't see each other. I'm really sorry your marriage didn't work. But what would it hurt to give it a chance?"

"I can't, Neal. Please don't ask me."

He slumped into the seat, his hands clutching the steering wheel. "It's strange. When Sandi died, I felt there was one thing I should have done, one thing I wanted to say. With you, I keep feeling there's something that must happen."

She gave a little shrug. "I guess the human heart always has a place for the special people in our lives. The lost loves, the lost ambitions, too. But look, we're making a mistake here, Neal. Running into you just opens old wounds, and there's nothing to be gained by it."

"Maybe for me at least, it could bring some closure."

"I don't want it to. I know I got into your heart a little, and I want you to always remember what you let go." There was a slight quiver of her lips as she reached for the door. "I have to go. Seems as if the last walk we took in the park wasn't so long ago. I've been married and divorced, and our hair is beginning to get a little gray. I like yours. Just think, it won't be long before Eddi'll be going to college. And then, what? Marriage? Children? And the process begins all over."

He started to protest, but in an instant she was out the door, walking quickly to her car. Her solitary yet resolute figure reminded him of that day he left Eddi at camp, and the loneliness he felt then. Kara was stronger than he was. He wished he were as capable of looking on pain as part of a growing process. He wanted to run after her and cry, "No, you're not going to walk out of my life again!" But he realized only pure selfishness would allow him to disrupt whatever healing process she was managing to pull herself through.

Chapter Thirty-Four

Eddi said, "I'm researching Furman and Radcliffe. And what do you think of William and Mary? That sounds like such a romantic place." At first she looked at colleges far away, attracted to escape, then she began more seriously to consider those within driving range, so she could come home often. "What about Georgia or Auburn? They're good schools."

This was an exciting time for her, but Neal had to hide how much he was dreading it. "You have my blessings," he said, "on wherever you choose to go."

"If I can get in. But don't worry, I'll get in."

Neal calculated that with the investments he'd managed — a few real estate holdings, some stocks and bonds — and with the increasing value of NEA Couriers, they were well off now. Whatever might happen, Eddi would be provided for. But these two decades of grueling work had taken their toll on him. It was harder to get up in the mornings, harder to settle in at night. He'd begun to feel tired, not so much physically tired as mentally and emotionally run down. Even the weather had become harder on him. As he met with business associates or dealt with employees — he now had fifteen — he experienced an increasing discontent with the routine, with the sameness of it all.

He got a little lift one day when once again his path happened to cross with Kara's sister Claire. They were in the shopping mall, he looking for a piece of jewelry for Eddi's going away present, Claire for a new outfit for herself. It had been years now since he'd seen Claire, but there was no mistaking the front profile and her dark eyes and rather pensive glance. They were both crossing the food court when he spotted her, called to her, and she stopped and smiled. They hugged and after a few minutes of casual talk Claire said, "Did you know Kara's back in town?"

Neal's heart skipped a beat. "No, I didn't know."

"Yes. At her old job."

"But — since when?"

"Oh, several months now. Her new position didn't work out and she finally decided to come home."

"I wish she had let me know," Neal said.

"She probably figured you'd find out in due course if you wanted to."

"Claire, I've never stopped caring for Kara."

"I knew you probably hadn't."

"What about Paul? Has she gotten over him?"

"I suppose. If you ever get over such things."

Neal shifted to one side as a young couple pushing a baby stroller came by. He followed the baby with his eyes before saying, "I'd like to see Kara, but I don't want to cause more misery."

Claire gave a shrug of her shoulders. "That's something for you to work out. Anyway, I knew you'd like to know. Take care, Neal."

As they parted, Neal tried to think what to do. Kara had been married and divorced. In the two times they'd met since she left ten years ago, she had said that all their meetings did for her was open old wounds. She clearly wanted closure on this part of her life. After struggling with it for days he decided to let it go. Still, to think of her so far yet so close . . .

In her senior year Eddi was elected to homecoming court. Except for a couple of setbacks, her school years had been fairly happy. "I won't be queen," she said. "You know who'll get that. Miss Society, from kindergarten. But I was chosen first runner-up. Do you think I could get a new dress?"

"I think so. What'll you wear?"

"We're all going to get together and decide."

The girls settled on long evening gowns, and Eddi asked him to go with her to choose her dress. They hit two shopping centers and half a dozen stores trying to find something she liked. In one of the stores they ran into another of the queen's court looking for a gown and the two girls stood chatting for five minutes while he and the mother, waiting patiently, became casually acquainted. He noticed Eddi glancing at the mother several times and there was no doubt in his mind that this was another of those moments when she yearned, perhaps subconsciously, for a mother of her own to help her choose an evening gown for her homecoming court. He sighed. Eighteen years. If one could only realize how quickly life passes . . .

The dress was selected at last and as it was placed carefully in a bag Eddi said, "I hate to ask you to spend so much, Daddy, on a dress I may wear only once."

"Well, I suppose every parent faces that."

"Maybe I'll get to wear it again some day in college."

On Wednesday before Homecoming, they were eating breakfast when Eddi glanced out the window. "Oh, no, look at the weather! What rotten luck."

The sky was dark and ugly, threatening rain. "Let's hope it clears," he said.

"Whatever happens we'll have to make the best of it."

Neal, too, was apprehensive for the girls. It was one of those flukes in the weather when it had become unseasonably cold, with a penetrating mist which produced moisture on car hoods and window glass. As he drove to the office he noticed how everything had turned ashcan gray — the landscape, the sky, even the daffodils looked faded. Workmen jack-hammering a section of asphalt at an intersection were all bundled up in heavy coats and hats with earflaps, orange outer vests blued by the steel-gray light. Even in the foggy warmth of his car he shivered and looked forward to his second cup of coffee in the office.

By Friday, the only thing that offered any splash of color was Eddi's beautiful long gown, pale blue satin with a fitted waist and bare shoulders. She modeled it for him, making little adjustments, her face glowing with excitement. "What do you think?"

Neal gasped. She looked so much like her mother it was heartbreaking. "I've never seen you prettier." He kept his voice steady with effort.

"Well, then, I'll see you at the game."

She kissed him goodbye and her escort, an old friend, whisked her away.

Neal collected his parka, had a quick cup of hot cider to protect him from the pervasive chill, and then drove to the stadium through the uninviting drizzle. His skin felt feverish, his shoulders ached and he pressed forward mostly on determination. He was hardly ever sick, and couldn't understand why he was feeling so wrung out. The weather didn't help, either. He parked and trudged with the crowd up into the bleachers. Everything was wet. Benches glistened under the lights and people pulled out plastic bags and cushions to sit on. There was a big crowd, but having arrived early, he was able to find a seat close to centerfield, where the homecoming court would be presented. It was a hometown game and the coronation of the queen made it all the more popular. People pressed close together, not so much to make more room as to help shield themselves from the awful weather.

As he scrunched down onto a bench he heard a female voice say, "Hello, Mr. Austin. Your daughter looks beautiful."

Neal did not see who spoke. "Thank you," he said. "I know they're cold."

It seemed forever before the teams and the cheerleaders ran onto the field to a roar of shouts and applause. There was a snappy pregame march played by the band. Finally came the coin toss, and to an increasing thunder of voices and drums came the kickoff, the home team first to receive. On the second play the ball was fumbled but fortunately recovered by the offense. "Watch it, butterfingers," a man behind Neal grumbled. Some parents took the game very seriously. But fumbles were unavoidable. The rain-soaked field wasn't kind to the players, and blue and white jerseys soon became a blur of muddy stains. A few passes were managed, but mostly it was a running game. When the crowd jumped up to cheer or to get a better look, Neal followed, but it became increasingly harder. There was a new aching between his shoulders and arms, and the skin along his spine felt taut and rigid. He felt as if his veins were full of some mercury-like substance, pumping sluggishly against gravity, less liquid than solid. Behind him, a little boy said, "Let's go home."

"Oh, we can't. Not until we see your sister." Apparently the family was one of the homecoming court, but Neal never turned to see whom it was or to introduce himself.

Finally, half-time arrived and one by one the girls were escorted out onto the wet field. They had all removed their wraps, determined to show their gowns. Each received a roar of applause. With a stab of pride, Neal wished Sandi could be here. It seemed to him that Eddi's greatest success was in the way she took it all in stride. This was her moment of glory, yet he knew she looked on her recognition as a passing success, keeping everything in perspective.

But he had his own moment of glory as he watched her walk onto the field. Off and on, the cold misty rain prevailed, and those people sitting in the crowded bleachers, all bundled up, kept moving closer together. None of the girls wanted to look less than their best and took their places bare-shouldered. He knew Eddi was freezing, and he grew colder and more miserable in sympathy, but he was struck by just what a young woman his daughter had become. She held the arm of her escort with poise and composure, and glided into her place with an air of confidence. Someday a man would fall helplessly in love with her, he knew, and would become her husband and lover. He was proud, anxious, and a bit sad. He hadn't realized just how much he dreaded the day she'd be gone.

Still, he saw himself presenting to the world something precious and unique. He had raised this sensitive girl who would soon go off on her own. How could he possibly have accomplished such a task? As she stood with her long dark hair ruffled by the wind, many unexpected things in himself seemed suddenly and unexpectedly fulfilled. Maybe this was his legacy after all. Maybe this was his contribution to making the world a better place, not that his daughter didn't have quirks and flaws, but that he had brought a special human being into the world and that he had been an imperfect but decent father.

Out on the field in their lovely gowns, all the girls looked beautiful, and something else occurred to him. Each one was precious. Every smile, every glance and arm and movement was to be treasured. He was sorry that modern culture so dehumanized the glorious gift of life. If only he could write something that would help lead people to love again. At least in his own daughter he knew his love was immortal. Despite the rain and the chill in his bones he felt refreshed and renewed.

But he was glad when the homecoming court walked off the field, and as the game resumed, he could see the girls pull their heavy coats over their bare shoulders.

Standing high in the bleachers, with the chill bearing down, he became dizzy. Though his flesh was cold, his head felt burning hot. Pressed in among hundreds of people, he felt curiously distant and isolated. This was the big event of the year and he wanted to be involved. He wanted to jump, shout, and cheer as much as anyone, but all he could do was fight the fear that he was going to be really sick.

Finally, the game was over and he trudged with the crowd down out of the bleachers and into the gymnasium. Here it was warm, and students and alumni, staff and parents pressed through the brightly decorated doors amidst the shouts and whistles of victory. Along with the rest of the court and the soon to be graduates, it was his daughter's moment to shine, a moment he very much wanted to share. But he felt crushed, as though there wasn't going to be enough air to breathe.

In the gym Eddi threw her arms around him. "You girls look stunning," he said. "I know you were cold, though."

"It wasn't so bad. Because we were excited, I guess." The light shone in her eyes. "Don't forget, Daddy, I'm spending the night with Lisa. We promise to come in by one, at least."

"Fair enough."

"You want to stay around for the dance? It'll be fun. We'll dance together."

"No, I'm heading home. You're so special to me, you know."

She looked at him closely. "You all right? You don't look so well."

"I'm fine. It's just a little stuffy in here, I guess."

"You're going straight home, then?"

"Yes. I'll see you tomorrow."

"Okay. G'night, Daddy. Thank you for everything."

He worked his way back through the packed gym. He was sorry he couldn't stay longer, but his own bed was what he needed now. Every minute or two he was stopped to shake a hand, to receive congratulations for his daughter's success. The walls and corridors were decorated with balloons and streamers and sparkled with the excitement of many young voices. But it all seemed to come to him in a daze. By the time he got to the car, plowing through another flash of rain, he felt feverish. He got in and drove home, one moment letting the window down to allow the wind in his face, the next pouring on the heat and shivering uncontrollably.

As he pulled into the garage, the headlights picked up glints and swirls which seemed like whirling ripples of confetti. He watched them with distracted fascination, feeling as if his own body were whirling. He sat in the car a moment, then started into the house. Somewhere along way he lost his keys. He discovered they were no longer in his hands, yet he hadn't heard them fall. In the rainy darkness, he looked around, but with no success. He felt he had to sit down a moment before resuming the search. The car was locked, so he made his way up the terrace steps to the gazebo. The cold rain lashed his face and there was no moon. He knew he must find his keys, but first he would sit a moment and rest. He hunched down on a bench, but the octagonal roof offered little protection and he felt the rain creeping into his clothes. He slipped lower onto the gazebo floor, away from the sides, which were partially sheltered. As he curled his legs up and closed his eyes, a malaise settled over him.

He wished he'd made it as a writer. He wished he hadn't squandered one life while waiting for another, and wondered, no matter how well things had gone, how different they might have been had he succeeded in what he'd set out to do.

But despite his failures he knew whatever happened, Eddi would be all right now. He'd given the world something fine and remarkable, someone who would never demand more than she was willing to return. She could make it now, he knew. He was willing to admit she was no longer dependent, but he was convinced she knew she could come to him for anything, as long as he lived.

He lay on the cold wood floor, knowing he must get up but not quite feeling up to it yet. He remembered the time he was sick in his little stucco house in St. Elmo. He was alone then, and he was alone now. He remembered his mother bringing him soup. He wished she were here at his side. It was funny that no matter how old one was in such moments, he often yearned for mothering.

He loved Eddi deeply, but he realized she couldn't fulfill his every need. There was a vacant place in his heart for companionship and for work, but he no longer feared the moment she'd be gone. He was too proud of what she had become.

He pulled his legs up closer to his chest, and he would perhaps have lain there all night had he not heard a car door slam and a while later, Eddi calling to him. "Daddy! Daddy!"

Suddenly there was a blaze of light all across the backyard, and Eddi bursting out of the house crying, "Daddy!"

By the time she reached the gazebo, he'd pulled himself up. Seeing him, she burst into tears. "Oh Daddy . . ."

"I'm all right . . . just lost my keys."

Someone was with her — Lisa, he thought, and a couple of boys. He felt himself helped up and half under his own power, with their help, he was taken into the house. "Why you here, Eddi? You're s'pose to . . ."

"Oh, Daddy, I came to check on you."

He heard a male voice ask about an ambulance, a doctor. Vigorously, he said, "No, no, I'm all right. It's nothing. A fever — maybe a little fatigue."

Eddi shooed them away, and helped him into bed. He remembered her voice drifting away into another room, and seconds later he gave in to the heaviness he'd felt for several days and fell asleep.

Hours later — morning, he surmised by the light on the window — he awakened to find her sitting in a chair, her arms folded on the bed, and her head in her arms. As he stirred, her head popped up and she blinked at him with wide, troubled eyes. She was still in her evening gown.

"Eddi, I'm so sorry I spoiled your night."

"I'm glad I came home, Daddy. I don't know what would've happened to you."

"But how did you . . ."

"I called for an hour. I knew you weren't well. Then when you didn't answer I came looking for you."

He lay comfortably, moving each part of his body experimentally. There was no particular stiffness from the cold gazebo floor and he could feel that his fever had subsided. "I've misplaced my keys, I think. When I couldn't get in, I decided to sit down awhile."

"I contacted call-a-nurse. She advised just keeping an eye on you, and if you weren't better by this morning, to bring you to the emergency room."

"I'm sorry, Eddi, this was a special night for you."

"What do I care about that? Of all times for me to be away."

"Well, soon that's going to become the norm."

"Oh, no, I'm never leaving you, Daddy!"

He laughed. "Of course you are. College beckons."

She looked at him a long moment, then her eyes filled with tears. "I was so scared."

He took her hand. "I'm all right now, though. Go and get some sleep."

"You sure? I haven't left you all night."

"Go get some rest. I'm fine now. I'll get up and make coffee."

"What do you think happened?"

"I don't know. Maybe my body telling me to slow down or something. Who can explain these things. I'll schedule a visit to the doctor."

"You promise?"

"Yes. But I don't think it's anything."

"Well, maybe you can stop working so hard now."

He considered this a moment. "Have I been so busy I've missed out with you?"

"Oh, no, Daddy, absolutely not. I can't think of one time you haven't been there for me."

"I could've been a better father, I know that. Still, I'm awfully grateful for the way you've turned out."

She smiled her sweet, innocent, slightly lopsided smile. "I'm grateful for you, too, Daddy. Honestly, not every girl can say that." She stood, stretched, and yawned. "I'm so glad you're okay. Should I call Tia?"

"No, she doesn't come in on Saturday. And neither do I. Not anymore. Now, you go get some rest. This is your day to sleep." She stood and he saw that her corsage was wilted and her gown rumpled from half dozing with her head on his bed.

As she pressed her cheek against his and went out, he lay thinking of what might have happened had he lain half conscious in the gazebo all night. He might well have contracted pneumonia or worse. He would have hated to be a burden for Eddi, or to have to give up on life as he'd planned it. There was plenty he still wanted to do. He'd like to see the directions she would take, the challenges she would meet and the choices she would make. It disturbed him to think he might not have been able to enjoy any of this. In his heart he still hungered for many things — he knew he wasn't ready to give up yet. He was sorry that he'd spoiled one of the highlights of Eddi's school life. But he remembered that standing in the bleachers, when he was happy and proud for her, he felt the presence of a thousand people, and in his heart an unwritten word, a longing which had never gone away, and a gratitude that in his daughter he had given something special to the world.

Chapter Thirty-Five

He looked down from the dorm window, watching Eddi gather a bundle of clothes from the van. As she stepped onto the curb and almost dropped her load, a fleeting expression of panic and determination crossed her lips. It was a look he knew well. In that instant she was his little girl again, just beginning to walk. They were on the patio, she playing around while he sat in a chair writing. A big truck descending a nearby hill roared explosively and he glanced up to see Eddi, her face fear-streaked, rushing to him as fast as her little legs could carry her. His heart, his life had been ensnared forever. He remembered it as clearly as when it had occurred nearly sixteen years ago.

She disappeared from his view, and entered the dorm a story below. He reminded himself that he must avoid all evidence of melancholy. From the window he could look over much of Auburn's pretty campus. Somewhere across green lawns was the English department, where young scribes soon would be learning their craft, passionate with creative urges. What remarkable works of poetry and prose lay ahead of them one could only imagine. He remembered that no fervor could have been greater than his at that age. He felt a pang of envy, but let it pass, knowing that worlds of experience separated them while his vision remained youthful.

In front of Eddi's dorm, cars were being unloaded. Just below, a mother, daughter and a small child transported armloads of clothes, seeming to float, disembodied, with eyes peeking through webs of hangers. Eddi had insisted on coming a day early, to claim her territory, he suspected. Before her roommate arrived, she wanted her own things comfortably arranged, her half of the space delineated in a way that would command neatness. She'd give a little, he knew; she would make concessions. But at least half this room would demand orderliness.

He heard her in the stairway, turned from the window and started down to meet her — his little daughter, running to him on chunky, unstable legs, entering her first year of college. How incredible! His nostalgia was confused with rushes of anxiety and pride.

Meeting her halfway up the stairs, he said, "I'm going down for another load. Where you'll put all this is beyond me."

"We'll manage, Daddy, not to worry."

"If Lisa brings half as much . . ."

"Oh, she will, you can be sure of that."

He'd offered to get her an apartment but she insisted she must live in a dorm at least a year. "I need to suffer," she laughed. "Besides, it'll be cheaper."

Down at the van, he gathered boxes under each arm and started back upstairs. As he pushed open doors with his hips, he noticed that one of the boxes was almost full of pictures. There was one of her mother, whom she'd known mostly through sixteen years of questions; another of Sandi and him when she was pregnant; friends from various stages of her life; and, unselfconsciously, a few of Eddi herself in successful moments — learning to skate, induction into Honor Society, homecoming court. As he ascended the stairs, various pictures jiggled to the surface like flashes from the past. Eddi favored him in looks, but it was her mother's nature he saw, as though the older she grew, the more like Sandi she became. In almost every photograph he detected a wan look of appeal as if someone was supposed to be there who wasn't.

"Knowing you," he had remarked as he watched her pack boxes at home, "when you go to college, you'll take thousands of new pictures. Why do you want to transport these?"

"Because they'll help keep me from getting homesick."

"Will they? Or will they only make it worse?"

"I'm familiar with them," she insisted. "There's only one thing. When I come home, my room will look so bare."

She had dropped in more unframed photos and looked up at him. "You'll be all right, won't you, Daddy? I know in a way it'll be a relief, but I keep thinking of those nights when there'll be no phones, no noise, no music." She began to tear up, perhaps because of the look in his eyes.

As he passed Eddi on the landing going down, and shifted the boxes on his hips so yet more pictures bounced to the top, he felt that somehow he was behind every scene, if not in image, in spirit: the birthday parties, the early boyfriends, the dance reviews and cheerleading and formals. The moments he felt had touched Eddi most were those when his presence was evident.

He'd miss these pictures from her room, he knew. The walls would be bare, the house empty without her. Still, there was a certain liberty in solitude, one he'd imagined often. As a child, he had sometimes wondered how it would be to have no parents, no siblings, to be utterly alone, answering to no one. Probably all children at one time or another imagined this. But of course no one would really choose to be alone at that age. Loud music, the electrified house, the unreasonable squabbles — he'd miss them all. But being alone wasn't necessarily the worst thing that could happen to a person.

Eddi came up behind, dropped two boxes, and began to arrange clothes in the limited closet and drawer space. "It won't be long before all this will need to come back and I'll have to have winter clothes. That's when it'll get really crowded."

As she arranged her drawers, he dumped the box of pictures on the bed and began to put them in some order. The parchment-colored walls were speckled with pinpoints of toothpaste left by previous occupants trying to disguise the little holes their pictures had made. Under the window, the heating system stood cold but ready to spin to life. The rooms were separated by a bathroom to be shared by four girls. After growing up with so much space of her own, he wondered how she could acclimate to it. One thing he knew — Eddi would defend her territory, but her style was to win over the competition. The personality who most rubbed her the wrong way was the very one onto whose bed she would flop down to discuss something they had in common. Soon all these dull rooms up and down the halls would be personalized with throw rugs, lamps and comforters, with curtains and valances and pillows, and with stuffed animals which would transform the cubicles into home.

After he'd fumbled with the pictures a moment, Eddi nudged him gently aside. "I'll arrange these, Daddy."

"The idea for now is to just put them somewhere."

"I'll do it, though. You don't know where I want them."

He stood watching as this menagerie of old scenes was placed on the bookshelves he'd built for her. Extracting a picture in a thin silver frame, she exclaimed, "Look, Daddy, remember this?"

"You can't possibly mean to keep that."

"I like it."

"It's probably the worst photo of me ever taken."

"I think it's adorable. All my girlfriends used to say, 'Who's that boy with you?' and I'd laugh, 'That's my Daddy.'"

"That was years ago."

"Not so long. I was thirteen. We spent a whole week at the beach."

"Thirteen," he mumbled.

With a stern gaze, she asked, "You aren't going to be sad, are you, Daddy?"

"Of course not. Why should I be?"

"I know you'll miss me."

"Yes, but I got you here. That's some accomplishment."

"I have all these opportunities ahead, but you'll go back to the same old things."

For a moment they stood together. Then he turned quickly toward the hall. "I'll bring another load."

Chapter Thirty-Six

Downstairs again, he forced himself to concentrate on the environment in which he was about to deposit his daughter. He himself could be quite comfortable here, he thought, with the expansive campus, the wide lawns, the early American brick and big trees everywhere. Eddi's own generous corner windows looked out on a park where students threw beach towels onto the grass and pigeons strutted around them.

As he gathered up a final armful of parcels and packages, a plastic bag fell over and out slipped her teddy bear. It was amazing how swiftly the nostalgia struck him. He'd had no idea she would ever consider bringing her old and bedraggled friend. He remembered well putting her to bed at one, two years old to the soft music of "Me and My Teddy Bear." As she fell asleep, one arm instinctively encircled her little companion to draw it into a close embrace. All his plans, all the pressures of his day were nothing as he sat on her bed until the music trailed off. And here she was, the two-year-old, a woman now, about to clear his protective harbor, bringing her compass along, her harbor light, her teddy bear.

Upstairs, he dumped the parcels and averted his face, making much of the act of depositing the load on her bed. But Eddi must have caught something in his glance, for she started to speak, hesitated, then grasped his arm. "Why don't we take a break now? Are you in a hurry to get back?"

"No, I'll stay as long as you like."

"Well, let's go and get some lunch, then." She flashed him a radiant smile. "I want us to do that often, Daddy. You'll come over and have lunch with me. It's not that far."

"You don't realize how busy you'll be."

"It'll be hectic for the first few weeks, yes, but that'll trail off." She found her purse and then in a determined way said, "Lunch is on me, for all the work you've done."

"I hate to see you spend your hard-earned money."

She laughed and slipped her arm through his. "Remember, I have an allowance to do with as I please."

"Within limits," he reminded her.

"Oh, yes, within limits."

They drove over to one of the campus haunts, a grungy-looking place known for its chicken fingers and cheeseburgers. All around the village was evidence that a new college year was about to begin — balloons and banners and several signs which said, "Discounts for freshmen." Eddi, he knew, had some hard studying ahead of her, moments of anxiety and of agony, decisions and choices, a few trials in human relations, probably. But she would do well, take it all in stride. In the noisy restaurant, they got a tiny booth and as they ate, she talked excitedly.

"Lisa's coming tomorrow. I'm glad she decided on Auburn, too. Just think how long we've known each other."

"You'll have the room to yourself tonight, then," he said.

"Except there'll be plenty of girls on the hall. Some of us will eat together, probably."

"Good. The idea's to surround yourself with friends."

They ordered, but when their food came she hardly touched hers. "Come on, honey, you need some nourishment."

"I thought I was hungry. Maybe I'll just take it back with me."

Her non-stop dialogue was evidence of anticipation and dread, he realized. His own appetite was limited, but they got through lunch and drove back to the dormitory. They parked down the street a ways, leaving space in front of the dorm for new arrivals with loads to carry up. As they ascended the one flight of stairs to her corner room Eddi said, "Help me make my bed, Daddy."

They arranged sheets, pillows — about six pillows of different shapes, sizes and colors — her teddy bear and her comforter. The impersonal, lifeless room became relatively warm and homey — evidence of Eddi's touch, anybody could see it. Then everything was done and it was time for him to leave.

She put her arms around him. "I don't want you to go."

"I know, darling. But I'm excited for you."

"I'm scared."

"Are you? Well, it's strange and unfamiliar now, but in a few days it'll seem like home."

"But what are you going to do?"

He laughed. "What do you think? Enjoy some freedom."

"I know you say that to make me feel better, but the house will seem so empty. Think of the space you'll have, though. You can do exactly as you please."

"So I've been telling myself."

"I'm coming home often, you know. That's why I decided on Auburn."

"I want you to, but not to check on me. I'll be all right."

She smiled brightly. "You can go into my room and think about me." She looked away a moment, and with trembling lips whispered, "I'm sorry you were never able to do what you really wanted, Daddy."

He was stunned. "What makes you think I haven't?"

"I used to hear you typing in the wee hours of the night. I've missed that in recent years."

"Well, it's not a priority now."

"Oh, but it should be, Daddy. Please don't give that up. It's so much a part of you!"

So Eddi had known all along, he thought. She had sensed his unrest. He should have realized there was little he could hide from her. . . . It settled things in a way. In another, he was sad for what she must have felt — that she both gave him purpose and deprived him of precious time. Looking into her wonderfully radiant face, her blue eyes which were his eyes, he felt as he supposed he would feel if he had created a literary masterpiece — a sense of elation and of letdown, of pride, yet of the loss of something, as though there were yet one word, one opportunity that had been missed. It seemed to him as if his creative nature separated him from the world, while his physical presence was so earthbound. He wondered if it were that way for many creative people. It was strange how much ballast Eddi gave to his life, while life itself seemed so distant and unsettled. But he had only to look at her to reduce all his frustrations to insignificance.

Something occurred to him then. What he had given Eddi and what he had received from her were so much more than the aspirations with which he'd begun. These unrealized dreams were reduced in value by the knowledge that no other living soul could have participated in this one special creation. No other living souls could have brought Eddi into the world and nurtured and tended her as he and Sandi had. Why hadn't he seen this before? Sandi had seen it. During her pregnancy she'd said, "You've always wanted to do remarkable things, Neal. Well, now you've created life. Doesn't that mean something?"

Then he thought of something else. Love is a light whose energy is kindled by the seeds of new generations. However he might measure up against the success of other men, however little he might leave the world of the things he'd hoped to, he wouldn't exchange anything for Eddi's love. Whatever his shortcomings, he could be at peace with the conviction that no other light in the world could have shone so purely through his own as hers did. She was his most lasting achievement. He would never have a highway or a hall named after him, and all the writing he'd done might someday become just fuel for a bonfire. He had wanted to produce one solid, notable thing. Now, at last, he felt liberated.

"Well, we'll see," he said. "Life's pretty much set me on its course, I guess."

"No, it hasn't, Daddy. You can do whatever you decide. You're the smartest man I've ever known."

It stabbed him in the heart. These were the exact words her mother had spoken. He drew her into his arms. They held each other silently a long time. Then he kissed her goodbye and was down the stairs and into his car without looking back.

He drove home, his chest bursting with pride and sadness. He fought back tears but they came anyway, slipping down his cheeks. He knew he must focus on the freedoms he could now claim, the choices to make on his own. He must resist the desire to turn back the clock, to seize one more chance, to recapture something that had slipped away. Certainly he wasn't the only person in the world who had started out on one road and for better or worse made a detour to another. But he could truly pity those who hadn't learned to love, who had for their life's work no more than success offered by an insubstantial world. But he . . . why, through his love for his daughter and her children and her children's children, something of himself became immortal!

He pulled into the driveway. The late sun struck the gazebo above the latticed brick terrace wall, the house before him curiously distant yet reassuring. He sat for a while unmoving. Finally, he took a deep breath and walked with determination across the lower patio and into the house.

The first thing that greeted him was music from Eddi's room. Accidentally, or perhaps intentionally, she'd left her player on, and instinctively he went down the hall to turn it off. As he entered her room, he stopped short. Right in the middle of her bed was a large, colorful poster which said, "I love you, Daddy." He stood staring and blinking. He remembered the time he'd taken her to summer camp and in his shaver drawer the next morning found a letter from her: "I love you, Daddy."

He turned away and walked back through the house to his home office. Abstractedly he began to arrange things on his desk, moving a stack of papers here, a pen holder, a phone index there. Then he put nearly everything back where they were. After a time the afternoon light slanting through the window faded and he left the office and went to his bathroom. He undressed, showered, and put on fresh clothes. In the kitchen, he tried to decide whether to make himself a meal or go out. It was entirely up to him, he realized. He had no one else to be concerned about. He imagined that just about now Eddi would be joining a contingent of new acquaintances, choosing another village hangout for a pizza or sandwich. She'd be homesick, he knew. It would take a while before she could throw herself into her new life. But she would be all right. That was a comforting thought. As long as she lived she would never cease to yearn for a mother, never cease to reach out to her father, but he knew she would fall in love, she would marry and the remarkable family process would begin again.

He set one place at the table, but it looked so unfamiliar he had no appetite. It occurred to him to call Kara. Of all the women he'd met through the years she was the only one whose face and figure and presence he could evoke in an instant — most of the rest he'd forgotten. But since that day in front of the post office when she said seeing him opened old wounds, he'd been afraid of hurting her again. Maybe she would simply think he was leaning on her because he was lonely. Still, perhaps there was something he could say, something that would be different or seem different. It wasn't impossible that they might discover something they hadn't seen before, even after all these years. The worst she could do was refuse.

He dropped down into his usual chair at the table, his arms folded across his chest. He wondered if Kara had met someone new. He wondered where she was. The only way he knew to contact her was through her sister. Somewhere he had Claire's number. He went back to his office and thumbed through his index until he found it. He picked up the phone, hesitated, hung up, picked it up again. Then resolved, he dialed Claire's number. A familiar voice answered.

"Kara! Is that you? I can't believe it!"

"Yes, it's me."

"You're at Claire's, then."

"Not for long. This is temporary. I'm glad you called, Neal. You've taken Eddi off to college, I guess."

"Yes. How did you know?"

"Oh, I know things," she said. "Remember?"

"So you do. I'm glad to hear your voice, Kara. It means a lot to me."

"Guess it's pretty quiet around there now."

"The place feels empty."

"I know you're proud, though," she said. "Still, it's a kind of starting over, isn't it?"

There was an awkward pause before he could say haltingly, "Kara, I was wondering . . . would you have dinner with me?"

"Oh, no, I don't think it's a good idea."

"Look, you said that before, and you see it would have been all right."

"How do I know it would have been all right?"

"Because you're still you and I'm still me."

"Yes, and you're lonely right now."

"That isn't why I want to see you, Kara."

"Why do you want to see me then?"

"I just do."

"I don't know, Neal. As you said, you're still you."

"Some things are clearer to me now."

She didn't speak for a moment. He wanted her to say yes, but he realized there was little reason she should. Quietly, she asked, "What did you have in mind?"

"Dinner. Tonight."

"You mean *now*?"

"I want to see you. It's that simple."

There was a long silence again and then she said, "All right, we'll see how it goes. Give me half an hour. But Neal?"

"Yes?"

"It's been twelve years. Things aren't the same."

"No, but like you said, it's a kind of starting over."

He went to change his shirt and decided he'd better shave, too. As he walked back to the bathroom, he realized he had never turned Eddi's music off. It filtered down the hall, reaching out. Perhaps he would just leave it on. There were harbors left. There were still things he could do.

Eddi would call tonight, he felt certain, and if not tonight, tomorrow night. When she did, he could tell her something that would make her happy. He could tell her he'd talked to Kara and that it was possible they were going to start seeing each other again.

Happy Lightning!

THE END

ALSO BY DONALD JORDAN

The Creation: A Letter

In THE CREATION: A LETTER, Donald Jordan inspires us to share our beliefs and faith, and serves as a model of how to do so. Coupled with short, illustrative anecdotes, Jordan's encouragement to be kind, responsible and honest, to express gratitude and to forgive, and most of all to love, provides genuine and humble guidance for readers of any age.

CPSIA information can be obtained at www.ICGtesting.com
Printed in the USA
LVOW08*1409150514

385917LV00003B/161/P